Michelle,
I hope y
Thanks fo:
competition.

£6
'5N
te
julie.

Bound

JULIE EMBLETON

Julie Embleton

Book 1 of the Turning Moon series

Other Titles by this Author

Turning Moon Series

Bound

Released

The Voyager Chronicles

The Dawning

Stand-alone

The Untitled

Visit www.julieembleton.com

Acknowledgements

First and foremost, I want to thank my family for their support, encouragement and belief. To my daughter I give endless thanks for inspiring me to be the best I can be, and for her gentle reminders that I need to step away from my laptop and back into reality so she can be fed and watered. To my team at Hillcrest Editing, thank you for all your hard work. I hate red pen. To my friends, thank you for your support and love. And finally, to my readers; those of you who are silent, and those of you who send tweets, comments, emails and general giddiness my way. Your words and support mean more to me than you'll ever know, and even though it's weird and entirely inappropriate, if I could, I would hug every single one of you. Stay giddy!

For Mary and Eric.

The words to express my immense gratitude

have yet to be created

ONE

Nyah Morgan kicked a fallen branch from the edge of her father's grave. A breeze whipped sharply around her, the crispness of late winter laced in its chill as it lifted strands of her jet-black hair and momentarily shrouded her view of the wilting wreaths heaped against the headstone. With the cuff of her sleeve she wiped the dampness from her cheeks and then tucked her loose hair behind her ear. Determined to behave stronger than she felt at that moment, she pulled in a deep breath and loudly sniffed away the last of her tears.

"Harper Morgan," she read out, wanting the words carved into the newly-placed stone to be spoken aloud so the surrounding earth would understand the importance of the man now resting in its depths. "Fearless leader, beloved husband . . ." Trailing off she dragged her gaze upwards and stared out over the other headstones neatly erected in the simple cemetery. It was a moment before she could release the breath burning her throat and force herself to look back down again. "Devoted father -," she continued, her voice now weaker, "- may he rest in peace."

Reaching out she traced her fingers over the carving that had been etched into the top right-hand corner of the headstone. A lone wolf stood proudly on the highest of three peaks, its neck carved into an eternal arch as it howled towards the moon. To the human eye, not that many ever wandered this deep into their territory, it was a simple carving. To her, and the other werewolves like her, it represented that her deceased father had been an Alpha. "I miss you, Dad," she whispered and then feeling her throat swell again gave her head a firm shake. "Enough," she muttered.

When the scent of Alan, the werewolf now set to take over from her father, reached her nostrils Nyah blew out a steadying breath and tried to put a blank expression back onto her face. She preferred to keep her moments of weakness to herself. Tears were best reserved for behind closed doors or huddled under the duvet, alone, at night, as was her preference.

"What do you think?" Alan said as he strode through the wrought iron gates that surrounded the cemetery. He came to stand beside her before reaching out to give the headstone an affectionate pat. "Jackson did a good job, didn't he?"

"He did," she agreed, "it's perfect."

Knowing that Alan hadn't come to the cemetery to share his thoughts on her father's headstone Nyah made a point of checking her watch. "I'm not late for the meeting, am I?" she asked, aware that she still had half an hour before it was due to begin.

"No," Alan said, "I wanted to talk to you about something before it began – away from prying ears."

"What's up?"

Alan nodded towards the open gate, inviting her to walk with him as if what needed to be said would disrespect the memory of his deceased Alpha. "Simon Northfell's attending the meeting," he told her.

Nyah let out an irritated sigh. Alan shared her less than pleasant opinion of Simon Northfell, in fact, the entire pack held little tolerance for him.

"I told him no," Alan said, following her through the small gate, "but as he constantly likes to remind me; I don't officially have the right to deny his attendance."

Together, they mimicked Simon's haughty drawl. *"You are not Alpha, Mr Stenson, the decision is not yours to make."*

"He's a royal pain in the ass," Nyah said, ensuring that the rusting gate latch had caught properly. "I wish he'd crawl back to whatever rock he's been hiding under for the last ten years."

"I doubt the rock wants him back either."

"Next Thursday can't come quick enough," she grumbled as they began strolling towards the copse of trees hiding the narrow pathway that led back towards the houses. "It's a pity we can't find a way to make you Alpha sooner."

Alan shook his head. "I don't think me being Alpha is going to change anything. He wants onto the council and he's going to fight tooth and nail to get it."

"He's nothing but a -," she began and then trailed off with a loud grunt of frustration. "He annoys the hell out of me," she said once her anger was in check. "I mean, really - who the hell does he think he is? He strolls back into Blackwater Ridge after a decade of absence and thinks that just because his great, great granddaddy's sister's cousin's nephew - or whoever it was that happened to be Alpha a gazillion years ago – has entitled him to involve himself in the pack council. He's deluded. His ancient, watered-down bloodline entitles him to nothing."

"Unfortunately, his ancient, watered-down bloodline does entitle him to something."

Nyah came to an abrupt stop. "What?"

"Yeah." Alan ran one hand through his wavy dark-blonde hair, a sure sign he was feeling frustrated with her. "I traced his bloodline and checked the statutes. He does have the right to be on the council."

"That is *not* good," she said after a short moment.

"I agree," he said darkly, shoving his hands into his pockets and staring blankly into the distance, "but there's nothing we can do about it."

They walked on, an occupied silence sharing their the narrow path and it was only when the first of the houses that skirted the edge of their small village were visible that Alan spoke again. "Nyah." He took hold of her arm, slowing her to a stop once more. "I've a bad feeling about all of this. Simon clearly has some sort of obnoxious plan formulating in his brain and I think that whatever it is he wants, he's going to announce at the meeting."

"Any idea what that is?" she asked hesitantly.

He answered with a 'you're not going to like it' grimace.

"Just say it, Alan."

"I don't - I mean, I'm not sure, and to be honest, I'm probably way off . . ."

"But?" she prompted.

Alan dismissed the subject with a sudden shake of his head. "Forget it," he said. "The guy rubs me up the wrong way every time I see him. His smug declarations about his anaemic bloodline are really starting to get on my nerves. And the way he assumes that he has the right to be on the council – if I hear him say the word 'birthright' once more, I swear, I'll . . ."

"But he does have a birthright," she reminded him.

"Yeah, unfortunately," Alan mumbled. "So look," he sighed, "at the meeting, he might say some things that are going to upset you, so I want you to be ready for it, okay?"

"Okay," she answered.

"Don't let him get to you," he warned.

"'Cos you don't?" she grinned, hoping a bit of humour might lighten Alan's dark expression.

"I'm just watching out for you is all," he explained and then nudged her along the path again, a smile finally widening his mouth, but not entirely reaching his brown eyes. "Old habits die hard, you know. And you've been through enough without that idiot upsetting you."

Nyah didn't dwell on it any further as they walked the final few metres of path. She was used to Alan's protective ways and his concern for her had gone into overdrive since her father had passed away. They had known each other for her entire life, Alan had once even declared himself as her substitute brother in the absence of her having any other siblings. "I'll be over in a few minutes," she waved after him as he jogged off in the direction of her father's house. Pack members were already gathering on the lawn outside for the meeting, prompting her to hurry up the path towards her own house.

Once inside Nyah quickly drank down a glass of water and then ran upstairs to freshen up. The last thing she needed today was a council meeting waylaid by Simon Northfell. Yesterday's crazed idea that she had been stable enough to start packing away some of her father's belongings had left her emotionally drained, meaning she now had nothing left in her reserves that a spat with Mr. Obnoxious would require. Wincing at the memory of how her tears had turned the entire packing operation into one big blurred, sobbing mess she pulled her brush through her hair to tidy it up. She'd dragged herself home last night, skipped dinner and undressing to fall straight onto the bed in a state that was beyond exhaustion, and when she'd woken up this morning she hadn't felt much better. Dark circles ringed her eyes when she took a critical look at her reflection in the mirror above the bathroom sink. "You're a mess, Morgan," she muttered before rolling her eyes and turning away.

Once back downstairs she kicked off her trainers in favour of a favourite pair of pumps that had been abandoned under the dining table, glancing automatically through the window that looked out onto the opposite side of the street as she slid them on. Seeing her father's house sitting in the dappled afternoon shade stilled her. She had lived in that beautiful house for nineteen years and she desperately missed everything about it; the comfort of its familiarity, the security that her father's presence used to bring, the scents that belonged solely to the old building, but more than anything, what she missed the most was the companionship. There had always been somebody rattling around that house. She couldn't recall a single occasion of ever being alone inside the sprawling place, and it was what she had loved most about being the Alpha's daughter. Her friends used to think that she was crazy when she said it. They used to wonder how she didn't go out of her mind when pack members were traipsing in and out of her house every day, and they had never understood when she'd tried to explain that it made her feel as if she had dozens of brothers and sisters when in reality there only her and her father. Now, of course, it was only her. Her mother was just a distant memory – a smiling woman in a lemon-coloured dress that her father had once told her was his favourite.

"Stop with the self-pity," she ordered herself, turning away from the window. Her new house was lovely. It was smaller, but easier to keep clean, and her housemate was easy and fun to live with. Karen was a widow - a young widow. At only twenty-five years old and a year into her marriage, her mate, Peter, had been killed in a car accident. Despite their marriage being cut short so cruelly, Karen had repeatedly told Nyah that it had been the best year of her life and nothing could ever take it from her. 'Just like nothing can take your memories from you,' she had consoled one night, '- so take your time grieving your father, but remember that everything that's up here -,' at which point she had tapped the side of Nyah's head, '- is yours to keep forever.'

14

She'd have to keep reminding herself of that when Alan and his family moved in to her old home next week, Nyah decided. It wasn't going to be easy to watch. Three generations of Morgan Alpha's and their families had lived under that roof and it was hard to believe it had all come to an end.

Alan was going to be a good Alpha she reminded herself, pulling the front door shut behind her. He was fair and honest, and, she had to admit, more open to change than her father had ever been. Perhaps now, she thought with a smile, they would finally be allowed internet access for their small settlement.

As Nyah crossed the street she saw Simon Northfell's grey-streaked hair marking his movements amongst some of the other pack members. Although the stiff shoulders and curt nods of those that he was addressing were subtle, the sense of her pack mates bristling at his presence was not. Their irritation prickled in the air like electricity. Simon was an arrogant and cold man, distrusted because of his long absence from the pack and the self-assured assumption held on his return that he could weave himself into the decision-making of the pack council. Purposely ignoring his obvious movement towards her she quickly ducked inside the house before he could corner her and start blabbing about his birthright again.

Nyah took her seat at the front of the large room reserved for pack meetings. Behind her, silently observing, hung a row of portraits displaying the former Alphas of the Blackwater Ridge pack. Her father's portrait had been hung on the same day as his headstone had been erected – exactly twenty-one days after his death – and as with the headstone, she didn't want to linger on the image of her father. It was hard enough that she saw traces of him every time she looked in a mirror and glimpsed her deep olive skin, warm brown eyes and black hair.

The scent of the stodgy oil paint hung heavily in the room and she briefly wondered if part of his spirit lingered too. She could almost picture him drifting above her, his arms folded and one finger tapping on his upper lip in his familiar 'pontificating pose' as she used to call it.

Alan's arrival broke through her musings. He pulled out the chair beside her casting a dark look in Simon's direction as he strolled confidently into the room. Sitting down, he turned to her a moment later, his warm smile back in place. "I meant what I said about you remaining on the council once I'm Alpha. You know we all want you to stay on, despite what tradition dictates," he said below the hum of voices.

"I know, and I've given it a lot of thought," she told him, "but I'd really like to take a step back for a while. The last few months have been so tough. I think I need a little time out."

"Of course – I'm not trying to railroad you into anything, I just want you to know that there's a place for you here, if you want it."

"I know, thanks."

"Are you still planning on taking the college course?"

Nyah couldn't hold back the beaming smile that spread across her face. "Yes, definitely. Registration takes place at the end of next month. I hope I can get a place."

"Sure you will, and before we know it you'll be a wealthy business tycoon," he grinned.

"I only want to open a single bookshop," she reminded him with a laugh.

"Ah, you say that now," he said wisely, "but when the money starts rolling in you'll be talking about expansion and profits and market-share."

"What's this about profit and market-share?" Michael, Alan's soon-to-be Beta, dropped into the chair beside Alan and leaned towards them with a blue-eyed conspiratorial wink. "Did someone say money?"

"Nyah's going to be a business tycoon," Alan announced. "Her college course starts next month."

"And how long will it take before I can start hitting you for a loan?" Michael asked her.

"Ooh, I'd say at least a hundred years," she replied.

Michael sat back, shaking his head with mock disappointment, but then remembering something else leaned forward again, his face growing more serious. "So, does that mean you're not staying on the council?" he asked quietly.

When she nodded in reply he glanced towards Alan for an explanation.

"She needs a break from us and the council," Alan told him. "I've told her that she's more than welcome to stay on, but deep down, I think she's just had enough of us."

"That's not true," she replied, knowing that although Alan was only joking, Michael didn't seem to be finding it very funny. "I enjoyed being on the council," she assured him, "and I know that, even though I won't be entitled to stay on after Alan becomes Alpha, there's still a place for me. But for now I just want to take a break from everything and try to figure out what I want to do with myself. Anyway," she smiled, relieved to see Michael's expression softening, "you know I won't be able to stop sticking my nose in; once an Alpha's daughter, always an Alpha's daughter."

Despite how authoritatively she stated her position, being an Alpha's daughter carried little weight. It was her father who had drawn her into the council in the last year, and he had stated in his Bidding Documents, the Lycan equivalent of a Will, that upon his passing she was to remain on the council and continue to be treated with the respect that his position had afforded her. Alan hadn't needed an official document to honour Harper Morgan's wishes, and seamlessly picking up where her father had left off he had continued to include Nyah in all of the pack business. But, despite Alan's request that she stay on the council she knew it wasn't truly acceptable. The only females that held any kind of authority were the wives of Alpha's. The daughters of Alpha's, although respected, were regarded more as window dressing, and if she did remain on the council she knew that in time, as the memories of her father faded for the pack, so would her influence.

The pack were all finally seated. Alan turned his attention to the crowded room and got straight down to business. The agenda was brief; patrol assignments, an update on the buddy system for the young pack members due their first change and a final run-through of Alan's inauguration ceremony which was to take place on the following Thursday evening.

Simon Northfell waited until then to slowly raise his hand from where he sat, wedged into the farthest corner of the room.

"Simon," Alan invited him to speak, with, Nyah noted, more than a hint of impatience.

Simon stood up, a worryingly smug smile stretching his thin lips. "I understand that the deadline for Alpha nominations is midnight tonight?"

"That is correct," Alan said tightly.

"And that any Lycan with an Alpha bloodline is entitled to put himself forward?" he continued.

A clearly audible wave of growls rumbled through the room.

"Also correct," Alan replied.

Simon cast a sneering grin at the scowling faces turned towards him and then spoke again. "I would therefore like to formally announce my submission for the position of pack Alpha."

Nyah's heart clenched painfully. Growls exploded into snarls and numerous pack members were suddenly jumping to their feet. She stared in a deafened shock as the men began gesticulating at Simon, their shouting voices not breaching the pounding in her ears as Simon continued to remain standing, a schooled expression of innocence plastered onto his face. This was what Alan had been trying to tell her earlier, she realized. He had guessed Simon's intentions but couldn't find the words to say it – not that it would've made any difference to how she was feeling at that moment; she wanted to phase, launch herself at Simon and rip his throat out. '*You* want to be Alpha?' she yelled at him in her mind, 'you think that *you* deserve to become Alpha of this pack? You want take the legacy that my father and his ancestors have lovingly and respectfully built and carry it on? You think you're good enough?!'

Alan shot to his feet beside her, one hand taking a firm grip of her shoulder as if aware that her wolf was trembling to burst free. He barked out a sharp order for silence. "Simon has every right to put himself forward for Alpha," he announced calmly. "The Show of Hands will take place on Monday night as has been arranged. The only change is that you now have two candidates to choose from. If there are no other matters I adjourn this meeting."

Nyah squeezed her eyes shut as she struggled to keep her wolf from taking over. The snarls and shouts were clearly audible to her now, but somehow, hearing others yell the angry words that screamed inside her own head helped. She stayed sitting at the table, each vicious shout appeasing her wolf until there was a complete silence, and it was only then when she lifted her head and opened her eyes. With the exception of Alan, the entire room had emptied.

"I wanted to tell you earlier," Alan said quietly, taking her hand from where it was still balled into a fist on her lap. "But a very small and stupid part of me hoped that the idiot wouldn't actually put himself forward."

"It's so, it's just so. . ."

"Disrespectful," Alan finished for her. "To return here after such a long absence and think he can take over as Alpha is nothing but pure contempt towards every member of this pack."

"Why would he do this? Why does he even want it? He's been gone for so long and he doesn't care for any of us! Why is he doing this?"

"I don't know," he answered honestly. "I really don't know. And it's not like he's even going to be voted in – hell, if he even gets one vote I'll be shocked. And a week from now, when I'm Alpha, everyone will be laughing at him."

"Maybe then he'll finally understand that no-one wants him here."

"I hope so. There's already way too much animosity towards him and after what he's just done it's only going to get worse."

To prove his point, Alan jerked his head towards the hallway outside. Nyah focused her hearing beyond the partly open door and immediately heard the savage threats rumbling between the men.

"Oh, Alan," she breathed, realizing how volatile the situation had now become.

"Hey," Alan gave her hand another squeeze. "It's not your problem, okay? I'll look after this."

She nodded tightly, happy to let Alan take control. Her mind was at breaking point. Too many thoughts were tearing around inside her head, ricocheting off each other in a panicked attempt to have themselves heard and although she longed to know why Simon wanted to be Alpha, she hadn't a single ounce of energy left to try to figure it out.

Slowly getting to her feet she followed Alan out to the hallway. Pack members were pacing the wide floor as they waited for him, tension rolling off them so dangerously that, for the first time in her life, Nyah didn't want to be in her father's house. Experience told her that the men would not leave here tonight, they would stay and talk until the small hours, heatedly. Suddenly, she wanted nothing more than to be inside her new little home, alone.

"Try and stay indoors for the next couple of days," Alan said as he walked her out onto the front porch. "I'm going to ask that everyone does the same. Until the Show of Hands on Monday evening I think it would be best if we all kept our distance from Simon."

"I don't want to be anywhere near him," she said hoarsely, her eyes flicking towards the sudden rise of enraged howling coming from the depths of the forest that surrounded their settlement.

Alan frowned in the same direction as her worried stare. "Go home, get some sleep," he said distractedly, already turning around to catch Michael's attention. "Everything will be fine," he added.

As she crossed the street a moment later Michael ran past her. She paused to watch him charge towards the forest, a flash of skin and fur blurring amongst the trees as he phased into his massive grey wolf form, a trail of tattered clothes fluttering slowly to the ground in his wake.

Nyah was quick to open her front door, slip inside and firmly lock it tight behind her.

Two

"Have you seen how quiet it is out there this morning?"

Karen slid into her chair at the breakfast table, jerking her head to where Blackwater Ridge was hidden behind the firmly-drawn curtains. "There's not a soul in sight," she said. "I looked out earlier and the place is deserted. It seems everyone's happy to follow Alan's request that we lie low."

Nyah lowered her coffee mug and glanced towards the covered windows. "What about tomorrow night though?" she wondered. "Everyone will be at the pack house to vote – what's going to happen then?"

Karen shrugged as she reached back to tie her glossy red hair into a pony-tail. "We just have to hope that Alan's demands for peace are kept."

Nyah didn't offer her thoughts on whether that might happen or not. Nothing Alan said, whether it be a demand or request, had to be obeyed, and a vengeful wolf heeded no order unless it came directly from the Alpha. Unfortunately, they had to wait another six days for that to happen. The Lamentation Phase practised after the death of an Alpha was an old and rarely observed tradition, but her father, being the stickler for tradition that he was, had requested it before his death, meaning the pack had to wait until the completion of one full moon cycle before Alan could be sworn in. Once every wolf had howled its dedication the mind link that connected the Alpha to his pack would be established. Then, Nyah assured herself, they could all breathe a sigh of relief and life would return to normal again.

"So, what to do when we're under house arrest?" Karen asked.

Now it was Nyah's turn to shrug. "Scrabble?"

"And wine?"

"I could go along with that," Nyah agreed.

Saturday and Sunday passed slowly, and thankfully, without incident. Nyah went no further than the opposite side of the street where she packed away more boxes to finally clear the house for Alan and his family. Karen had insisted on helping and she had been glad of the company. With the tense silence hovering in the deserted streets outside she didn't want to be alone in the house that she had only ever known as her bustling haven.

When Nyah woke to a pale, buttery light on Monday morning a tangible sense of relief was spreading with the sun's rays. The Show of Hands was now only hours away and once it was official that Alan was going to be their next Alpha she hoped that Simon would scuttle back to whatever dank hole he had come from.

Energised with optimism, Nyah had half the contents of the fridge spread across the breakfast counter when Karen got back to the house, a container of fresh milk in one hand and a newspaper in the other.

"What's all this?" Karen laughed.

"I'm going to make us a huge brunch," Nyah announced. "It's my way of saying thanks for your help yesterday and a way of using up the last few hours before the Show of Hands."

"I like your plan, girl," Karen smiled, sliding onto one of the stools at the counter. "Good thing I got us some milk."

"Anyone out there?" Nyah asked, taking the carton and slotting it into the fridge door.

"I met Michael in the supermarket, and guess what? Apparently, Simon left on Friday night after the meeting and he only came back this morning."

"Where did he go?" Nyah asked.

Karen shrugged. "Michael said he didn't know, or care, only that he wished he hadn't bothered coming back. And he said he's never been so disgusted in his life. He said that Simon putting himself forward is a complete insult to the memory of your father."

Nyah replied with a short, humourless laugh. "I think that was Simon's intention."

"And Michael also said that your self-control on Friday night was to be commended," Karen reported with a meaningful nod.

"Believe me," Nyah said, "I was barely keeping my wolf from taking over."

"Well, everyone is on your side," she declared, grabbing the cookbook that Nyah had set out. "So if you do happen to lose your control later this evening I don't think anyone will be rushing to stop you from hurting Simon – me included. Now," she grinned, tapping the page open before her, "would it be rude for me to request cinnamon pancakes?"

"Not at all," Nyah laughed, "they'll go perfectly with the waffles, scrambled eggs, bacon, muffins and fruit salad. We're going to consume our weight in food today."

Karen groaned and pointedly looked down at her stomach. "Goodbye flat stomach, it was nice knowing you."

Nyah took back the cookbook and waved her away from the counter. "It'll be a while before the banquet is ready," she told her. "And as it's for you I'm not allowing you to help, so go and relax."

"I have a better idea," Karen said hopping off the stool. "I'm going to go for a run. Then I can enjoy our feast guilt-free."

"Do a lap for me!" Nyah called after her as she ran upstairs.

"Wow, something smells good!" Alan said, inhaling deeply when Nyah opened the front door to him a while later. "Please invite me to stay for whatever it is you're baking," he pleaded.

"Brunch," she smiled, "and you, Tanya and little Jack are more than welcome."

"Thanks," he grinned, "but as I much as I'd love to, I can't. There's a lot I need to get done today." He followed her into the kitchen. "Did you say brunch or bake sale?" he laughed, seeing the table laden with freshly-baked treats.

"It's a thank-you for Karen," Nyah explained, wrapping some warm muffins in a napkin and handing them to him. "She helped me to pack the last of the boxes yesterday and I wouldn't have managed it all without her."

"That's one of the reasons I came over," Alan said, "Tanya and I both want to say thank-you, but we also want to say that there was no rush with clearing out Alpha Morgan's belongings. Really, we were both happy for you to take as long as you wanted with packing everything away."

"I know," she said, crossing back to the stove to check on the bacon, "but it had to be done, and putting it off was doing no-one any favours. Anyway, you need all the bedrooms free before Jack's little brother or sister arrives."

"Well, thanks," Alan said again. "I know it wasn't easy for you."

Nyah gave a quick nod. It hadn't been easy, but at least now it was all done. "So, what else did you want to talk to me about?" she asked, flipping over a few crisping pieces of bacon.

"Tonight," Alan said. "I think it would be best if you left it until the last minute to arrive for the Show of Hands. There's still a lot of anger and if Simon so much as looks crooked at you there'll be trouble."

"I was thinking the same," she admitted. "I just want to arrive, vote and leave. I don't think I can even bear to be in the same room as him."

"Leave it 'til after eight, then," he agreed. "And if it's okay with you, I'd like Michael to bring you over and back."

Nyah nodded. Michael was as wide as he was tall. With any luck she could hide behind his massive back and avoid being seen, or indeed, see a certain someone.

Alan held up the parcelled muffins and winked. "Thanks, I'll see you later, okay?"

"Yep, I'll see you later," Nyah answered, just as the sound of the front door opening sounded out.

Nyah leaned over the counter to see Karen back from her run. "Good timing, Karen," she said.

"Morning, Karen," Alan greeted. "Good run?"

"Mm hmm," Karen replied, brushing straight past him and heading for the stairs.

Alan watched her walk up the stairs before turning to Nyah with a questioning frown. 'What's up with her?' he mouthed.

Nyah answered with a shrug.

"See you later," he said quietly, thanking her once more for the fresh muffins before leaving.

Nyah let fifteen minutes pass before calling up the stairs. It was strange for Karen to disappear when it had been obvious that the food was ready. "Karen? You ready for our feast?"

It was a moment before Karen came to the top of the stairs. "Yes," she said, flatly.

"Okay." Nyah turned back to the kitchen with a frown, reckoning that Karen must have come down with a dose of crankiness or something. But whatever that something was, Nyah couldn't figure it out. The thank-you brunch was going down like a lead balloon. Karen sat quietly picking half-heartedly at whatever Nyah offered, her face emotionless and any attempt at conversation shrugged off.

Eventually, Nyah couldn't take the strangeness any longer. "Are you okay?" she said, putting down her fork. "Did I do something to upset you?"

"I'm fine," Karen replied indifferently.

"You sure?" Nyah pushed. "You seem a bit . . . quiet."

"I'm fine," Karen repeated.

"Are you worried about tonight?" Nyah prodded.

"I suppose I am," Karen said, a welcome flash of emotion suddenly visible in her eyes.

"It'll be okay."

"Only if he wins."

"Of course he'll win. Everyone wants Alan as Alpha."

"It's not Alan I'm talking about."

For a second, Nyah thought Karen was serious; the tight set of her mouth and the piercing glare she flung at her certainly gave that impression. "You had me going there," she laughed forcefully, but when Karen's hard expression didn't melt into a smile Nyah felt her face slacken. "Karen?"

"Why shouldn't Simon be Alpha?" she demanded.

"What?" Nyah gasped.

"Why shouldn't Simon be Alpha?" Karen repeated, louder this time. "He has a strong bloodline and he wants to dedicate himself to this pack. He should be given the opportunity to prove himself."

Nyah didn't answer - she suddenly couldn't work her mouth.

"And he has plans for our pack that could see us growing to be the largest and most powerful pack this continent has ever known. Our potential is incredible," Karen gushed.

"Your words are incredible," Nyah said with disgust. "Can you hear yourself right now? Do you actually hear what you're saying?"

Karen blinked once in reply.

"You support Simon?" Nyah asked, leaning towards her. "You want that deserter leading our pack?"

"Simon has plans for our pack that could see us growing to be the largest and most powerful pack this continent has ever known. Our potential is incredible."

"You said that already," Nyah snapped, pushing away her plate and standing up. "What has gotten into you?"

Karen stared blankly up at her.

"Why are you saying this? Simon serves no-one but himself, if he becomes Alpha -."

"Simon has a strong bloodline and he wants to dedicate himself to this pack. He should be given the opportunity to prove himself," Karen cut in.

"Stop saying that!" Nyah yelled. "What is wrong with you?"

"I'm fine," Karen answered robotically.

"You're not!" Nyah backed away from the table. "You're far from fine. Why else would you be saying all this stuff about

Simon? He's not good enough to be Alpha; he could *never* be good -."

"Simon has plans for our pack that could see us growing to be the largest and most powerful pack this continent has ever known. Our potential is incredible."

Nyah clamped her mouth shut and stared at Karen. Her face was lifeless, her eyes vacuous. It was as if she was staring at a shop mannequin.

"Simon has a strong bloodline and he wants to dedicate himself. . ."

Nyah didn't want to hear the rest of the sentence. She already knew it.

Turning, she fled, pounding up the stairs into her room where she slammed the door shut and threw herself onto her bed. Was this who Karen really was? Had Nyah been sharing her home with a woman who actually wanted that heinous man leading their pack? What about the things she had said when they'd been filling the boxes with her father's belongings only yesterday? 'Simon would never have dared to return while Alpha Morgan was still alive; he's such a coward, isn't he? I hope Alan's first act as Alpha is to kick him out of the pack.' Was that the same person who now sat at the table in the kitchen below?

Nyah grabbed her pillow and jammed it over her head. She felt sick. What Karen had said, what Karen believed, it made her stomach roll.

From under her shelter she heard the muffled thud of Karen's bedroom door closing and she rolled over to turn her back to their adjoining wall. She couldn't make sense of what had just happened. Never before had anyone ever defended Simon Northfell, even when she had been younger, when Simon had left the pack, she could remember the talk drifting around her house. Everyone was glad that he had left. Comments such as 'good riddance' and 'let's hope he stays away' echoed for days after his sudden departure and even years later, whenever his name came up in conversation the reaction would always be the same; hatred, distrust and a fear that he would return.

Karen believing that Simon Northfell should be Alpha was terrifying. And what if she wasn't the only one?

THREE

When the drifting smells of the spoiled brunch began to irritate Nyah she rolled off her bed and went back downstairs.

"What a waste," she muttered, grabbing plates off the table and letting them land with a loud clatter against the granite worktops.

Her anger began to build as she scraped the cold bacon straight into the bin. A mountain of congealed scrambled egg followed and she slammed the empty dish down onto the worktop, scowling at the building pile of wasted food.

When the sound of Karen's feet landing on the bedroom floor above sounded out Nyah gritted her teeth and finished clearing off the rest of the table. She didn't know how she was going to even look at her when she came down.

"Nyah, I'm so sorry. Why didn't you wake me?" Karen groaned sleepily as she came down the stairs.

Nyah remained silent as she dumped the dirty dishes into the sink, repeatedly telling herself that everyone was entitled to their own opinions – even if they were ludicrous.

"Why didn't you wake me?" Karen asked again, briskly rubbing her upper arms as if she were cold.

"I don't need your help; I can clean up by myself."

"I don't mean cleaning up – I mean why didn't you wake me for brunch? Nyah, I'm so sorry – and all the trouble you went to." Karen rounded the counter and came to stand beside her.

"It's fine."

"It's not fine, you're angry with me. I didn't mean to – will you stop!" Karen grabbed the plate of muffins that was about to be tipped into the bin. "Stop throwing out all the food!"

Nyah abruptly lifted her foot away to purposely allow the lid of the bin to slam shut.

"Okay." Karen put the plate of muffins down and held up her hands in surrender. "I am so very, very sorry. I was really looking forward to our brunch – I don't even know why I fell asleep – I'm sorry Nyah. Don't be -." Karen's words ended with a sudden grunt as she pressed the heels of her hands against either side of her head. "Man, I have such a headache."

Nyah drew in an impatient breath and returned to cleaning up. How could Karen behave as if everything she had said didn't count, didn't hurt?

"I hate that you're angry with me," Karen said after a long silence.

"Maybe you shouldn't have announced your undying devotion to Simon, then," Nyah answered, forcefully scrubbing a handful of cutlery.

"What?"

When Nyah turned around to face her, Karen had a genuine look of puzzlement on her face. It made her temper flare again.

"Eh, rewind – my *what* to Simon?" Karen spluttered.

Nyah flung the cutlery back into the sudsy water and fixed the most venomous stare she could manage at Karen. But then something about Karen's demeanour registered with her.

Karen was pale. Her face was coated with a light sheen of moisture, and her hand, as she lifted it to massage the side of her head again, was shaking. "Are you okay?" Nyah asked, suddenly concerned.

"No, I don't think so, actually." Karen leaned back against the counter and closed her eyes. "I really don't feel well. My head is throbbing."

"Did something happen to you on your run?" Nyah asked, quickly peeling off the rubber gloves and coming to stand before Karen. She took hold of her face and gently lowered it as she searched her head for signs of an injury. "Did you fall? Did you get into a fight?" she asked, feeling a little panicky.

"No, I , I don't think so," Karen answered.

"Can't you remember?" Nyah released her head and stepped back to look her over. It was only then she realized that Karen was still wearing her running gear. There was mud on her knees. "Did you not even phase?"

"I. . ." Karen looked down at her tracksuit pants and shrugged. "I can't remember."

"What do you remember?" Nyah said, taking her arm and leading her over to the couch.

"Um. . ." Karen sat down heavily and then leaned her head back, squinting up at the ceiling as she struggled to recall what had happened. "Um, I remember leaving here, and then I remember crossing the street and walking down the side of Billy's house towards the forest. I remember walking into the forest . . .but, then. . .um . . . "

"You don't remember anything else?"

Karen shook her head. "No, it just skips to when I woke up. It's . . ." she paused. "It's weird."

"Are you sure you didn't fall or something?"

"I don't think so," Karen said slowly, still squinting up at the ceiling.

"And you don't remember what you said earlier, about Simon?"

"What did I say about Simon?" she said hesitantly, lowering her head to look directly at Nyah.

Nyah shook her head. "Nothing. Rubbish, you were talking rubbish."

"I feel rubbish," Karen moaned.

Nyah looked down at her. Werewolves rarely became ill and if they did it was never a good thing – her deceased mother was proof of that. "When did your headache start?" Nyah asked. "Before or after your run?"

"Just now, when I woke up," Karen answered pushing herself away from the back of the couch and leaning forward. "You know, I think I'll just go back to bed for a while."

"Are you sure? I could get the doctor for you."

"No, I think I'll be okay. It's probably just the stress of being cooped up for the last few days."

Nyah helped her to stand and followed close behind her as she climbed the stairs.

"Just make sure to wake me before the Show of Hands, okay?" Karen asked as she reached her room.

"Of course, I promise. And if you need anything just shout."

"I will."

Karen closed over her bedroom door and Nyah went back down to the kitchen. A bitter mixture of relief and worry was creeping through her and as soon as she had finished tidying up the last of the brunch she crept back up to Karen's room to check on her again. A light shade of pink had returned to Karen's cheeks when Nyah leaned over to look at her. She was breathing evenly in her sleep too. Perhaps it was just stress, she decided, backing out of the room. Being locked inside for the last couple of days had also meant keeping their wolves bound - not something any Lycan should ever do.

"That's all it was," Nyah muttered to herself as she sat onto the couch. "She'll be fine."

There were still another four hours to go before the Show of Hands and not feeling like she could cope with anything more strenuous Nyah turned on the television, keeping the volume low in case Karen called out for her.

Just before eight o'clock Karen emerged from her room.

"Hey, how are you feeling?" Nyah asked, taking her arm as she came down off the last step of the stairs. She lead her to stand under the overhead light.

"I'm okay, a bit better," Karen answered, wincing under the glare of the light as Nyah peered closely at her. Her porcelain skin still seemed a little too pale for Nyah. "My head still feels a bit cotton-woolly, but not as bad as it was earlier."

"I have to wait for Michael to bring me across to vote, why don't you come with us?" Nyah said.

Karen shook her head. "No, I'll go now; it'll only take a few seconds."

"You sure?"

"Yes, Nurse Nyah," she said, with an attempt at a grin. "I'll be straight back."

Nyah watched from a slit in the curtains as Karen walked across the street. She disappeared into the house and then re-appeared a few minutes later. She was rubbing her temples again when Nyah opened the front door for her.

"You okay?"

"Uh huh." Karen came inside and flopped onto the couch.

"What's the atmosphere like over there?"

"Hmm?" Karen looked up, her drooping hazel eyes looking feverishly glazed. "Over where?"

"In my house – I mean, the pack house. What's it like? Tense?"

Karen stared sleepily towards the window and shrugged. "How would I know?"

"You've just been in there, voting. Are there many there?"

Karen frowned. "I haven't voted yet. I'm going to go now in a second."

"Oh no," Nyah murmured.

Karen began to slouch over to one side as if intending to sleep on the couch. "I'll go in a minute. I just want to rest for a second. I need to work up the energy to peel myself off the couch."

"Why don't you go back up to bed?" Nyah said lightly. "There's plenty of time to vote. I'll call you in a while."

"Would you? That'd be great." Karen stuck out her hand and Nyah heaved her off the couch. "I have to vote, it's important – the future of our pack depends on it," she sighed rubbing the sides of her forehead again as she began to climb the stairs. "Stop hovering," she demanded as Nyah walked right behind her. "I can walk up the stairs on my own, I'm not that bad."

"I don't want you to fall," Nyah pointed out as Karen's hand missed the banister and grabbed at nothing but air.

"I won't," Karen assured her with a slurring smile that suggested she was drunk as opposed to ill. She gestured towards the front door. "Michael's coming, go and answer the door to him and stop fussing over me."

"Fine," Nyah relented, as Michael's knock sounded out. She waited until Karen was off the top step and safely onto the landing before turning and running back down the stairs.

"Ready?" he asked as soon as she opened the door to him.

"Yeah, let's hurry, though," Nyah urged and stepped out onto the porch with him. She quickly told him about Karen as they walked across to the pack house and he agreed that if she was no better in the morning the doctor would need to be called. "It's probably nothing," he assured her. "Everyone's wound up in one way or another, she'll be fine."

"I hope so," Nyah replied, purposely moving closer to him as they approached the front door of the house.

"Simon's been and gone," he said quietly as she stepped inside. "Not without a bit of trouble, though," he added. "Blake and I had to break up a few scuffles."

The regular front room layout for pack meetings had been cleared to allow one large table holding the ballot box to be placed at the top of the room, while another table, equipped with blank squares of paper and a box of pens, was surrounded by a screen that sat in the far corner. Contrary to what the Show of Hands title suggested it had been decades since packs had voted that way.

Nyah quickly slipped behind the screen, grabbed a pen and clearly wrote 'Alan' on a piece of paper. She folded it in half and then came out from behind the screen, crossed the room and placed her vote into the ballot box being watched over by three pack members. They each gave her a respectful nod and Michael put his arm around her shoulder as she turned to leave.

"We're all here for you, Nyah," he said, giving her a gentle one-armed hug. "And no-one wants the memory of Alpha Morgan disrespected. Simon hasn't a hope in hell, don't you worry."

She was back inside her home moments later wishing that she could enjoy seeing the look on Simon's pinched face when the pile of white slips with Alan's name sat beside a space that held nothing with his name. She checked her watch. At nine o'clock, fifty minutes from now, the result would be known. With only thirty-two members in their pack, the counting of the votes would take just minutes, then, as was customary, the pack was going to gather outside the pack house and the name of the next Blackwater Ridge Alpha would be announced. It couldn't come soon enough she decided, perching on the arm of the couch to count down the minutes.

Karen was still sleeping at nine o'clock and Nyah let her be. Gently closing the front door she sat down on the top porch step to wait for Michael. He came across to her just as Alan and Simon appeared from her father's house. Taking her hand he walked with her onto the pack house lawn where they stood at the back of the gathered group, out of Simon's view.

Blake had stepped onto the porch to stand beside Alan. "The tally of votes for the Show of Hands has been completed and verified," he announced.

Nyah inched out from behind Michael's back to peek at where Blake stood. "The tally is as follows: Alan Stenson, twenty-eight votes, Simon Northfell -."

Simon's tally wasn't heard. A massive cheer went up and immediately people ran forward to drag Alan down from the porch steps. He was lifted onto two sets of broad shoulders as whistles and cheers rose into the air.

"Four votes?" a voice close to Nyah said. "Who in the hell voted for Simon?"

Nyah wondered the same, but at that moment she didn't care. She released a long, slow breath and for the first time in three days felt free again. When she stepped out fully from behind Michael's back Alan had been set down and she watched as Simon strode up to him and held out his hand in congratulations. When their handshake ended Simon gave one last lingering look at the pack, flashed a brief agreeable smile and then walked proudly through the parting crowd. Even though he cut an isolated figure as he disappeared into the night alone, Nyah continued to feel nothing for him but complete hatred.

"Alpha Female," Nyah whispered as she hugged Tanya. "How does it feel?"

"A little overwhelming," Tanya admitted. "But I'm so happy for Alan and I'm so proud of him."

"We all are," Nyah grinned as Alan, Michael and Blake approached. When Alan opened his arms wide towards her Nyah gladly stepped into his embrace. "Congratulation, Alpha Stenson," she smiled up at him once they broke apart.

"Thanks, Nyah," he said, giving her shoulders a gentle squeeze.

"You too, Grizzly Brothers," she said to Michael and Blake, using the nick-name that had followed them from childhood. With their equal bear-like height, build and identical curly brown hair, it was hard to believe that Alan's next in command weren't brothers.

"Maybe things can get back to normal around here now," Blake said, jerking his head to where Simon had faded into the night. "That's his plan scuppered."

"Thankfully," Tanya murmured, an involuntary shiver shaking her small frame. Alan put his arm protectively around her shoulder and drew her in closer to him. He pressed a lingering kiss to the top of her head before turning to Michael. "Michael Vincent, your first act as Beta is to escort my mate home," he declared.

"It would be my pleasure," Michael smiled, holding out his arm to Tanya.

Before she could move away Alan kissed his fingertips and pressed them to Tanya's swollen middle. "Goodnight, my little pup," he said softly. "Don't keep your Mama awake with your kicking tonight."

As they watched Michael lead Tanya away Nyah turned to Alan. "You know, I think I'll sleep better tonight than I have in a long while."

Alan nodded, releasing a breath that suggested he was enjoying the growing relief of his being elected too. "Four votes," he said quietly. "I was prepared for one, 'cos obviously, Simon was going to vote for himself - but four?"

Nyah glanced at the pack members still gathered on the lawn. Faces were lit with happiness, voices were full of optimism, relief was emanating like heat from the sun. There wasn't the faintest sense of disappointment. "I don't know," she said with a shrug. "But it doesn't matter; come Thursday night you'll be Alpha and that's all that matters."

With a final quick hug she said goodnight and left Alan as he was drawn back into another round of congratulations.

People continued to linger outside the pack house, glad of the freedom to be outside again. Chatter and laughter had replaced the eerie silence that had hung in Blackwater Ridge for the last few days and Nyah savoured the excited atmosphere, feeling a sudden wave of lightness rush through her. The sense of stasis that the Lamentation Phase had pressed upon them was finally lifting and the sense of liberation was exhilarating.

So it came as a surprise to her, as she crossed the street towards her house, to hear the angry whispers of an argument coming from a couple standing farther down the street.

In the pool of light cast by a street lamp she recognised the curly, wild hair of Leanne Stone who was jabbing her finger into the chest of her mate, Eddie, who stood with his hands pressed against the side of his head.

"You'll be thrown out of the pack if they hear you!" she hissed. "Shut up!"

Nyah ducked her head, not wanting to intrude on their privacy, but even as she turned into her driveway the voices continued to reach her ears.

"No." Eddie flatly answered Leanne. "I won't shut up."

"Yes you will!" she replied, "Say one more word about him and you'll have more than a blinding headache to worry about!"

"He wants what's best for this pack," Eddie said calmly, "and his bloodline is strong."

Nyah's feet came to an involuntary stop and she spun towards the direction of Eddie's strangely monotone voice.

"Our pack could grow to be the largest and most powerful pack this continent has ever known," he said, echoing Karen's exact words from earlier. "Our potential is incredible."

FOUR

Nyah tilted her head towards the night sky. They couldn't have wished for a more perfect night. The depthless, inky black sky was smattered with winking stars and not a single cloud dimmed the brilliant light of the full moon.

Closing her eyes, she welcomed the change into her body. Heat coursed through her, followed by a sharp flash of pain as her muscles and bones twisted into shape. Seconds later she was on all fours, shaking out her thick black coat.

The ground was warm under her paws as she padded deeper into the forest. Ferns brushed against her fur and she breathed in the familiar scents of her pack as they moved through the forest alongside her. When she emerged into the bright, moon-lit clearing Alan stood proudly on the jagged chunk of rock that sat alone in the centre of the mossy ground.

He was a massive wolf, his ashy blonde fur glistening in the silver light as he silently watched his pack gather at the foot of the rock.

When the entire pack was before him he allowed a long moment of silence to pass before he lowered his head towards them and let loose a snarling, vicious bark.

Immediately, the pack cowered low to the ground, symbolizing their acceptance of his supremacy and command. His snarls cut into the still air surrounding them, the pack continuing to remain pressed low against the ground, their eyes averted. The ferocious sounds came to a stop and then he threw back his head to release a long, soulful howl.

The pack responded in like. Doleful howls soared towards the moon as each wolf arched its neck to cry out acceptance of the new Alpha.

Nyah felt the power of his domination rush through her as she howled her subservience, and within moments, the Alpha mind-link had been established.

"Do you vow to serve me?" Alan's voice rang out in her mind.

"Yes!" she and her pack responded, "we serve you, Alpha Stenson!"

FIVE

"What do you think?" Tanya performed a slow, measured turn to show off her dress. "Do I look enormous?"

"You look beautiful, not enormous," Nyah corrected from where she sat on the edge of Tanya's bed. "The dress is perfect."

Tanya sank onto the chair of her dressing table and gave her baby bump an affectionate rub. "He's some kicker," she sighed. "Hey, I'm excited about tonight, are you?"

"Yes, I am," Nyah answered. "The last time we had a Pack Welcoming night I had just turned seven."

"That long ago?"

"Yep. And the Carverbacks and Greycoats were only half the size they are now."

"Alan mentioned that earlier," Tanya said, tweaking disobedient strands of her hair. "He said there's over one hundred in each of the packs at the moment."

"That's a lot of wolves," Nyah said.

"You mean - a lot of chances," Tanya told her.

Nyah frowned at the reflection of Tanya's pointed expression in the mirror of her dressing table.

"What do you mean?"

"A lot of wolves means a lot of chances for you to find your mate."

Nyah groaned at Tanya's wiggling eyebrows and flopped backwards onto the bed. 'Let's find a mate for Nyah' was Tanya's pet project and no matter how big or small the event Tanya was always brimming with hope that it would provide the 'magic moment'.

"You'll be twenty in a few months; it's high time you found your mate," Tanya declared in her all too familiar lecturing voice.

"Mm hmm."

"Don't mm hmm me. You know I'm right."

"And you know I hate talking about this."

"Well, it's going to happen sooner or later and pretending that it won't isn't going to change the fact," Tanya warned.

"But it's such a big deal," Nyah said, propping herself up on her elbows, "and I don't know if I'm ready."

"You'll never be ready," Tanya said wisely, turning away from the mirror to face her again. "Trust me; nothing will ever prepare you for the moment you find your mate."

"Especially if it's in the frozen aisle of the supermarket?" Nyah grinned, knowing that if she distracted Tanya enough she wouldn't have to listen to another lecture about how super fabulously wonderful her life would become once she found her mate.

Tanya's face melted into a dreamy smile. "I still get chills when I walk down that aisle, you know. I'll never forget that day."

"Tell me about it again," Nyah asked, "I love hearing about how you and Alan met."

"It was eleven fifteen on a Wednesday morning," she began immediately, not needing any persuasion to tell her story, "and I was in the fruit and veg aisle trying to decide if I wanted two melons for the price of one or six grapefruit for the price of four."

The opening lines of Tanya's account were so well known to Nyah that she could have said the words for her. *'All of sudden,'* she narrated silently, the story committed to her memory.

"All of a sudden," Tanya continued, "I got the most delicious, toe-curling, stomach-knotting scent, but when I looked up there was no-one in the aisle with me. So – I dropped the fruit back onto the display, grabbed my trolley, stuck my nose in the air and began to follow the trail. I walked up the cereal aisle, down the biscuit aisle, up one chilled aisle and then down another before I rounded the corner of the frozen aisle where I clapped eyes on the most beautiful wolf ever made." Tanya sighed dramatically and Nyah rolled her eyes. "The moon Goddess was in a good mood on the day she created my Alan," she breathed. "He stood in that aisle, shaggy blonde hair hanging over his eyes, a tight white t-shirt clinging to his body and a pair of jeans moulded to his perfect, perfect ass."

"I wonder what our new Alpha would say if he knew his wife was talking about his behind in such a way," Nyah laughed.

Tanya dismissed Alan's probable horror with a quick wave and carried on. "I thought I was in heaven – until of course he got my scent and looked up at me. I tell you, Nyah, it's the most powerful thing in the world. Even more powerful than the moment you lay eyes on your new-born baby. It's so incredible. In that one second, when our eyes met, I felt as if an invisible rope had suddenly been tied around the two of us and it was tugging hard, trying to draw us together. When you find your mate you never feel fully content unless you're right beside him, physically touching him in some way. When Alan isn't close to me I feel distracted, on edge. It feels like everything's off kilter until he's beside me again."

"That there is why I'm so nervous," Nyah confessed sitting up straight again. "I don't know if I'm ready for those all-consuming emotions. I mean, I'd like to meet my mate, but I don't want it changing who I am or what I want to do with my life. Sometimes I worry that finding my mate will morph me into a completely different person."

"No, no it won't," Tanya assured her. "The emotions are all-consuming, but in a good way, a positive way. And it doesn't change who you are, really." She smiled at Nyah again. "You'll find out for yourself soon," she promised. "Although he'll have to fight his way through all the admirers that'll be gathered around you tonight," she said seriously, pointing towards her dress. "You look stunning."

Nyah slid off the bed and stood up. "Thanks, it's been so long since I've had the chance to wear something as nice as this." She smoothed down the front of her skirt. The dark green silk clung to her figure and when she looked back up, catching a glimpse of her reflection in the mirror, she barely recognized herself; her usual attire was jeans, t-shirts, hoodies and trainers.

Tanya stood up too. Her loose, flowing dress reached to the ground, the sand-coloured fabric a perfect contrast to her deeply tanned skin and thick glossy chestnut hair. "I'm a bit nervous about meeting Alpha Black's wife," she admitted in a whisper. "I hear she can be a bit aloof."

"Yeah, I've heard that too," Nyah said, "but if you get stuck with her just fiddle with your necklace and I'll come and rescue you."

"Deal," Tanya smiled, "and you do the same with your bracelet if you get landed with an over-zealous pup and I'll come and rescue you."

When Nyah stepped out onto the porch of the pack house it was as if she had somehow been transported to another territory. Blackwater Ridge had been transformed for the night. Paper lanterns were strung from the trees, mismatched sets of tables and chairs were set out on the lawns and in the middle of the street, the wide rectangular area marked out with a jumble of tall potted plants, there was a dance floor – complete with flashing lights and a mirror-ball dangling from the overhead street light.

"Courtesy of Blake," Tanya revealed as Nyah stared open-mouthed at the sparkling globe. "Apparently, he 'just happened to have it stashed in his garage'."

"Good – they've the barbeques fired up," Alan said appearing behind them, just as the first mouth-watering smells of barbequing meat drifted around them.

"Settle down," Tanya whispered, gently rubbing her hand over her stomach. "I swear this pup can smell meat," she said.

"Well he wouldn't be mine if he couldn't," Alan laughed, sliding his arms around her. He kissed her cheek, but then lifted his head suddenly, turning towards the east of their territory. "The Greycoats are here," he said, "and the Carverbacks too," he added a second later when Blake announced their arrival by mind-link. "I'll go and meet them." He gave Tanya another kiss, whispered something in her ear that made her blush and then jogged off.

"You ready?" Tanya winked at Nyah.

"As I'll ever be," Nyah said.

"Oh, my poor, poor feet," Karen moaned, flopping onto the bench beside Nyah long after midnight had come and gone.

Nyah held up her shoeless feet and wiggled her bare toes. "Put them on the cool grass and feel the relief," she smiled. "I think I've danced holes in the bottom of mine."

Karen's eyes fluttered with pleasure as her throbbing soles absorbed the chill. "Perfect," she sighed.

"This is turning out to be some night," Nyah said. "The atmosphere is electric."

"Did you hear that three of ours have met their mates?"

"Three? It was two less than an hour ago."

"Now it's three," Karen sang. "Love is in the air."

"I should say so," Nyah agreed. Although Karen would never experience a mate connection again, she and a very handsome member of the Carverback pack had been dancing together all night, and as Karen continued to enjoy the relief from the cooling grass, Nyah saw her Carverback admirer hovering patiently at the edge of the dance floor, polite enough not to disturb Karen while she sat with her friend, but eager enough not to take his eyes off her.

"Mr Tall and Handsome is waiting for you," Nyah whispered.

Karen blushed and ducked her head. "Isn't he though?" she said just as quietly, hoping the loud music would drown out their voices. "He's got the brownest eyes I've ever seen. I've been dancing with him all evening."

"I noticed. I think he's got a great big crush on you."

Karen's blush turned a deeper crimson.

"What?" Nyah laughed. "Don't be embarrassed!"

"I can't help it." Karen pressed her cool fingers against her hot cheeks. "I never thought I'd feel attracted to anyone again after Peter died. I feel kind of guilty . . . and yet, I really want to see Tom again after tonight," she admitted. "Is that bad of me?"

"No, of course not," Nyah answered. "You deserve to find someone. Peter would have wanted you to be happy."

"Tom lost his mate too," Karen revealed in a low voice. "So we're both kind of in the same situation."

"And maybe he wants to see you again too," Nyah said.

Karen chewed on her bottom lip. "I wonder?"

"Well, judging by the way he can't take his eyes off you right now I think that would be a yes," Nyah said, subtly nodding in Tom's direction.

"What about you?" Karen asked, taking a sweeping look around the crowded street. "Anyone for you here?"

Nyah shook her head and Karen's shoulders sagged with disappointment. "Aw, that's a pity."

"It's fine, I'll meet Mr Wonderfully Fabulous when the time is right," she comforted her, "and I'm having a really good time tonight so I'm not bothered about it one bit."

Karen stared determinedly into the crush of people on the dance-floor as if hoping to spot the mate that Nyah had somehow missed.

"Okay, that's it," Nyah laughed, pulling her attention back. "Tanya is bad enough, I don't need you joining forces with her, and anyway, you really need to go back over there – Tom's in a knot waiting for you."

Karen did her best to hold back the huge smile that lit her face as she slipped her feet back into her shoes. Giving Nyah's hand a quick squeeze she skipped off, Tom immediately dropping his pretence of casual lingering to meet her halfway across the lawn.

With her attention focused on Tom's adoring looks towards Karen, Nyah missed the approach of a figure from behind the bench. By the time she had become aware of his presence, Simon had already taken a seat beside her.

"May I say that you look absolutely beautiful tonight," he smarmed.

"Thank you." Nyah made to stand up, but his hand was quick to whip out and take hold of her arm.

"Please, for a moment, grace me with a little conversation."

Gritting her teeth, she stilled. If he wanted conversation he could do the talking, she had nothing to say to him.

"Are you enjoying your evening?"

As tempting as it was to say 'up until now, yes', Nyah gave him a simple 'yes' instead.

"I admire Alpha Stenson's hospitality. Expanding our pack is something we must consider."

Nyah continued to stare ahead, hoping that someone would see who had cornered her.

"I take it by your unaccompanied presence on this bench that you did not meet your mate tonight?" Simon queried.

"No, not tonight," she replied, seeing Michael's curly hair amongst the dancers.

"All in good time," he said, sounding annoyingly patronizing.

Michael had the attention of some females from the Carverbacks and was not likely to lift his gaze off them anytime soon. Nyah began searching for Karen instead.

"And for the sake of our pack I hope that your mate will be deserving of your bloodline," Simon continued.

Nyah involuntarily whipped her head around to face him. "What do you mean by that?"

"Your bloodline is a pure and powerful force," he replied, as if it was the most obvious thing in the world. "To join it with anything less would be a crime."

"Whoever I join with," she answered, "will be none of your business."

"Perhaps not, but I hope that Alpha Stenson makes it his."

Nyah leaned away from him in disgust. "It's nobody's business. No-one gets to pick and choose my mate."

"Despite what a poor matching would mean for our pack?"

When her mouth failed to work Simon was quick to carry on. "You should consider your future with a little less selfishness, Nyah. Do you not think that you owe it to your pack to find a mate who can equal the strength of your bloodline? Should you really allow chance to select your mate and risk diluting the power of your heritage?"

"Arranged bondings are a crime," she snapped at him. "Forcing non-mated wolves into a union is forbidden."

Simon held up his hands. "I am merely giving my opinion on your duty to produce pups of -."

"Keep your opinions to yourself," Nyah hissed, jumping up. "My mating is none of your business."

"It should be somebody's business," he said calmly, rising to his feet also. "Your father -."

"Don't you dare speak of my father!" she spat. "And don't even try to suggest that he would have wanted an arranged bonding!"

"He would have wanted what is best for this pack."

"Which is something you have no concept of!" With rage scalding her veins Nyah knew it would be best to leave before she said something she'd truly regret, but when she began to turn away from him he quickly grabbed her arms and held her in place.

"Don't disrespect me, Nyah," he warned menacingly, his beady black eyes narrowing as he pushed his face closer to her. "I have -."

Two large hands suddenly ripped Simon's bony hands off her. Being released so abruptly made her stagger backwards, but instead of falling onto her ass she crashed against a hard wall of muscle. "I've got you," Blake's voice reassured.

Michael gave Simon a hefty shove. "Leave Nyah alone," he warned, but before she could hear Simon's reply Blake was already wheeling her around and hauling her away. "Let's go, come on."

Michael and Simon's growls were quick to fade as Blake hustled her through the crowds. "Damned idiot," Blake muttered.

"Why is he even still here? Why hasn't he been kicked out?" she griped, allowing Blake to steer her amongst the visitors.

"Because technically, he hasn't done anything wrong," Blake answered. "He hasn't hurt or threatened anyone."

"Isn't it enough that he pisses everyone off?" Nyah snapped.

Blake gave a deep chesty laugh. "I wish it was," he chuckled.

Once they were on the far side of the dance floor and well out of Simon's sight, Blake released Nyah's hand. "I think I'll stay with you for the rest of the night," he decided. "Simon isn't one to take no for an answer – what did he want anyway?"

Nyah allowed a shiver of repulsion to roll through her. "He's decided to take an interest in who I mate with," she answered. "I think if he had his own way he'd be handpicking mates for me based on the strength of their bloodline."

"That's none of his damn business!" Blake said, an appalled expression twisting his face. "He actually said that?"

"Oh, he's all on for arranged bondings. I mustn't dilute my heritage, you know."

"That's disgusting."

Nyah shivered again. "He's disgusting."

"Alan will be furious – Simon has absolutely no business talking to you like that."

"Let's just leave it for now," Nyah said taking his hand again. "Come and dance with me for a while."

Blake was still frowning as they squeezed onto the dance floor, but when his favourite song blasted out from the speakers he perked up and shouted over the heads of the bouncing crowd to Michael, who, judging by his thumbs up and massive grin, liked the track too. Michael made his way over to where they danced, his adoring fans following him, and realising that there were far more pleasant things to be thinking about she shunted her encounter with Simon aside. Alan would deal with it, she told herself, and with any luck it would involve him handing Simon an empty suitcase and detailed directions to somewhere very, very, far away.

Six

At first, Nyah had thought that the appalling scream had been part of her dream, but when it shrilled out again she woke abruptly, jerking upright in her bed with the sheets clutched to her chest. "Karen?"

A thud from the room next door sounded out before Karen burst through the door, her scared eyes wide open. "Did you hear that?" she whispered, "did you hear a -?"

The scream rose again, a wailing cry this time, the sense of loss and pain in its timbre clear to comprehend. Nyah jumped out of bed, grabbed a sweater and followed Karen downstairs. When they flung open the front door and ran out onto the porch, Billy and Leo were running by, heading directly towards Alpha Stenson's house.

"What's wrong? What's happening?" Nyah called out.

Before either of the men could answer another wail rose and Karen involuntarily grabbed Nyah's arm. "That's Tanya," she gasped.

Tearing across the street they ran through the open front door of the pack house.

Tanya was on her knees on the kitchen floor, tears streaming down her face, her eyes wide and desperate as she rocked agitatedly back and forth. Leanne was there too, trying to soothe Tanya, her hands fluttering about aimlessly as nothing she said or did appeased Tanya in any way. Nyah skidded to a stop, dropped to her knees and grabbed Tanya's shoulders. "What is it? What's happened?"

"He's dead!" Tanya screamed. "He's dead!"

"Who's dead?" Nyah looked down towards Tanya's stomach. "The – the baby?"

"No!" she wailed back. "Alan! Alan's dead!"

Nyah tried to say 'what?' but all that came out was a choking breath.

"Alan?" Karen whispered. "Alpha Stenson is dead?"

Tanya cried out again and then doubled over, collapsing onto Nyah's lap.

"No," Nyah said, shaking her head. "No, it can't be true, it's not true."

"He's gone," Tanya sobbed, her voice lost in her huddle. "I can feel it, he's gone. I've lost him."

"No," Nyah said, staring at Leanne and then turning to the others now gathered in the kitchen. "No, she's wrong. Tell me she's wrong. Where's Alan? Where are Michael and Blake?"

"Eddie's gone looking for them," Leanne replied. "We don't know where they are, but – he's, he's looking."

"Michael and Blake left with Alpha Stenson about fifteen minutes ago," Billy cut in. "I was coming back from a run and I saw them leave here and heading towards the forest."

"Who else was with them?" Nyah asked.

"They were alone."

"Has someone gone after them?"

"I, no, I -."

"What about Rob? Where's he?" Karen asked. Rob was the packs Delta and if not already somewhere in the forest, the only one who would be able to mind-link with Alan. No-one in the kitchen knew where he was, and as Nyah looked from one startled face to another she began to feel sick.

"Has someone contacted the patrol?" she asked swallowing back a wave of nausea.

Again, the strained faces shared a despairing look.

"For the Goddesses' sake, someone do something!" she shouted, feeling queasiness, panic and anger swirling into a burning ball inside her stomach. "Someone needs to go out there and find out what the hell is going on!" she yelled.

"I found Rob!" Eddie's voice suddenly hollered from the hallway. "Rob's here!"

"Take Tanya upstairs, "Nyah ordered Leanne and Karen as Rob and Eddie rushed into the kitchen. "And somebody get the doctor for her – now."

As soon as Tanya was helped to her feet Nyah stood up, her own legs feeling rubbery and in need of support. "What's happening?" she asked Rob.

"I can't link with Alpha Stenson," he said desperately. "I lost the connection a few minutes ago. They were close to the north border when I last heard from him, but they were running, so I don't know where they are now."

"Why were they running? What happened?"

"Alpha Stenson said there were rogues circling our boundary line."

The small group gave a combined start.

"Rogues?" Eddie said.

Rob nodded. "It happened so quickly. Alpha Stenson linked with me about five minutes ago to say that rogues had been spotted. He, Michael and Blake were running to meet up with the patrol and he was ordering me to gather more men and send all the women and children to the pack house. The last thing he said was that they were nearing the north border, then it just, he just. . ."

Tanya let out another strangled cry and Karen urged Leanne to move her faster towards the stairs.

"We need to find them." Nyah pushed past Rob and ran back out onto the porch. More of the pack had been woken; lights were blinking on and doors were being opened along the dark street. Figures were beginning to emerge from their houses and Nyah called out to them. "We need everyone's help!" she cried, running down the porch steps and onto the grass. "We need to find Alpha Stenson, our Beta, and our Gamma. The mind-link has been broken and there are rogues on our land!"

"Bring all the women and children here!" Rob added jumping over the porch railing and landing with a thud beside her. "Hurry!"

Rob took Nyah's arm and turned her towards him. "Nyah, I think Alpha Stenson is dead," he said hoarsely. "The link severed so abruptly, I've never felt anything like it."

Before the enormity of what Rob was saying could have a chance to sink in Nyah found herself hurrying alarmed women and children inside the house while Rob organized the men on the lawn.

"Four groups," he shouted, quickly dividing up the men. "North," he ordered the first group, "south," he said to the next, "east," he continued, hustling another man sideways.

"Rob." Nyah grabbed his arm. "Rob, look."

Rob stopped, looking first towards Nyah, but then turning to follow where her pale face was aimed towards the dark street to their left.

A silhouette, bulky and deformed, was emerging from the shadows of the forest. For a short moment the group held silent and still, unsure of what they were seeing, but then the hulking shape reached the circle of illuminating streetlight and Nyah felt her insides knot.

It was Blake and Michael shuffling towards them, their movements heavy, laboured, weighted.

"No," Nyah choked when she saw what their burden was. Alan lay limp in their arms, his head slumped against Michael's bloody chest, one arm swinging lifelessly towards the ground.

The pack broke, swarming forwards to surround the three men, but Nyah found she couldn't follow. Her body froze in place, her eyes the only part of her that would move as she looked between the desolate faces of Michael and Blake.

"No," she said again, refusing to believe what she was seeing.

"Is that. . .?" another voice said beside her. It was Karen. "Oh, no . . ." she whispered.

Nyah could only recall blurred, confusing moments of what had unfolded around her that night; Tanya's hysteria, Alan's son, Jack, crying for his daddy, Michael and Blake, angry and vicious one minute and then guilt-ridden and pitiful the next. She remembered vengeful groups of wolves tearing into the forest to look for the rogues only to return unsatisfied. And smothering it all, pressing down upon her all night, the flash of triumph on Simon Northfell's face when he had wandered into the pack house and briefly rested his approving gaze on Alan's lifeless body.

Night dissolved into a dawn that dragged a dull, grey day behind it before exhaustion drove Nyah to bed. She and Karen took a spare room in the pack house where, although Tanya was sedated, they were unwilling to leave her.

It was late afternoon when Nyah woke from an agitated sleep. Blackwater Ridge was obscured by a misting rain that clung to every surface, echoing the despair that saturated her entirely. It wasn't possible that Alan was gone. She couldn't accept that she would never see him again. Alan had been a constant in her life and trying to fathom how her life could carry on without him was impossible.

Tanya's bedroom door was ajar when she came out onto the landing and Karen called out softly to her, asking her to come in.

When she eased open the door Karen was sitting on the side of Tanya's bed, one hand slowly stroking Tanya's tousled hair.

"How is she?" Nyah whispered.

Karen wearily shook her head.

Tanya lay on her side facing Nyah, but her eyes just stared blankly into space, blinking with a drugged weightiness every few moments.

"She had to be sedated again?" Nyah asked, coming over to kneel at the side of the bed to take Tanya's clammy, limp hand.

Again, Karen shook her head, and when Nyah saw how Karen's empathetic gaze rested on Tanya she felt her heart crumpling inside her chest. Only Karen could understand the level of pain that Tanya was suffering.

"This is the easy part," Karen whispered, "right now a part of her is still fighting to believe that Alan isn't dead. She's still got a tiny bit of hope that it was all just a big mistake and she's clinging onto that with everything she's got."

Nyah took in Tanya's eerie calmness and then looked back up at Karen.

"Once she accepts he's gone, she'll . . . then it will . . ." Karen pressed her lips together and squeezed her glistening eyes shut. She drew in a jagged breath and then blew it out slowly, quietly clearing her throat before she spoke again. "Tanya's sister Keera will be here this evening. She's going to bring Tanya and Jack to Colorado once Alan is buried."

Nyah nodded, the hard ball of sorrow in her throat restricting her breathing.

"How are you doing?" Karen asked after a moment.

"Feeling kind of numb," Nyah answered truthfully. "It's like I'm dreaming – it's all so surreal."

"I know," Karen agreed. "I keep thinking that I'm going to wake up any second – at least, I wish I could wake up any second." She tugged the sheet further up onto Tanya's shoulder and returned to stroking her hair.

"Have you eaten yet today?" Nyah asked.

Karen grimaced. "I'm not hungry."

"Can I get you some coffee?"

"Sure, okay."

Blake arrived as Nyah came down the stairs. He looked up at her, the watery smile he tried to give lasting for only a few short seconds. They shared a long hug before Nyah broke away from him, wincing at the bruises on his cheek.

"How are you?" he asked.

"Okay," she answered, "you?"

Blake shrugged and pulled her into his arms again, pressing a kiss firmly onto the top of her head. "Not good," he admitted, squeezing her tight. "Every time I shut my eyes I can see the rogues attacking Alan. I can't get it to stop."

Nyah returned the pressure of his hug.

"Is Karen still here?" he asked after a moment.

"Yeah, she's upstairs with Tanya." Nyah stepped back when Blake loosened his hold and he cleared his throat in an attempt to strengthen his voice.

"There's a pack meeting at seven tonight. Will you let her know?"

"Sure."

"It's at Michael's house – he doesn't want to disturb Tanya."

"Okay."

Blake looked completely lost as he stared aimlessly around the hallway. "Okay, well, I'll see you later. I need to go and let everyone know about the meeting."

Nyah followed him to the door, watching as he crossed the lawn and moved onto the next house. His steps were laboured and his shoulders rounded heavily towards his chest as he tread across the grass. "Please wake up," she begged herself, closing over the front door. This was all a dream. It had to be, because it wasn't possible that her real life could shift so violently and fling her into such a bleak and wretched place.

The rain had stopped by the time Nyah and Karen left for the pack meeting, but the dampness clung to everything. Even though it only took a few minutes to walk to Michael's house Nyah felt as if her bones had managed to soak up buckets of the clammy moisture. She shivered hard as they took their seats in the small room that had been cleared for the meeting, Simon's presence in the seat directly behind her causing the tremor to linger.

"This will be a short meeting," Michael announced. He looked as bad as Blake, if not worse. His left eye was swollen under a huge purple and black bruise and a thick wad of bandages were taped to his neck. Nyah looked away, flashes of bared fangs and bloody claws flickering through her overwrought mind.

"Firstly, I want to confirm that there have been no more sightings of the rogues," Michael said. "I've spoken to the Greycoat and Carverback packs and they haven't seen or heard anything of them either. The patrols are being doubled for the next week and I want everyone indoors before sundown until further notice. No-one is to run in the forest alone, please run in packs of three or more and make sure that plenty of people know where you are going and what time you expect to be back."

There were a few murmurs of agreement in the room, but Nyah doubted anyone was going to want to run in the forest for the next while.

"Alpha Stenson's burial will take place tomorrow evening at four o'clock."

Michael's announcement brought a painful silence upon the room. "With the patrols doubled at the moment I need some volunteers to help with preparing his grave."

Immediately, every person who was not involved in patrolling raised their hand.

"Thank you," Michael said softly. He gestured towards the four men seated near the front. "Come to me afterwards and I'll let you know what I need."

"Finally," he said wearily, "we need to hold another Show of Hands. Alpha Stenson had not fully completed his Bidding Documents, but he had written that on his death he did not wish for the Lamentation Phase to be honoured. Therefore, a new Alpha must be sworn in before midnight tonight. To ensure the border remains protected we will hold the Show of Hands in two phases, the first . . ." Michael trailed off as he registered Simon Northfell getting to his feet.

"A Show of Hands is not necessary in our particular situation," Simon stated. "Lycan laws declare that if a newly sworn Alpha who was challenged for leadership dies within his first moon-cycle the pack member who received the second highest number of votes is entitled to his place."

An appalling silence swelled through the room as gratification twisted Simon's mouth into a deadly smile. "Which means the Alpha position is rightfully mine."

"Over my dead body," Michael snarled.

Karen grabbed Nyah's hand as the room erupted around them.

SEVEN

"This can't be happening."

Nyah was pacing the length of Michael's kitchen. He and Blake hovered agitatedly near the door, the steady rise and fall of murmured confusion travelled in from the meeting room where the pack waited for their Beta to contest or support Simon's leadership.

"There must be something we can do!" She threw another desperate glance at both their faces as she stalked by them again, her knotted fists jammed deep into the pockets of her hoodie.

"We're bound, Nyah. Lycan Laws are clear on the matter. Simon has the right to become Alpha."

"But - but he can't!"

"Nyah - ." Michael dragged his two hands down his face and sighed heavily. "You don't seriously expect me to stand in front of our pack and repeat what you just told me? No-one is going to believe a word of what you're saying – you said so yourself – it sounds ridiculous."

"I know it does," she snapped, coming to an abrupt stop in front of him, "but, Michael, something strange *is* going on. How else can you explain Karen and Eddie's behaviour? Karen doesn't even remember that day now; it's like the whole twenty four have been erased from her mind, and I bet if you were to ask Eddie he'd say the same. And what about last night? I saw the way Simon looked; he was the only person that wasn't shocked about Alan's death. I'd swear it was like he'd been expecting it."

"So you want me to stand before the pack and accuse Simon of having something to do with Alan's death, even though I have no proof? You want me to say that he did something to Karen and Eddie that gave them both headaches and made them say the same things?" Michael grabbed hold of her shoulders as she opened her mouth to answer. "I know you dislike him, hell, most of us do, but, Nyah, you're beginning to sound like a crazy person."

Nyah roughly shook off his hands and stepped back. "I'm not crazy. I'm not. Simon Northfell is up to something and allowing him to become Alpha of this pack is the worst thing that can happen!"

"It's not a case of whether we *allow* him or not!" Michael barked, wheeling away from her to grab a cloth-bound book sitting on the work-top. Snatching it up he thrust it towards her, jabbing a finger against the cover. "Section eighteen, paragraph three. It's there in black and white. Simon has the *right* to be Alpha. In fact, he already is. The second Alan's heart stopped beating the title fell to him. There's nothing we can do. All your speculating and suspicion is nothing without hard proof that he's threatened or killed a member of the pack!"

Michael slammed the weighty book back onto the counter. "Simon Northfell is Alpha," he said hoarsely. "We may not like it, but that's just the way it is. So I'm going to go back into the meeting, and as Beta of this pack, I'm going to be the first to submit to him."

Michael pushed past her and strode out of the kitchen, allowing the door to slam loudly behind him. Nyah turned her watering eyes onto Blake.

"I can't disagree with him," he answered her with a weary shrug. "There's no proof, Nyah. We can't contest Simon because of a gut feeling." Forcing himself away from the support of the counter he crossed to where Michael had flung down the ancient book. He slowly curled his hand into a fist and rested it gently on the cover. "Michael's right. There's nothing we can do to change any of this. We are bound."

When Blake left her alone Nyah wanted to snatch up the book and rip it into shreds. Instead she allowed a few tears of frustration to roll down her cheeks before roughly brushing her face dry and steeling herself in preparation for what she was about to do.

Karen was huddled in the corner of the hallway when she emerged from the kitchen. "Michael submitted to Simon," she said quietly. "He wants us all to follow."

Nyah looked towards the front door. Those that had already obeyed Michael were slinking towards it, their shoulders hunched and their heads bowed as they left. "Don't submit," Nyah whispered.

"What?"

"Don't submit. Refuse to serve him."

"Are you out of your mind?" Karen hissed. "If I don't submit I have to leave the pack. I don't want to be a rogue."

"Go to Tom," Nyah said suddenly. "He'll speak to his pack on your behalf – they'll accept you."

"And what do I say? I turned my back against my new Alpha because he doesn't give me the warm and fuzzies? I'd be torn to shreds."

"So you *want* to serve Simon?"

"No!" Karen pushed Nyah away from her. "How can you even say that?" she asked. "Of course I don't want to serve him, but what choice do I have?" she asked desperately.

Nyah couldn't answer her. Karen had no other choice. None of them did.

Karen stalked away, throwing her one last look of frustrated desperation before she joined the reluctant members trailing into the meeting room. Nyah remained in the hall, one hand tightly gripping a railing of the staircase as pack members began to leave the house, their heads ducked low, their eyes not lifting from their feet. She could feel Simon waiting for her, and the growing satisfaction that rolled from him with every minute that slid by made her stomach churn.

When Karen crept out from the room Nyah called softly to her, but she refused to answer, she didn't even turn to look at her before she hurried out the front door.

"Ah, Miss Morgan," Simon crooned when he saw her hovering hesitantly in the doorway. "Saving the best for last, are we?" She was the last. With the exception of Michael and Blake the room was empty. "This isn't right," she said through a thick throat.

"Lycan laws are quite clear on the matter," Simon replied patiently. "Should the new Alpha pass before -."

"You received four votes," she ground out.

"Exactly," Simon smiled. "And it was four more than . . . wait - who was it again? Oh, yes. No-one." He raised a single eyebrow, daring her to continue arguing with him. Instead she looked to where Michael stood behind his new Alpha. He gave her a warning shake of his head. Blake simply stared at his feet.

"Leave us," Simon commanded the two men and they immediately obeyed, snapping the door shut firmly behind them as they left the room.

Nyah felt suffocating heat and clammy coldness colliding in her body. This could not be happening. Simon Northfell could not be Alpha.

"Miss Morgan?" his enquired silkily, indicating the empty space in front of him as he crooked his finger to invite her forward.

"Why are you doing this here?" she asked suddenly, trying to stall the inevitable. "Why aren't we gathering at the moon rock in the traditional way?"

"You would rather I threaten the safety of this pack by bringing them into the rogue-infested woods?" he answered with faux horror. "I thought you cared more for your pack."

"I do, which is why I don't agree to you taking leadership."

"You seem to forget that you are no longer in a position where your opinion is of any value, Nyah. And let me tell you; dragging my Beta and Delta into the kitchen in an attempt to have them revolt against what is rightfully mine was your final act as the daughter of a very dead and buried Alpha. From now on no-one is going to listen to your opinions."

"I don't need to warn them anymore. They'll soon see I was right when they realise what a pig you are," she spat.

"Don't hold your breath," Simon replied moving towards her when it was clear she wasn't going to approach him. "I can keep this pretence running for as long as it takes."

"As long as it takes for what?"

Simon came to a stop directly in front of her, but Nyah fought the urge to move back. Instead, she lifted her chin defiantly and kept an unwavering stare pinned to him. His narrowed eyes ambled leisurely over her face before sauntering down her body. "That is not your concern right now," he said, an amused laugh erupting from his sneering mouth when he brought his gaze back to her scowling face. "All I need from you at this moment is your vow."

"No." She shook her head and stepped back. "I will not vow to serve you."

"Because I'm not perched on the moon rock like your daddy and Alan were? Regardless of which form you take, Nyah, a vow is a vow. Besides –." Simon leaned towards her and lowered his voice to a whisper. "I would rather hear the words of servitude falling from your pretty lips than having to listen to your little wolf howl."

Her arm shot out to strike him but he had grabbed it tightly before her fist could land. "You will vow to serve me!" he snarled. "Bow before me you mutinous bitch! Right now!"

The command could not be ignored. Now that the entire pack had succumbed to his leadership her refusal was only nudging her closer to rogue status. For a moment she struggled against his grip, her wolf whining quietly inside.

"Bow before me!" he yelled again.

Every cell in her body wanted to disobey him, but his power as Alpha had already been established and the effort it took not to lower her head and say the vile words made her limbs shake.

"Say it!" he demanded, tightening his grip and digging his nails into her skin.

"I serve you, Alpha." The words leaked from her mouth despite the effort she put into keeping her lips pressed together.

Simon released her arm.

She felt as if she was going to throw up, right there on his shoes. She wished she could.

Simon reached out and traced a cold fingertip along the line of her jaw before lifting a strand of her hair away from her face and draping it behind her shoulder. "I have wonderful things planned for you, Nyah," he said, victory brilliant in his black eyes, "and it is best for all our sakes that you remember your vow to me. Do you understand?"

EIGHT

Nyah heaved herself out of bed and wearily pulled up her blind. A brilliant blue sky hung above the blooming cherry blossoms, and in the sun-drenched gardens below, birds twittered happily, darting from branch to branch in a random spring dance.

She wrenched the blind back down with a grimace. Not even a perfect spring morning could lift her spirits. Four weeks had passed since Simon Northfell had become Alpha and although life in Blackwater Ridge had sputtered back into some semblance of normality, she knew that it was only a matter of time before he would show his true colours.

The new Alpha had so far managed to convince the entire pack that he was a pleasant, caring leader, and with such efficiency that Michael was barely speaking to her because her insistence that Simon was only biding his time was becoming more ludicrous by the day. He had angrily sent her away from the pack house the previous day, warning her that if she didn't drop her notions he'd tell Simon and let him deal with her himself. That had silenced her pretty fast, but it didn't dampen her determination.

"So, today's the day," Karen reminded Nyah when she wandered down to the kitchen a while later. Karen had already been for a run and was spread out on the couch with her feet up.

"Yeah," Nyah yawned. "Today I sign up for my course."

"Excited?"

"Suppose so," Nyah answered, flopping down onto one of the stools at the kitchen counter.

"Wow, rein in the enthusiasm," Karen said.

Nyah leaned her elbows on the counter and dropped her chin onto her upturned palms. "I am excited. I'm just tired, that's all."

"Well," Karen threw her legs over the side of the couch and hopped up. "You'd better get used to it. Once you complete this course you'll be ready to set up your own business and then you'll be up at the butt-crack of dawn every morning moaning about deliveries and staff and whatever else business owners get to moan about."

"If I'm lucky," Nyah warned her. "Blake told me yesterday that Alpha Northfell wasn't too keen on the idea of me opening a bookshop in the town."

"Why? You could make good money. There are no other bookshops in the town."

Nyah shrugged and stifled another yawn.

"Do you think he follows your dad's beliefs that we should keep to ourselves?" Karen wondered, crossing into the kitchen where she flicked on the kettle. "I hope he doesn't. If we don't integrate ourselves more with the locals we're denying ourselves the opportunity to expand and progress. We'll stay the smallest pack in the country if we don't make some changes."

"And that's the one thing Alpha Northfell doesn't want," Nyah said. "He's always banging on about increasing our pack size."

"So why be against your bookshop idea?"

"Because he's Simon Northfell," Nyah murmured, "And it probably doesn't fit in with whatever *his* plans are."

Before Karen could reply a knock landed on their door. Michael was standing on the porch when she swung it open.

"Alpha Northfell would like you to meet him in his office in an hour," Michael announced before she could draw a breath to say hello.

"For what?" Nyah asked slowly.

"I don't know, Nyah," Michael answered, impatience quick to coat his reply. "Just be there, okay?"

"Fine," she murmured to his back as he spun around and marched off.

Nyah frowned at her watch as she crossed the street towards the pack house. It was just before eleven o'clock. Registration for her course was at midday and she had to get to the bank before then to withdraw money for the fee. With a sigh she yanked her sleeve back down over her watch. Whatever Simon wanted to waffle about had better be rattled off quickly. If she missed registration she'd lose her place on the course.

Blake was standing to one side of Simon's office door when she came to the top of the stairs. "Am I too early?" she asked, knowing that an Alpha only posted a watch on his door if there was someone of importance inside the room with him. Or someone who posed a threat, she remembered, glancing nervously towards the closed door. There was no scent of a strange wolf in the air.

"No, you're on time," Blake said, opening the door to allow her enter. Nyah hesitantly walked by him, her curious glance being met with a blank expression.

"Nyah." Simon was bent over his crowded desk, but immediately pushed his chair back and came out from behind it to invite her further into the room.

"Alpha Northfell," she greeted him distractedly, glancing around the room that had once been her father's office. Simon had swapped most of the furniture around and it didn't look anything like the room she had known so well.

"Sit," he said warmly, pulling out the chair that sat on the opposite side of his desk. "So, how are you today?" he asked, returning to his own chair.

"Fine, thank you," she answered, realising just how much she hated his fake Mr Nice tone of voice.

"Good."

The scent of a stranger became apparent to her just then and she automatically turned to look towards the adjoining door that led to another smaller room on her left.

"I called for you because I need to discuss something with you," Simon said, drawing her attention back.

"I thought my opinion was of no value," she replied lightly, turning back to face him.

"I don't need your opinion," he answered good-naturedly, "I need your help."

"My help?"

"Yes, your help. Well - to be more accurate, the pack needs your help."

At that moment she felt like a reluctant donkey strapped to a heavy cart – a smart donkey that knew damn well how the tempting carrot being dangled before it would inch back as soon it moved a hoof forward. Subtly pulling in an impatient breath she shifted on her chair. "Is something wrong?"

"No, nothing is wrong as such, but . . . there are concerns developing." He paused to let his statement take effect, but she remained passive, forcing him to carry on. "We need to increase the size of our pack. Now -," he held up his hands as if expecting her to roll her eyes and comment on how he sounded like a broken record. "I know this is something I talk about constantly, but with each day that passes the fears I have for our future grow."

Nyah allowed herself to relax a little. The subject matter was nothing new. Why he thought she could help was beyond her, but if he wanted to rattle on about it yet again she'd let him.

"Increasing our numbers is something that I want us all to work towards," he carried on, "but it's a slow process and, one, which I have to admit, I don't have the patience for." Distractedly, he plucked a pen off the desk and began twirling it between his fingers. "There is also the issue of the unique element that is contained within our pack." He glanced up at her, his expression suggesting that she knew what he was talking about and would she offer an opinion on it.

Reluctantly, she asked him to elaborate.

"Wolves respect power," he said, dropping the pen, hopping up from his chair and coming around the desk to perch himself on the edge right in front of her. "We are drawn to it. It is in our nature to seek this power, find a place within in its ranks and serve."

Nyah continued to sit in silence, unsure of whether he expected her to reply to his eager little proclamation or not.

"Should our pack, small as it may be, resonate with an unassailable might we would have wolves howling at our boundary, begging to join us. If we were to accept them we would soon have a magnificent pack, maybe even the largest on the continent."

Nyah found she had to clear her throat before she spoke. "Why would we want to be the largest pack?"

"Opportunity," he replied, his beady eyes shining as he got up from the edge of the table and walked behind her chair, placing his hands on her shoulders before leaning down to whisper in her ear. "Something you are striving to take hold of, I believe."

"My course?" she realized, suddenly wondering how it fitted into his Master Plan.

"Yes. When I heard of your aspirations I finally came to appreciate how intently you want what is best for your pack."

Nyah had the urge to shake out her shoulders when Simon finally lifted his hands away. He crossed over to the window behind his desk, lifting the curtain aside with one finger so he could look out at the view. "I admire that in you, Nyah," he said, almost as if it pained him to admit it. "I know you distrust me, but I have to admit, when I heard of your intentions I felt a swell of pride."

Nyah frowned at his back. Now she was totally confused. Did he want her taking the course or not? And what in the hell had it got to do with increasing the pack?

"Whether you are prepared to admit it or not, we both seek the same future for our pack," he informed her, his voice slightly muffled as he remained facing the garden below. "We are working together, you know."

"I just want to take a college course," Nyah said.

Simon dropped the curtain and turned to face her. "No, you want to create an opportunity for yourself and your pack."

She kept her mouth shut. It was what she wanted, but not in the fanatical way that Simon was suggesting.

"And I think it's admirable. As I said, it makes me proud." He came to sit on the edge of the desk again and as he settled into position, his hands clasped loosely in his lap, Nyah inched deeper into the chair.

"It makes me wonder about you and me," he admitted, wistfully, the words hanging in the air like a bad odour.

"You and me?" Nyah repeated, when it became obvious he wasn't going to say anymore until she spoke.

He nodded once.

"I, I don't follow, Alpha Northfell."

"We are more alike than you think. We want the same dream, Nyah. If we were to work together, my hopes for our pack would be realized."

"Work . . . together? I, I don't understand. Do you mean start a business together – once I've completed my course?"

Simon gave her a patient, kind smile as he shook his head. It did nothing but increase her confusion. "Forget the college course. I have something far better to offer you. What I can give you – and what it allows you to give to your pack in return – outreaches anything you aspire to right now."

"I -," she began again, and then paused as a suggestion came to her. "You mean . . . a job? You have a job for me? "

"'Job' is not the word I would use," he smiled down at her.

"What word would you use?" Her wolf had started to growl, a low grumble that Nyah had to block out by giving her head a quick shake.

"A calling, perhaps."

"A calling?"

Simon lifted his hands and pressed them together before resting the edge of his steepled fingers against his lips. He looked as if he was about to burst into prayer. "When your father was Alpha you always did what you could to assist him, am I right?"

Nyah barely nodded in her confusion.

"And yet, you always felt as if you were on the periphery. You were always side-lined, simply because you were a female. Which – and I feel very strongly about this – was incredibly unfair." Simon leaned towards her, letting his hands fall into his lap again. "And why? Because as a female, Nyah, you have so much to give this pack."

Despite the back of the chair already digging into her shoulders, Nyah pushed herself farther away from him.

"Now is your time, Nyah," he blathered on. "Now your calling can be answered. Now you can do something for your pack that no-one else can."

She stared wildly at him, her wolf now growling louder and causing the hairs on the back of her neck to prickle. "What can I do?"

"Ensure your magnificent heritage does not die out."

"What?"

"Your bloodline is the unique element that I spoke of, a strength that wolves crave, a power that is absent from most packs. If you were to mate with an equally powerful bloodline the pups would be unique. This is your calling, Nyah. This is how you can help your pack."

Nyah couldn't believe he was back to this subject again. With a jaded sigh she leaned towards him. "Alpha Northfell," she began, but he cut across her.

"You want to help your pack, don't you?"

"Yes, of course I do, but -."

"But you are not prepared to make the necessary sacrifices?"

"Sacrifices? Um, I . . . Alpha Northfell," she faltered, "I, I really don't understand what it is you're trying to say to me."

As if dealing with a small, confused child he gave her another supercilious smile. "Nyah," he soothed, "I tried once before to explain this to you. Don't you remember?"

She paused for a moment, the distant memory of a conversation quickly replaying and leaving her struggling to believe that he was actually serious about an arranged bonding, but when she forced herself to study his tight, thin face there was a look of unwavering determination cemented into his piercing eyes. "You're . . . I'm not . . ." Shaking her head forcefully she moved to the edge of the seat. "I won't allow you to do that," she said, grabbing the armrests as she began to stand up.

"Allow?" he smirked, lunging towards her and slamming his hands over hers. "Who said I needed your permission?"

Nyah fell back into the seat. For a short moment she felt a thrill of victory in knowing that she had forced his fake niceness to fray and could already hear herself singing a smug 'I told you so' to Michael, but the triumph was swiftly replaced with fear as Simon continued to loom over her, a look of pure disdain twisting his mouth. He dragged his contemptuous gaze down her body before casually lifting his hands off hers and straightening up. What sounded like 'insolent brat' was muttered as he moved away from her and began to saunter about the office.

"Lycan Laws have forced us into a situation that threatens the future of this pack," he informed her, his voice suddenly doused in grating pleasantness again. "It surprises me that you're not prepared to ignore these binding rules for the sake of your kin."

"I obey Lycan laws," she reminded him sharply.

"Yes, I suppose you do," he agreed, spreading his hands out to indicate the office he now held, "but allowing your powerful bloodline to be willingly diluted is against Lycan law."

"No Lycan Law dictates that," she replied confidently, twisting in her chair to follow his progression around the room.

"The pack Alpha retains the right to contravene Lycan Law when the well-being of his pack is under threat," he recited.

It was a wonder that he hadn't had the statute cross-stitched and framed on his office wall with the apparent sentiment he held towards it she thought, before replying with a curt "We're not under threat."

"That's not the way I see it," he replied lightly.

Simon completed his lap of the room before he came to stand behind her. When she moved to twist around and face him he clamped his hands onto her shoulders and held her in place. "I'm disappointed in you, Nyah," he breathed into her ear. "I would have thought that an Alpha's daughter would have held more regard for her pack."

"I hold regard for my pack," she said, squirming under his grip, "in the same way that I hold regard for Lycan Laws. And it doesn't matter what way you paint it, forcing me to mate with some random stranger is against our -."

"Is that your worry?" he interrupted, sounding uncharacteristically concerned as he abruptly released her shoulders so he could scurry around the chair to face her. "You don't want to mate with a stranger?"

"I don't want to mate with anyone who's not my - ."

"Because it won't be a stranger," he cut in again, taking hold of her chin. "I wouldn't allow some undeserving whelp to mate with you; it will be somebody worthy. Nyah –," he said determinedly, "I want you to bear my pups."

It took a few seconds before the words that carried on his sour breath registered with her. "You want me to what?"

As if already anticipating her reaction he stepped aside smoothly as she jumped up from the chair and backed away from him.

"You want me to bear your pups? You think that I'd let you . . . allow you to -." Nyah stumbled against something at the side of his desk and changed course, still backing away from him. "No. Absolutely no way. You're not coming near me. I won't let you."

"You can't stop me. I'm your Alpha."

"I am not mating with you!" she yelled. "I will not carry your pups!"

"What about the future of our pack?"

"No! You're crazy! I won't do it. I'll bear pups for my true mate, no-one else, especially not you!"

"I won't allow you to diminish your blood-."

"What do you think that mating with you would do? Your bloodline's as weak as water! You have no power in your bloodline, not a single drop of it!"

"My position as pack Alpha says otherwise," he replied slowly. "I didn't get where I am today with a weak bloodline, and how dare you disrespect me in such -."

"You didn't get your position by entitlement," she cut in with a bitter laugh, "and well you know it."

"I was voted in -."

"Voted?" she spat at him. "Voted? You cheated – you lied – you -."

"I attained this position through the fair and just -."

"No!" she yelled, jabbing one finger towards him. "You murdered Alan!"

Her words obliterated the final remnants of his fading act. Simon Northfell fell completely still and she suddenly found herself motionless too, 'Murdered Alan!' echoing inside her head like the reverberation of a gunshot.

"And there it is," he said calmly after a short moment of awful silence, folding his arms and leaning back against the wall. And just like that, Simon Northfell, the caring, pleasant Alpha evaporated before her eyes and the real Simon Northfell appeared in his place. "There it is," he repeated, his voice even sounding like she had remembered. "I was wondering how long it would take before the big white elephant in the room would be acknowledged."

"You murdered Alan," she ground out, not caring how much trouble she was now in.

"I most certainly did not kill him," he replied with such conviction that she realized she had simply worded her accusation incorrectly.

"You *ordered* his death."

"And can you prove it?"

When she didn't answer he flashed a short sneer. "I thought not."

Simon unfolded his arms and rolled out his shoulders as if relieved to be free of the weight of pretence he'd been carrying for so long. "Sit down," he ordered with a flick of his fingers as he strolled back to his desk.

Nyah obeyed, but only because her shaking limbs were threatening to crumple her onto the floor at any moment.

"Clearly, being nice was a waste of my time," he declared gathering up the papers on his desk and sliding them into a drawer. "I should have known. You're as stubborn as your damned father was." He slammed the drawer shut on the word 'father' and she flinched. "Let me tell you how it's going to be, Nyah," he said, sitting down and leaning back with a sigh. "This afternoon I am going to announce to the pack that you and I have decided to mate. I will tell the mongrels that we both want what is best for this pack and are prepared to make the necessary sacrifices to achieve it. Anyone who questions our bending of the Lycan Laws will have me to answer to."

"I won't do it," she said quietly. "I will not allow you to take me as your mate."

"Yes, you will," he replied, sounding completely bored. "You will have no choice."

"My wolf won't allow it. She'll fight you – hard."

Simon laughed and it was the guffaw of someone who already had what they wanted and knew that all the threats in the world were just wasted air. "Cassius?" he called out.

Nyah had forgotten her earlier sense of a stranger nearby. The door to the adjoining room opened and a man stepped through, his eyes briefly flicking towards her.

"Nyah, meet Cassius Ochre," Simon said.

Cassius Ochre looked to be in his late fifties. His copper-toned skin was lined with age and sun, but his hazel eyes were bright and lively, almost childlike, despite the obvious fear glistening in them at that moment. A deep sense of competence radiated from him, but that wasn't what made Nyah's eyes linger on his lanky form. Something else about the man notched up her level of panic; he possessed an unearthly sense of power - supernatural power - stronger than anything she or Simon were endowed with.

Instantly threatened, Nyah stood up. Cassius Ochre held something more potent than Simon Northfell, yet, as she watched him sidle along the wall, his eyes darting nervously between her and Simon she felt her adrenaline spike hotly inside. When the scary things were afraid it was time to run.

"Sit," Simon snapped at her.

"No," she shook her head, her whole body trembling as it fought against her disobedience towards her Alpha's order and the primitive urge to obey the flight directive of her burning adrenalin.

Simon forced out a heavy sigh. "Why must you always insist on fighting me?"

Leaving her to hover uneasily at the back of her chair he rose from his own with a mutter and walked across the room. A wide cabinet was positioned against the wall, an antique dating back to her great-grandfather's time. When this had been her father's office the surface had been covered in framed photos of the family. Now it was bare except for a clunky scotch decanter. Simon dallied over pouring himself a generous measure of the amber drink. "While I find your comment about my weak bloodline wholly disrespectful, Nyah, I am not foolish enough to believe that it's as strong as yours," he announced, swallowing back the entire contents of his glass in one mouthful. "The passing of generations has, naturally, weakened it considerably, however, purity remains." He turned back to face her, his glass refilled. "Cassius has kindly agreed to temporarily restore that strength and that is when we shall mate."

Nyah snatched a glance at where Cassius remained standing. He didn't have the demeanour of a man who had kindly agreed to anything. His mouth was set in a grim line and breaths came through his nose in tight, shaky rushes.

"And," Simon continued, swallowing back half of the scotch, "we're also going to add something else. An extra special ingredient for an extra special . . . bite."

Cassius made a strangled noise. His obvious apprehension of Simon's intended mutation of the recipe made Nyah swallow tightly. "What is the something extra?" she asked warily, tearing her stare from the mute Cassius back to Simon again. "What do you mean?"

Simon tipped back the remainder of his drink and sat the glass back down. "Nothing you need to worry your little head about," he replied. "All you need to understand and be grateful for is that you shall be the mother of a new breed of Lycans."

"I won't do it," she said, her shaking voice in total contradiction to her determination. "I won't carry engineered pups for you. It's disgusting!"

"Because we're not in love?" he whined scornfully. "Because I don't make your heart flutter whenever I look at you? Because you want to find your true mate and live happily ever after?" With a loud snort he threw her a look of disgust. "Our lack of connection is a small sacrifice to make, and a sacrifice I'd have thought that you'd bear with dignity."

Simon pushed himself away from the cabinet and aimed a dismissive wave in her direction. "But, clearly, dignity will not be exhibited on your behalf," he said, "which is why I have brought him here today."

Cassius kept his eyes stuck hard to the floor as Simon came to his side and gave his shoulder an encouraging squeeze. "I know you have a penchant for drama, Nyah, so I feel it would be in the best interests of all concerned if you were to be . . . well," he gave a short bark of a laugh, "muzzled is such an uncouth expression to use, but it's all that comes to mind right now." With a flash of a smile he slapped Cassius hard on the back. "She's all yours," he announced in a forced whisper.

Nyah moved back as Cassius took a step towards her.

"You will not move," Simon ordered lightly, returning to his desk. "You will not cry out, you will not fight, you will kneel and remain silent and still."

Immediately, Nyah's knees loosened and she found herself on the floor. As much as she wanted to shift and smash her way out of the room her body did as he had commanded. She was silent and still.

"Good girl," he crooned. "It's so much easier when you play nice."

Cassius approached her, drawing a bunch of withered stalks from the satchel he had strung across his body. When she recognised the poisonous wolfs bane flower her mouth opened to cry out, but all that sounded was a breathy gasp. Simon sniggered.

Cassius laid the stems at her knees and then began lifting other items from the satchel. Tears began to spill from her eyes, blurring the actions of his shaking hands as more unidentifiable objects were placed in a circle around her. When Cassius returned to face her she looked up at him. His lined face was creased with pity, but when his eyes flicked towards Simon she could see that his fear greatly outweighed any compassion he might have had for her.

A knotted length of rag was the final item that he took from his bag. He lit the top end and once it began to smoke he began wafting it about her body. Spicy brown smoke curled around her face, stinging her eyes and burning her nostrils but Simon's order had her trapped in place, unable to even cough as the acrid smoke scratched her throat. It was then that she began to feel the room spin. Rushing blood hissed through her ears and as the ground before her began to dim she felt her wolf suddenly writhe inside. Her mournful cry was the last thing that Nyah heard before she lost consciousness.

NINE

When Nyah woke it was to unexpectedly familiar surroundings. She was in her old bedroom in the pack house, but nothing about the room felt right anymore. She didn't feel right either.

Her head was pounding and her throat felt scratched and dry, but it wasn't that which had jerked her awake from a black, shadowy sleep. Dragging herself up she swung her legs over the side of the bed and looked down at her clothes. Something bad had happened. Her fuzzy brain was struggling to recall exactly what, explain why she felt different, and not a good different, a bad, frightening different.

Fisting her hands she drummed them against the side of her tender head. "Come on," she muttered, "wake up, wake up."

She remembered then. It came back to her, what Simon had done, what Cassius Ochre had done.

"No!" Jumping to her feet she clutched at the front of her t-shirt as she realized what was wrong. "No, no, no!" she wailed, staring frantically into space as she searched desperately within. The emptiness she found was overwhelming. Her wolf was gone.

Nyah fell heavily to her knees, her arms instantly wrapping themselves around her middle. It's too late, she thought, there's nothing to protect, she's gone!

"You're awake."

The shock of hearing Simon's voice threw her backwards and she collided into the side of the bed. She hadn't heard him come into the room, she couldn't even catch his scent as he loomed over her – what in the hell had he done to her?

A pleasant smile was pasted onto his face as he moved to lean towards her. Instinctively, she scrambled away from him. "What did you do to me?" she gasped. "Why can't I feel my wolf? Why can't I feel anything?"

"I have silenced your little wolf, Nyah."

"You . . . did what?"

Simon rolled his eyes impatiently. "Don't get hysterical, it's only temporary." He waved an irritated hand at where she was cowering on the floor. "Get up from there and sit on the bed."

Immediately, her limbs responded and she clumsily moved to a seated position on the edge of the bed.

Simon made a tight noise of satisfaction. "Wonderful," he smirked.

"You -," she began, but he cut her off with a loud 'shh!' "Don't speak or move," he ordered.

The abuse she was ready to hurl at him died somewhere in her throat and her tongue went limp in her mouth.

"A few house rules," he announced pleasantly, folding his arms across his chest. "Firstly, you will tell no-one of what happened in my office this morning, but you will freely tell anyone who is prepared to listen that you and I have agreed to mate for the well-being of our pack. Secondly, you will behave as if you are fully amenable towards our arrangement. And finally," he smirked, "you will not leave this house or the pack territory unless I give you permission."

With a smile that brought the same comfort as a slap across the face he moved back towards the door. "As you'll be living here with me from now on I have asked Karen to bring over all of your belongings. I would like to dine at seven this evening. Everything you need is in the kitchen. And wear something nice when you join me."

The door closed and all Nyah could do was stare dumbly at where he had been standing.

Puppet. The word echoed over and over in Nyah's head. For hours after he had left her in the bedroom she had remained frozen on the edge of the bed, her body unable to move until he had come back in the early evening and had ordered her to go down to the kitchen and prepare their meal. She had then watched in a disbelieving stupor as her hands had peeled, washed, chopped, stirred and prepared an entire meal completely independent of her brain. Then she had gone back upstairs, showered and changed and had returned to the dining room where she had served him his meal and had then taken a seat opposite him as instructed. He had ordered her to eat every bite of her meal. She had obeyed.

Now she was back in her bedroom, curled into a tight ball under the duvet, tears streaming down her face as she cried silently into her pillow.

This was how it was going to be, he had told her. Until their ceremony on Saturday afternoon, (she was refusing to allow herself hear his use of the word 'marriage') she would be kept hidden in the house. He had to keep her separate from the pack, he had declared, she was a precious little thing to him now and she may as well get used to it, because once she was carrying his pups she'd be kept under lock and key. After all, he couldn't risk something happening to her once his 'special' babies were growing inside her. 'And before you wonder about the pack being alarmed by my desire to protect you,' he had calmly added, 'you'll be delighted to know that they have taken the news of our arrangement with respect and gratitude, and -,' he had announced with a syrupy smile, 'all are looking forward to Saturday.'

He had then proceeded to explain how Cassius would return on Saturday night to 'assist' with their mating and it was then that she had tried to block his voice out. She didn't want to hear any of the appalling details. But he had blabbered on of course, until she had gagged, prompting him to quickly order that she not vomit at the table. It was an order she was happy to allow her body to obey.

'And you'll get your wolf back,' he had said flippantly as she had sipped on her glass of water, the only words of the entire day that she had wanted to hear. 'Cassius Ochre, my concerned Shaman insists on it – says you'll be dead within no time if I don't.'

Now as she lay sniffing into the pillow she reminded herself that that was what she needed to focus on. Once Cassius returned her wolf she'd have a chance to fight back. She had six days to wait for that, though, and in the meantime, she was his puppet – and no better than a human. Simon had said it himself; 'The slightest little incident could see you snap a bone or catch one of those wretched diseases humans tend to drop dead from. And your healing abilities are gone, too, so please be careful with the kitchen knives.'

Wishing he had ordered her to have a good night's sleep she rolled onto her back to stare up at the shadowed ceiling.

The pack house was silent and empty – to her, at least. With her wolf gone she couldn't hear beyond a few feet, she couldn't smell anything unless it was smack bang under her nose and she knew by the way that she had struggled to carry an armful of firewood into the living room earlier that she was as weak as a fly. All of that though, however alien it felt, was bearable; the absence of her wolf was not. Words such as 'hollow', 'abyss' and 'fathomless' couldn't even come close to describing the appalling emptiness she felt inside.

Panic began to creep through her again and it was a struggle not to hear the warnings that cried out in her mind; 'Without your wolf it's going to be impossible to escape Simon! You're trapped in this house, unable to let anyone know what's happening! Simon's orders have you completely bound to his will! How are you going to break free of him? How are you going to stop him?'

Thoughts of what would happen on Saturday night began to seep into her mind then, images of Simon approaching her, leaning over her, his hands on her skin . . .

Nausea rolled through her and she bolted upright in the bed. 'Don't' she warned herself. 'Don't let that bastard do this to you. Stay calm. You'll get yourself out of this – you will.'

'What if he marks you?' the louder, anxious part of her mind butted in. 'What if he bites down on your neck and brands you?' She shook her head and pulled her knees up, huddling into a tight ball. A male wolf only marked his true mate, and it usually happened during their first mating. If Simon marked her she would be tarnished, maybe even enough for her true mate to reject her if she was lucky enough to find him. And if she bore pups for Simon? Her stomach clenched again. That would be like a death sentence. No male would ever come near her if that happened.

A sweaty coldness rose inside her and she drew in a deep breath. Simon Northfell was not going to make her throw up. No way. She would get out of this situation. She would. She was going to stop panicking. She was going to lie down and go to sleep.

Slowly, Nyah lowered herself back down onto the pillows.

There. That was better. It was all going to be okay.

No. No it wasn't.

Nyah grabbed the pillow out from under her head and clamped it down over her face. She wanted to scream, but her obedient mouth remained shut tight.

TEN

"This beef is overdone." Simon dropped his knife and fork onto the plate with a clatter. "I can't stomach it. What else is there to eat?" he whined.

"Salmon, Alpha Northfell."

"Fish? Is that all?"

"Yes, Alpha Northfell."

Sighing like a petulant child he threw his napkin onto his loaded plate. "Clean up here," he ordered, "and stop biting your nails," he snapped as he pushed back his chair to stand up. "It's a disgusting habit."

Nyah whipped her hand away from her mouth and buried it between her knees. She hadn't even been aware that she'd been biting her nails. The habit, although short-lived, had begun in the weeks after her mother had died, and only for the gentle persistence of her father she had learned to stop.

Simon left the dining room and she got up from the table, quickly clearing away the dishes and carrying them through to the kitchen as had been ordered. Her own dinner had been barely touched and now she'd have to watch it slide off the plate and into the trash as her body obeyed the clean up command.

"Nyah."

The wobbling stack nearly fell from her grasp when she looked up to see Michael coming in the back door.

"Hey," he smiled, crossing the kitchen towards her so he could unload her hands. "How are you? I haven't seen you in days."

"I'm great," she lied smoothly, as had been instructed.

Michael gave her a careful look. "Really?"

"Yes, really."

"Okay, good," he said, sounding totally unconvinced. He carried the plates over to the sink and she followed him, desperate for her body to override Simon's orders so she could alert Michael to her situation.

"So . . . em, you and . . . Simon?"

114

"Mm hmm," she replied breezily. "As it turns out, we both want the same thing, so it seemed only natural that we work together to achieve it." Her voice sounded so light and matter-of-fact when inside she was hysterically screaming for help, begging Michael to see what was really happening. He was the first person that she had laid eyes on since Simon had trapped her in the house and having her body obey Simon while her mind thrashed and screamed for help was torment.

"It's, well. . . it's surprised us all," he admitted leaning against the counter beside the sink where her hands began to calmly stack the dishes. "You've done a complete one-eighty on Simon. Only last week you were calling him the devil incarnate and now. . ."

"And now I can see what is best for this pack and I will do what I can to achieve it." As the words spewed from her mouth she suddenly knew what it felt like to be possessed. She wanted her hands to grab Michael and shake him or even gesticulate in some way that would alert him to how she was being controlled, but they remained obediently and frustratingly occupied with the tap and detergent bottle.

"My darling Nyah," Simon crooned coming through the kitchen door. He must have flung himself down the stairs when he had sensed Michael in the house. "She's a credit to her father, isn't she Michael? He would be so proud to see her acting so selflessly," he beamed.

Nyah returned the watt filled smile.

"Did you want to see me, Michael?" Simon asked lightly.

Michael pulled a set of folded papers from his back pocket. "Patrol schedules," he said handing them over.

"Thank you." Simon didn't look at the papers, instead he fixed an expression that clearly said 'is that all?' onto Michael, who, receiving the message loud and clear, said a quick goodnight and ducked back out into the dark garden.

"Lock that door and then bring some tea to my office when you're done cleaning up," Simon ordered.

"Yes, Alpha Northfell," she replied.

As soon as he left the kitchen she sagged over the edge of the sink. She wasn't trapped, she was entombed, slowly suffocating in this coffin that used to be her home. The words she had said to Michael had come from a place inside of her that she couldn't control, a filthy, dark place that she wanted gone. She wanted her wolf back, she wanted her life back. She wanted Simon Northfell shredded to pieces.

It suddenly occurred to her, as the sounds of furious breaths hissing through her nostrils registered, that something was different; she was angry. For the first time since she had woken in her old room five days ago she was feeling something besides fear. She was sick of Simon manipulating her, sick of bowing and scraping to him, sick of making his meals, cleaning his house, being powerless to act when he decided he wanted her silent. Her knuckles turned white with the force of her grip on the edge of the counter and she revelled in the sensation of the fury rushing through her. Simon was everything an Alpha should never be – even his control over her; it wasn't the kind of power an ordinary Alpha could wield. 'You stole the Alpha position!' she raged silently, 'and now you can't even maintain it without cheating! Your hold over me isn't even your ability – it's Cassius Ochre's!

The wrath felt good, it felt natural. For the last five days her emotions had been on a plateau; she'd been living with an unvarying level of anxiety inside and it was a relief to finally have it swamped by something more powerful.

Nyah tutted when she saw her hand reach out to lock the back door. As usual her body was obeying Simon's orders. When was this going to stop? And harder still to figure out, how was she going to stop it?

"What in the hell am I going to do?" she muttered at her reflection in the small square pane of glass in the back door.

Nyah frowned as her mumbled voice reached her ears and she glanced down towards her mouth. What she saw mirrored back made her eyes widen in shock. She was biting her nails.

Snatching her hand away she spun around, afraid that Simon had already caught her disobeying his order, but seeing that she was still alone in the kitchen she turned to face the glass again.

He ordered you not to bite your nails, she reminded herself, staring hard at her reflection. Alpha Northfell said you must not bite your nails. He ordered you. You cannot disobey an order.

Nyah lifted her hand, held one finger to her lips, slid the jagged nail between her teeth and bit down.

Eleven

It was an effort to keep the crockery from rattling on the tray as Nyah climbed the stairs to Simon's office. She moved with what she hoped was an innocently measured pace, unable to decide if the trembling was due to fear or excitement.

Another brief experiment had proved that Simon's control over her was malfunctioning; he had ordered that tea be brought to his office and without a single moment of hesitation during the few minutes it had taken she had made him coffee instead.

"Come in," he answered when she knocked gently on his office door. She entered the room and without a word set the tray on the table before him and then filled his cup.

She was almost out the door before he called after her. "Did I not ask for tea?"

She turned to face him, allowing confusion to crease her forehead as she stared at the steaming cup of liquid. "I, I, you said coffee, Alpha Northfell."

"Well, I meant tea. Take that away and bring me tea."

"Yes, Alpha Northfell."

It took supreme control not to charge back down the stairs, fling the tray onto the kitchen counter and do a victory dance. Repeatedly telling herself to stay calm she quietly entered the kitchen, poured the coffee down the sink and turned the kettle on. Then instead of dancing, she paced.

Tomorrow was Friday, which meant the next day, Saturday, was their 'special day'. It didn't leave much time to carefully plan her escape, but it was going to have to do.

With shaking hands she made a pot of tea and just as she was about to sweep back out of the kitchen she paused. With a sly smile she placed the tray back onto the counter, plucked the lid off the teapot, formed a juicy ball of spit in her mouth and then carefully released it into the pot before popping the lid back into place. Childish, she told herself as she climbed the stairs, but so deliciously enjoyable. With any luck she'd already caught one of those nasty human diseases meaning Simon would die a pox-ridden death.

Nyah didn't sleep for a single second that night. Inky blackness melted into a pale, pink light as she set her plan, picked it apart, reworked it and then layered it with so many back-up plans that her head ached when she finally sat up in the bed to smack the alarm into silence. Simon's snarky comment about how nicer everything was when she 'played nice' had popped into her head hours earlier and that was all she had to remember for the next few hours. Play nice.

With his breakfast served Nyah took her seat at the opposite end of the table. Thankfully, he hadn't ordered her to remain silent for the meal and not wanting to provoke him she hadn't uttered a single word while he had been stuffing forkfuls of bacon into his mouth as he read the newspaper. Drawing herself out of an enjoyable fantasy that centred around him violently choking to death on the bacon she had cooked him, she drew in a steadying breath. "Alpha Northfell?"

"Yes?" he replied after a long pause, not lifting his eyes from the paper.

"I, I was wondering if you would give me permission to go to Blackwater today so I can buy a dress for tomorrow." Keeping her eyes fixed on her plate as she spoke, she hoped she had worked just the right mixture of pitiful hope into her tone.

"You have dresses."

"I, they. . . I wanted something new."

"Wear that green dress you wore on the night of the Pack Welcoming. I liked that one," he ordered, flicking over the page.

"Yes, Alpha Northfell." Pressing her lips together she picked up her knife and fork and began to eat again.

"You don't like the green dress?" he asked after a moment, forcing her not to smirk.

"I do, it's just that I wanted something . . . special for Saturday. It's not how I thought that my . . . wedding would be, but I still want to. . ." she trailed off with a disregarding shake of her head, remembering to keep her eyes lowered. She then let a few seconds pass before loudly pulling in a determined breath. "I don't expect you to understand, Alpha Northfell, but women notice these kinds of things and they'll have a greater belief in me if they see I want this to work."

"And a new dress shows that?" he asked, unconvinced.

Nyah nodded briskly. "We always want a new dress for a special occasion." To finish, she allowed a small trembling smile to escape as she shoved her breakfast around on her plate.

There was a weary sigh. "Fine. You may go to Blackwater for one hour."

"Thank you, Alpha Northfell." Nyah finally allowed her grateful eyes to lift towards him. It was just a brief look, but she filled it with as much doe-eyed sweetness as she could muster.

Blake was standing in the hall when she came down the stairs at midday. She hadn't seen him since the day she had arrived at Simon's office and the urge to run down the stairs and fling her arms around him was overwhelming. "I will bring you to Blackwater," he announced, emotionlessly.

"Yes, Alpha Northfell told me," she replied, slowly coming down off the last step. Blake's face was blank and when he looked down at her his eyes didn't even seem to be focused. "Blake?" she whispered.

"Yes, Miss Morgan?" he replied, sounding just like Karen had on the day of the Show of Hands.

"Nothing."

Blake opened the front door for her and she stepped out onto the porch. Michael and Rob were standing either side of the doorway, but neither of them reacted when she looked at them. Instead, they stared blankly towards the distance, their faces impassive and lifeless. It was the same with another two pack members that she met as Blake walked her the short distance to his car. She addressed them, but they didn't reply. The only reaction she got was a terrifyingly vacant look. "Karen," she murmured, when the familiar face of her friend sitting in the passenger seat of Blake's car became visible. Nyah hurried towards the car, but even before she could reach out to grab the door handle she could see that Karen had been turned into a robot too. Her warm, funny friend simply stared out the windscreen as if she was day-dreaming. And not a pleasant day-dream.

The drive to Blackwater passed in complete silence. It wasn't until they got out of the car in the parking lot that Karen spoke. "You have one hour," she announced, looking at her watch. "Then we will return you to Alpha Northfell."

"Aren't you coming with me?" Nyah asked.

"I will accompany you," Karen confirmed robotically. "We are to stay together at all times."

Blake was to stay with them, too, she discovered as they entered the small mall and began walking towards the first boutique. She had expected as much, so she walked on confidently, fully prepared for having bodyguards shadowing her as she set her plan into action.

"What do you think?" Nyah held up the first dress that she laid her hand on. "Or maybe this one, it's a nicer colour."

Karen remained silent. Nyah hadn't been expecting a comment, but she had decided to stick to her plan of 'playing nice'. It was entirely possible that Robot Karen had been ordered to look out for suspicious behaviour, so being anything but enthusiastic about her shopping expedition could land her back in Blake's car.

Moving further along the rail she grabbed another dress. "Oh, now, I like this one. And I think Simon likes blue. What about this?"

Again Karen said nothing. Nyah smiled anyway and hung the dress back onto the rail sneaking a quick glance at Blake who hovered close to the store entrance.

"This one," she declared, holding up a garishly frilly green mess of ribbons and lace. "I think I'll try it on – and this one too," she decided, grabbing a pretty pale blue dress, just in case.

Karen followed her into the changing rooms and stood right on the other side of the curtain while she changed. Nyah made a show of asking her opinion on both dresses, taking her time with twirling around in them and wondering aloud about shoes and how she would wear her hair. When she was tired of her own theatrics she decided on the pale blue dress.

"Okay," she smiled, shoving the dress towards Karen. "You hold this while I run over to the cash machine – I didn't bring enough money."

Before Karen could refuse Nyah hurried from the store. Blake stuck to her heels as she approached the cash machine, but hung back far enough to miss the fact that she withdrew way more cash than she would have needed for a single dress. Quickly tucking the money inside the pocket of her jeans she flashed him a smile and returned to the store.

"I'm getting married tomorrow," she gushed to the store assistant as the dress was rung through the register.

"Congratulations," the woman replied, "that's so exciting!"

"I know." Nyah sighed, wistfully. "Tomorrow is going to be such a memorable day for me and my groom."

The first spasm of nerves hit Nyah as they left the store. Karen had mechanically reminded her that she only had thirty minutes of her allotted time left and Nyah told her that she wanted to go to the accessories store at the far end of the mall. "I want to get something pretty for my hair," she explained as they walked along, "and this is the best store here for that."

The store was quiet and Nyah moved along the displays with Karen close behind her. She quickly picked out an elaborate hair clip and then headed towards the register via the stand with the lengths of hair extensions.

"Damn . . ." The clip hit the floor and skittered right under the display unit. Bending down, Nyah purposely allowed her purse to slide from her shoulder, knock the handle of the dress bag off her wrist and drag it to the ground where her purse strap then conveniently snagged around her ankle as she attempted to untangle herself from the awkward mess. Karen agitatedly pushed her aside, dropped to her knees and stuck her hand under the unit, blindly feeling around for the clip as Nyah quickly straightened up and whipped a hair extension packet off the display and dropped it into her bag.

It was stealing, but she'd already held a mental debate about the whole thing sometime around three-thirty that morning and had made peace with her decision.

Karen stood up and handed her the clip.

"Thanks."

"Fifteen minutes," Karen replied. An odd-looking necklace had fallen free of her top when she'd bent down to retrieve the hair clip. Nyah had never seen Karen wear it before and its thin leather cord, with what appeared to be a knot of dirty feathers hanging from it, was definitely not Karen's usual style.

With the hair clip paid for Nyah left the store where Blake took over time-keeping announcements to advise her that she had twelve minutes left.

"I'm done now," Nyah announced, seeing that Blake was wearing a necklace that smacked of Cassius Ochre's handiwork too, "but I do need to use the restroom. Where's the nearest one?"

Nyah made a point of pivoting around to look for the restrooms even though she knew exactly where they were – or it, to be exact. They were standing in the farthest corner of the mall and unlike the main section the only restroom available was a disabled one. With a window.

"There it is," she smiled, heading in its direction. "Oh." Nyah frowned and took a quick look up and down the empty hallway where they stood. "It's for disabled use." Neither Blake nor Karen offered an opinion on the matter so she pushed on. "How many minutes do I have?"

Karen checked her watch. "Nine."

"Oooh, I really need to go," Nyah groaned, "and the other restrooms are way over the other side of the mall." She threw a questioning glance at Blake and Karen who continued to wear dead expressions on their faces. "I'll just be a minute, okay?"

Blake simply blinked at her.

"Thanks," she smiled, taking his muteness as a yes. "I'll be quick – here." She held out the bag towards Karen.

"I must come in with you," Karen said, her hands remaining by her side.

"I don't think so," Nyah said calmly. "I'm not going to pee with you watching me."

"I must stay with you at all times," Karen reminded her.

"I don't think Alpha Northfell would be too pleased to hear that you watched his future wife using the toilet," Nyah warned.

There was a long silence throughout which Nyah could feel beads of sweat forming on her forehead. She had a back-up plan if this one was about to implode, but it meant crossing to the other side of the mall and time was definitely against her now.

Karen looked at Blake. Blake just stared back at her. Obviously, Simon had neglected to give instruction on what to do in the event of a pee emergency.

"This is ridiculous," Nyah said, hoping she sounded like an authoritative soon-to-be Alpha's wife. "I'll be two minutes."

She dangled the bag in front of Karen again. "Please hold this for me."

Some part of Karen's voodoo-drugged brain must have reacted to her commanding tone because she reached out and took the bag.

"Thank-you," Nyah said curtly before opening the door, ducking inside and locking it.

Nyah pressed her back to the door and looked up. Once, many moons ago, Karen had told Nyah the story of how she had been trying to escape the attentions of a persistent boy from her school who had taken to following her around like a love-sick puppy. In between fits of laughter Karen had detailed her find of this very bathroom and how a hard tug of the air-vent above the sink (too hard a tug for human hands) had granted her a perfect escape and finally driven the message home to the smitten boy that she wasn't interested. Karen's presently drugged brain obviously didn't remember the story, or at least, Nyah hoped that was the case as she clambered onto the sink and eased the tips of her fingers under the metal surround of the vent.

Seconds later she had clambered out and was tearing across the back end of the parking lot, her purse clutched tightly to her chest as she sped towards the neighbouring bus station.

She didn't know how long it would take before Karen and Blake would realize that she was gone, but she only needed seven minutes before the bus for Phoenix would whisk her away. It was going to be the longest seven minutes of her life she realized as she joined the small queue at the ticket counter.

Knowing that whoever was going to track her would end up in the bus station at some stage she paid for a ticket that would take her all the way to Phoenix even though she planned to get off way before that final stop. With the ticket purchased she dashed into the poky ladies' restroom and pulled a t-shirt from her purse – a bland grey one that wouldn't stand out. The opposite of the bright red one she had purposely worn. After shoving the red one in the trash can she scooped her hair up onto her head, unwrapped the stolen length of blonde hair, clipped it to the back of her head and then held it in place with a baseball cap that had also been stashed in her purse. After a suffocating dose of perfume was sprayed all over her clothes she slipped back out into the waiting room.

The bus was already loading. Scanning the parking lot for two searching figures she shuffled into the queue, climbed the stairs and took a seat halfway down the bus. Her heart was banging against her ribs and her fresh t-shirt was already growing damp under the arms as she forced herself to slouch back in the seat and nonchalantly gaze out the window. There was still no sign of Blake or Karen.

Nyah watched with gritted teeth as passengers meandered out of the station and strolled towards the bus. 'Hurry the hell up!' she wanted to scream as they chatted carelessly with the driver who seemed to be taking forever to load their bags into the luggage compartment.

With her foot shaking violently from side to side she crossed her arms and dug her nails into her skin. This was taking too long. Any second now Blake was going to come tearing across the lot and yank her off the bus. 'You're not going to make it' she warned herself, squeezing her eyes shut, 'this isn't going to work!'

A loud slam made her jump hard in her seat, but when she opened her eyes, fully expecting to see Blake slamming a fist against the window where she sat, she saw that the driver had just closed the luggage compartment. She didn't have to worry about her plan failing she realized, trying to catch her breath – she was going to die of a heart attack before the bus even left the damned station.

The driver ambled on board and took a moment to wave and say hi to all his passengers, and then slower than she would have thought possible, he settled himself into his seat, fiddled with his switches, twiddled with his seat belt, fished out the key for the ignition, messed about with the seat position and then finally, finally, stuck the key into the ignition and started the engine.

'Come on', Nyah begged, as he then began to adjust his mirrors, 'just drive – please, just drive the damn bus away!'

Tearing her eyes off his painfully slow movements she glanced out the window. Blake and Karen were in the parking lot, Karen's red hair glinting menacingly in the strong sunshine as they stood motionless on the black-top, staring straight at the bus.

Nyah ducked forwards, pretending to tie the laces on her sneakers. Her fingers shook violently as she bent low, her mouth silently forming the words 'please drive' over and over as she waited for Blake's holler to reach her ears. When the bus lurched forwards she moved with it, banging her head off the seat in front of her, but she stayed down, her eyes squeezed shut, not caring what the other passengers might think.

'Please, please, please,' she begged silently, already anticipating the brakes coming on, the door sliding open and Blake's heavy feet marching down the aisle to where she sat. But the bus kept moving. It trundled along, the welcome sound of shifting gears making her drop the knotted laces and cautiously lift her head.

Nyah breathed out a slow, shaky breath as the bus rolled out onto the main road, picked up speed and left Blackwater, Blake and Karen shrinking in the distance behind her.

TWELVE

Thirteen days passed in a forced state of complete randomness. Nyah travelled by whatever means possible, sometimes doubling back on her route or even journeying in a complete circle. Even though her unique scent had almost disappeared she wanted to be sure that if Simon was only hours behind her the way that she had criss-crossed her own path over and back would confuse the hell out of him. Tracking her had to be next to impossible, and ironically, the only advantage to having her wolf gone. The disadvantages to having her wolf gone however, were numerous – and overwhelming. She couldn't hear properly, couldn't see beyond her own nose in the dark, couldn't run with any kind of speed and was unable to pick out a single scent that would alert her to the presence of other werewolves. Worst of all was the feeling of emptiness. The silence that occupied the vacant space inside her was abysmal. Now and then she would make a decision about her next move and forgetting about her loss would automatically pause to feel her wolf's opinion. In those hollow seconds after, the sense of being severed from her own self was so acute that she found herself wrapping her arms around her ribcage as if trying to hold herself together.

And not only did she have to deal with all of that – now another more worrying side-effect had taken hold.

At first, she had assumed that the weighty tiredness she had been experiencing was due to the come-down of her regular adrenalin rushes, but when the grogginess began to seep through her during moments when she wasn't freaking out, she began to wonder if Simon's comment about how her bound wolf would eventually kill her was true. She wasn't exactly knocking on death's door; the weariness was more a nuisance than anything else, but now that she had begun to monitor the episodes of feeling deflated it was obvious they were occurring more often and lasting for a little longer each time. And what she was going to do about it she had no clue.

'Just like everything else', she reminded herself, flinging her bag down onto the motel bed. She landed beside it a moment later, stretching out on her back as she blew out a deep breath.

When she had fled from Blackwater her plan had not stretched beyond safely escaping Simon, and too frantic to figure out what she would do once she achieved that she had left the worry about the next step of her plan tucked into the back of her mind somewhere. But now that she was free there was nothing stopping the bucket-load of questions from tipping out at regular intervals. 'What are you going to do now? How are you going to get your wolf back? How are you going to help your pack?'

Nyah threw one arm across her face and groaned quietly. She had spent hours dwelling on every question and all that she had managed to come up with so far was a big fat 'I don't know', so she had decided that all she could do was to keep moving. Sooner or later she'd have to get help, that was inevitable — trying to achieve anything without her wolf was pointless — but the problem was who could help, and who would want to? No-one in their right mind would want to come within a thousand miles of Simon Northfell and the only people that could restore her wolf were of Cassius Ochre's kind, and how trustworthy were they? If she did manage to find a Shaman chances were they would deliver her straight back to Simon.

Nyah was too exhausted to navigate the labyrinth of her complicated situation. It had been a long day. Her crappy sense of direction had left her walking for miles along an endless stretch of road so void of passing traffic that she had wondered if she had somehow missed mankind coming to a sudden and silent end. When a truck had eventually rumbled into view she had been quick to wave the driver down and accept his offer of a ride, but no sooner had she clambered up into the cab and dumped her bag at her feet than she had regretted her actions. Anyone that opened a conversation with a lip-licking 'You look just like my dead wife' was not the kind of company that you let your guard down with, and she had spent the subsequent hours so alert to every move the creepy driver had made that by the time she had slid down from the intense atmosphere of the humid cab every nerve in her body was ready to snap.

Scary Widower had dropped her on the outskirts of a town called Shoreton and after a short walk she had found The Leaning Pines Motel. It was only gone six-thirty in the evening when she had stuck the key into the door of her room, but she was so exhausted that even the thoughts of having to chew food made her want to cry. She was starving, though. And clothes needed to be washed. A motel stay was a luxury; she avoided them as best she could for financial and security reasons - some owners were just downright rude they asked so many personal questions - so whenever she did fork out her precious cash for a room she made sure she got her money's worth by availing of all the facilities; hot water, free soap and the occasional breakfast buffet that she had become scarily skilled at discreetly fleecing and cramming into her bag.

Heaving herself upright she dragged her bag onto her knees and began pulling the contents out. She possessed only a few basics, bought hurriedly the day after she had fled Blackwater. Her biggest expense had been the pair of sturdy walking boots that had replaced her favourite but flimsy sneakers, and aware that her few hundred dollars had a long way to stretch the only other clothing items she had allowed herself to buy were three t-shirts, a pair of jeans and some underwear. Her vital toiletries collection was stuffed into a plastic bag and she tipped out the various bottles and tubes onto the bedspread, rooting for the travel-size bottle of clothes detergent. She may have been running loose like a wild animal, but she sure as hell wasn't going to end up stinking like one.

Grabbing the items that needed washing she moved into the bathroom and filled the sink with water and a blob of detergent and then left the items to soak. She could wait another day before hitting a launderette. Washing and drying jeans by hand was no joke.

Returning to the bedroom she kicked off her boots and sitting back down onto the bed with her left boot in one hand she stuck her hand inside and retrieved her cash. Hitching rides, stealing from breakfast buffets and sleeping under the stars had saved her a lot, but no matter how frugal she forced herself to be, the wad of bills was going to continue shrinking. Three days ago she had withdrawn the last of her savings from the bank in a state of complete paranoia, where the teller, unable to ignore her slick brow and shaking hands, had been quick to ask if she was okay. 'Food poisoning' Nyah had lied, furious for allowing attention to be drawn to herself in such a public and CCTV'd place. Ducking out of the bank in a frantic state of panic she had taken a bus back to her departure point in the neighbouring state from two days previous, hoping desperately that her need for cash wouldn't be what led Simon to her.

Maybe Simon wasn't even looking for her she thought, returning to the bathroom to scrub at the socks soaking in the sink. Or maybe he had tried, but had given up after realizing that she was too clever to be caught. Maybe he had turned his attention to someone else in the pack, found another victim to work his disgusting -.

Sucking in a deep breath Nyah refused to let the thought expand. She couldn't allow herself to think about her pack. She may have turned rogue, but the sense of ownership that she still felt for everyone in Blackwater Ridge hadn't diminished. If she dwelt long enough on what could be happening to them her fears for them would drag her back. 'And you can't do that,' she told herself sternly. 'Not until you have a way to fix all of this.'

Strangling the last few drops of water from her socks she shoved aside the questions before they could flood her mind again. There were only three things she had the energy to do right now; shower, eat and sleep.

The pine trees that prompted the motel's name were clear to smell in the night air when Nyah left the 'Patriot Diner', a cosy, friendly establishment that kept its promise of 'delicious home-cooked fare'.

Drawing in deep breaths of the warm, clear air she crossed the empty street towards the motel, slowing her pace to allow herself a short moment to enjoy the scent. Shoreton was a quiet place. There was no hum of traffic, no yapping dogs and as she wandered across the motel parking lot there wasn't even the muffled rise and fall of television noises coming from any of her fellow guests' rooms. The only sound that drifted lazily about her was the mournful whine of a distant freight train.

She turned to face the source of the sound, her memory suddenly recalling a movie scene where a girl and a guy on the run from something, or someone, had jumped a freight train. The romantic vision of them sharing an empty box car as they trundled through an inky black night wasn't what brought a smile to her face at that moment. A freight train could carry her hundreds of miles – free of charge. Yes, it could be risky, and she'd have to be organised; food, water, something to pee in, but it would be free travel.

The wail faded as she took a keen look towards the forest rising like a black mountain over Shoreton. She was pretty sure that the sound had come from that direction, meaning she'd have to trek through the forest to reach the tracks, but it was definitely worth a try. There and then she made a decision. She'd return to the Patriot for a big breakfast, get some food to-go and then head into the forest. But before marching off she'd take her sweet time in the diner to watch the other customers come and go, because, as she squinted into the dark navy light, she came to realize something: Shoreton was prime werewolf stomping ground; a medium-sized town in a remote place surrounded by forests and a low-lying mountain range. The chances of her being the only Lycan in town were fairly slim and the last thing she needed to do was to find herself tramping through Lycan territory on her quest to find the tracks.

'It would be game over if she wandered into Lycan territory, she warned herself, turning away from the looming view to slip back into her motel room and lock the door. The severity of that potential outcome made her pause in the centre of the floor, briefly making her reconsider the plan, but then she shook the doubt off. Simon Northfell was hunting for her. Nothing could be any worse than him finding her.

As planned, Nyah dallied over her breakfast the following morning, furtively taking in every person who came and went from the diner. The only company she had shared with her dinner the previous night had been the waitress and a young couple who had argued a lot during their short meal, but now that more of the locals were milling about it would be easier to get a sense of whether Shoreton was home to werewolves or not. Even though her now absent wolf would have alerted her to other werewolves before she could have even laid eyes on them, a part of her was still able to pick them out.

Werewolves carried themselves proudly and confidently. Their scent was impossible for her to discern, but their presence wasn't. Even humans were aware of it, albeit at an unconscious level. She had often noticed how humans would find themselves drawn into lifting their heads and turning towards a figure entering a room for no particular reason. Eyes would linger as they appreciated the obvious physical attributes when in reality it would be the unseen essence of the werewolf that had caught their attention. At that moment, as if to validate her point, a woman sitting alone at a booth near the door suddenly perked up when a man pushed open the outer door and stepped inside.

Nyah immediately ducked her head, angling her back slightly towards him as she pretended to be engrossed in the local newspaper that had been left on her table. She kept her pose for a few minutes before casually straightening up and glancing around, hoping her wandering gaze appeared innocently distracted.

His back was turned towards her from where he sat at the diner counter, one hand cupping a mug of coffee, the other occupied with the same paper she was pretending to read.

'*Shoreton residents reject re-zoning*' the headline read. She briefly wondered if the rejected re-zoning threatened Lycan lands as she looked him over. As with most males, he was tall and well-built. He wore a pair of jeans and a lumberjack-style, blue-checked shirt. The sleeves were folded halfway up his arms, held in place with the cuffs of a long-sleeved white t-shirt. She watched cautiously as he raised a distracted hand and ran it over the top of his tightly cut, dark hair.

He's relaxed, she decided, slowly settling herself back into the seat. Although why wouldn't he be, she reminded herself crossly. "You're practically human," she muttered into her coffee mug.

He took his time with his coffee, lazily flicking through the entire paper before leaving payment on the counter and waving a thanks to the waitress.

"See ya round, honey!" she called after him.

Nyah drank back the last of her coffee and watched him head towards the east of the town. Her plan to find the train tracks was still on, but she'd have to be careful. There was no doubt in her mind now that Shoreton's forest was home to werewolves.

THIRTEEN

"Damned, stupid, rubbish human hearing," Nyah spat, tripping over another rock as she hacked her way into the sprawling forest of Shoreton.

When she had stood in the motel parking lot that morning, stuffing fruit and water into her bag, she had naively admired its jade depths as it sat neatly in the distance. The words 'jaunty saunter' had even tripped through her mind as she had pranced towards it. In reality however, it was a massive expanse of dense, lofty trees that constantly whispered their amusement at her pathetic attempts to track the sound of the trains that sporadically rumbled somewhere far, far ahead of her.

"And damned, stupid, rubbish plan," she muttered, heaving herself up onto another bank, the roots of some ancient tree providing a welcome foothold for her mud-encrusted boots.

She'd been tramping through the forest for hours, the trains sometimes sounding promisingly close and then, more often than not, frustratingly far away. She wasn't going to give up just yet, though. There were still another good few hours of daylight left, and further ahead, the light twinkling between the trees was full of encouraging brightness. Perhaps she'd almost reached the edge of the forest. Perhaps the train tracks were just a short distance away. And perhaps there'd be a stream – she'd run out of water ages back and thirst now had her tongue sticking to the roof of her mouth.

Another stumble-filled while later, just as she had guessed, the trees began to thin and she found her pace increasing. It had been almost half an hour since she'd last heard a train, but she kept pushing forward, hoping that she was still heading in the right direction.

When a faint wail eventually sounded out, she grimaced. Coming to a stop she tilted her head towards the east. She was off course again. Way off. "Dammit!" Without her wolf she was useless.

Curbing the urge to kick out at the nearest tree she pulled in a calming breath, leaned against the hefty trunk for support and shut her eyes. "Okay," she ordered herself crossly, "just listen. If humans can do it, so can you."

Holding completely still seemed to help. The train was already fading into the distance, but she could now pinpoint the direction: North east.

Nyah opened her eyes and stared without seeing towards the sloping ground at the foot of the tree as another whistle blast considerately lingered for a few seconds longer. Yes. That was definitely north east. Definitely. Smiling, she allowed her eyes to refocus and check in with her brain again, but as soon as what lay at her feet registered with her she froze. "Oh no, no, no, no . . ."

In the loose, dry earth scattered around the bottom of the tree were some clearly defined and instantly recognizable paw prints. Nyah was on Lycan territory. "No, no, no," she muttered again, slowly turning to stare into the surrounding forest. She had been looking out, she had, she had been checking constantly for signs of wolves, even going to the trouble of occasionally examining branches at lower levels for traces of snagged fur. How the hell had she missed it?

Nervously glancing over her shoulder she realized that she now had a decision to make; turn back or carry on. It wasn't too hard to choose. Carrying on would only bring her deeper into the territory, whereas turning back would mean that, although she'd lost pretty much the whole day, she'd stay safe.

Reluctant to move for another moment she took another careful look through the trees. Regardless of her easily-made decision, it still didn't change her current situation; she was still on Lycan territory. It was possible that she may have just reached the boundary line – or maybe she hadn't even crossed it. "Or maybe you're knee-deep in their land," she muttered back to herself, squinting at the patchy light dancing between the trees that suddenly didn't seem so pretty and innocent any more. There was no way to know for sure, but the fact that she was alone – well, seemed to be alone – was a good sign.

Hitching her bag tightly onto her shoulder she stepped away from the tree, placing every step with infinite care as she inched back towards the direction of the dark, compact forest. Her eyes constantly darted between the ground littered with crunchy twigs and pine-cones to the pools of speckled light that were splashed amongst the trees around her. Half of her wanted to just bolt and barrel through the forest in the vain hope that she could outrun whoever might already be following; the other half was frozen, wanting to remain rigidly fixed to the one spot until she was absolutely sure she was alone.

It occurred to her later that it was her sudden vigilance that had probably given her away. If she had carried on with her muttering and marching the patrolling wolf that had found her might have just let her carry on, assuming from her appalling trekking skills and weak scent that she was human, but when his voice had called out the order for her to stop she had obeyed immediately, even bowing her head in submission. If he hadn't known she was a werewolf up to that point, she had just given him the first reason to question it.

"Turn around."

Nyah did as asked, slowly turning until she was facing the tree where she had spotted the paw prints.

The owner of the voice stepped out from behind the wide trunk. Instantly, she recognized the blue shirt and tight hair; Diner wolf. He took a short moment to look her over, his stern expression giving nothing away.

"You're trespassing," he announced.

"I'm sorry. I didn't realize this was Lycan territory. I'll leave straight away." She wanted to kick herself when his eyebrows twitched up in surprise. Dammit – she was a blabbering idiot!

"I can't allow you to leave," he replied, coming closer and not bothering to disguise the fact that he was trying to find her scent.

"But –."

"No." He shook his head as he sniffed the air around her. "Rogues must be presented to the Alpha. You know the Law."

"But I haven't threatened any members of your pack," she reminded him.

"Which means your life will be spared," he reminded her in return, "but if you attempt to escape or shift I will assume it as a threat and - ."

"I know," she muttered, cutting off his warning. "I know the Law."

"Good. This way, then." He gestured for her to walk ahead and with a muted sigh she obeyed.

The first long moments passed in silence before she decided to try to plead her case. Diner Wolf had started out walking behind her, but was soon forced to step in beside her, the need to continually grab at her arm whenever she stumbled becoming more embarrassing by the second. No matter how hard she begged though, he remained stoically mute; the only time she saw the faint whisper of a waver was when she turned on the waterworks.

Eventually, she gave up, deciding instead to embrace the worry about what was going to happen once he handed her over to his Alpha.

Lycan Laws were pretty black and white when it came to trespassing rogues, which meant that the very first thing the Alpha of Diner Wolf's pack was going to do was notify her pack of her capture. Then, if Simon wanted her returned, guarded transport back to her territory would be arranged. If for some bizarre reason Simon didn't want her back, Diner Wolf's pack had the choice of allowing her to stay or letting her go free – unless of course she threatened or harmed one of the pack – then Diner Wolf's Alpha had the right to kill her on the spot.

She didn't want to die. But she didn't want to go back to Simon either. And the chances of her escaping were somewhere between fat chance and no chance.

She needed time to think, but Diner Wolf was marching her far too energetically through the last of the thinning forest. As the outskirts of what looked like an enormous pack village came into view she began to slow her pace, pulling against Diner Wolf's grip.

"I can't let you go," he reminded her, stopping as she dug her heels in and stared anxiously ahead.

"Please," she begged, her eyes tearing up for real this time. "I got lost was all; the last thing I wanted to do was cross onto Lycan land. Please, let me go."

Diner Wolf shook his head slowly. "I have to present you to my Alpha – you know that." He held out his hand to request that she walk again and she realized that he was being as nice as he could be under the circumstances. Any other wolf would have just hauled her ass straight out of there and yelled at her to shut the hell up.

Shut the hell up.

There was her answer.

Diner Wolf's Alpha couldn't contact her pack if she kept her mouth shut. Okay, eventually, he would just pick up the phone and start ringing around until he found out, but keeping her lips zipped would buy her some time. And if she'd had the wherewithal to think before opening her mouth to Diner Wolf she wouldn't have been in this mess in the first place. With her wishy-washy scent she could have easily led him to believe that she was a half-breed and unaware of her werewolf genes. It wasn't uncommon for half-breed children to never learn of their hidden animal and a fraction of composure on her behalf could have fooled him into believing she was an unsuspecting hiker. Instead she had panicked and shot her mouth off.

It won't happen again, she decided firmly, as Diner Wolf took a gentle hold of her arm and began leading her towards the village.

FOURTEEN

Dean Carson, Alpha of the Carter Plains pack, had only savoured two bites of his steak dinner when his Beta, Nick, mind-linked with him. Nick had found a rogue on their territory and was on his way back to their village with the rogue in tow. 'There's no threat,' Nick had assured him before breaking the link, 'this one's definitely not a typical rogue. Believe me when I tell you that the word strange doesn't cover it.'

Strange or not, Dean still bristled. Flinging his cutlery down he got up from the table, stalked from the kitchen into the hall and wrenched open the front door. Drawing himself up he watched them approach, scowling hard as he sized up the rogue that had crossed into his territory.

Nick was right. This one definitely didn't fit the rogue mould. First off, the rogue was female; ninety-nine per cent of the time rogues were male, and secondly, she didn't behave like a rogue – not when compared to the aggressive and threatening ones he had encountered in his time. Stumbling alongside Nick with her terrified eyes as wide as the moon, he wondered if Nick had mistakenly picked up a human. There wasn't a whiff of rogue swagger about her.

Pretty, though, he thought, admiring her long black hair, toffee-toned skin and doe-like, brown eyes which briefly met his stare before darting to the grass again. Dean cleared his throat. Physical attributes aside, she was a rogue on his land, and that, he didn't like.

He widened the front door as Nick brought her up the porch steps and once she was standing in his hallway he followed them inside, making a point of slamming the door behind him. She flinched and Nick's voice popped into his head. 'See what I mean?'

Dean circled her once, noting how her head and neck tried to shrink themselves into her shoulders as he looked her over. "Where did you find her?" he asked Nick emotionlessly.

Nick's account was thorough, to the point where his description of how she had been constantly tripping over her own feet brought a flush of embarrassment onto her face. She fidgeted nervously with the strap of her bag, struggling to hide the horror of hearing just how long she had been followed and just how clearly Nick had heard her frustrated mutterings.

"No threat was made at any stage," Nick finished up.

"I heard you the first time," Dean replied flatly, continuing to stare hostilely at her, but allowing Nick to hear the laugh that echoed inside his mind.

'And there were tears,' Nick added silently, 'when's the last time you saw a rogue bawl?'

'That would be never,' Dean chuckled back before speaking aloud, his Alpha tone full of authority. "Thank-you, Nick, you may leave now."

"Yes, Alpha Carson."

As the door clicked softly behind Nick, Dean heard her swallow nervously. Continuing to nail an intimidating stare on her he allowed a nice long moment of awkward silence to pass before he spoke. "What's your name?"

"Taylor," she replied.

"Your real name."

She shook her head.

"What pack are you from?"

Again, she shook her head.

"Why are you on our territory?"

"It was a mistake. I didn't know I'd crossed the border."

"You were three miles beyond the border – how deep into our land did you need to travel before working it out?" When she didn't answer he moved a step closer. "Why is your scent so weak?"

She visibly bolstered. Mashing her lips together in a tight line she drew in a breath and pushed back her shoulders. Getting answers wasn't going to be easy, he realized. "Tell me why your scent is so weak."

No reply.

"Are you a half-breed?"

Her blank expression suddenly shifted and she flashed a violent stare at him before quickly dropping her eyes to the patterned rug under her muddy boots. The sound of her teeth being ground together reached his ears.

"Why were you in the forest? My Beta said you appeared to be looking for something – what was it?"

She was counting the geometrical shapes woven into the border of the rug. He watched as her eyes flicked from one shape to the next, her mouth remaining clamped shut and her forehead creasing with determination.

"Is someone looking for you? How long have you been rogue?"

She was now completing a second lap of her count.

"Have you been staying in Shoreton?"

Her lips almost vanished with the effort she put into keeping her mouth shut.

"Are you alone?" He finally let an impatient sigh fill the silence she refused to break. "Are you going to answer any of my questions?"

"Let me go," she suddenly blurted out, abandoning the rug to look directly at him. "I mean no harm to you or any of your pack. Please, let me go and you'll never see me again."

"Lycan Law states -."

"You don't need to quote me Lycan Law," she cut across him, "I know it better than you think. I'm asking you – I'm *begging* you, please, just let me go."

Dean shook his head. "You're not going anywhere until your Alpha is informed. If he doesn't want you back I'll decide what to do with you then."

Her vigour faltered. Dean watched closely as she swallowed nervously again, distractedly readjusted her bag on her shoulder and took a second to carefully word her next sentence.

"Look . . . I, I turned rogue for a good reason, and all I'm asking is that you let me leave your territory. I won't tell anybody I was here – believe me, I don't *want* anybody knowing I was here . . . and it really would be better if you just let me go."

"Why would it be better?"

Her mouth tightened and once again she dropped her eyes to the floor.

"Tell me why you abandoned your pack," he demanded.

Her head whipped up. "Me? Abandon my pack? I'm not the one who abandoned anything," she snapped.

"So someone abandoned you?" he surmised. "A lovers tiff?"

"Oh, you got me," she answered sarcastically, waving her hands as if surrendering. "I turned rogue because my mate forgot what my favourite flower is."

"Maybe you should remind him when he gets here."

A strange expression replaced the derisive look on her face. "What? When who . . . comes here . . . ?"

"Your mate. No doubt he's going to come looking for you."

There was a pause in which he heard her breath loosen. "I don't have a mate."

"So who abandoned you then?" he pushed, aware that he had stumbled close to whatever had her running rogue.

"I – it's not. . . ."

"Someone made you run," he realised aloud.

Her mouth slammed shut and the sudden determination not to utter another single word stiffened her entire body.

"For the love of . . . this is ridiculous," he said, his patience unravelling. "You need to start answering my questions."

This time she challenged his stare. He wasn't her Alpha so she didn't have to bow down and show him respect, but nonetheless, there must have been a pretty monumental struggle going on inside her. No wolf, regardless of whether it was a rogue or not, could confront an Alpha as effortlessly as she appeared to be. With one hand perched on her hip, her head tilted to one side and her eyebrows raised in an expression that smacked of 'wanna bet?' he had to agree when his own wolf gave a growl of outrage. It's a defence mechanism he appeased his snarling wolf, now even more curious as to what had forced her into this oddly impressive behaviour.

"You need to let me go," she said calmly.

"Okay then," he answered after a moment, wondering if what he was about to do might answer one question for him. "You want to leave?"

"Yes . . . " she replied, warily, but judging by the tone of her voice, hopefully, too.

"Go then." He jerked his head the door. "The door's not locked. Just open it up and take yourself off my land."

She didn't move immediately. Instead, she frowned at him and then swapped her bag onto her opposite shoulder.

"It's a one-time offer," he warned.

Cautiously, she stepped towards him. He didn't move. She skirted around him, he didn't move. She rested her hand on the door handle, he didn't move.

"Go ahead," he encouraged. "Open it."

She turned the handle and slowly opened the door. He didn't move.

No sooner had her first foot landed on the porch boards than two of his men rounded the side of the house and gave her a warning snarl. She jerked so hard with the fright that she dropped her bag and let out a startled yelp.

Question answered. Dean grabbed her by the arm and hauled her back inside before she could catch her breath. "You need to tell me what the hell is going on!" he demanded, flinging her bag down. "You had no idea those two were out there. You didn't sense them!"

"And you had to make a science project out of it?" she yelled back, jerking her arm free of his hold.

"You can't sense them," he repeated. "And you have a scent that's as weak as tap water. What in the hell is wrong with you?"

Her now familiar clammed up expression was enough to snap the last of his patience. Snatching up her bag he threw it hard at her, expecting that she would catch it effortlessly. Instead, it smacked into her stomach and she stumbled back against the door.

He shot to her side, quick to apologise as she coughed breathlessly. "I thought you'd catch it," he said, ignoring her attempts to shove his hands off her arms. "Are you ill? Is that what's wrong with you? I'll call the pack doctor, you need help, I'm going to -."

"There's nothing wrong with me!" she yelled, another hard shove against his chest making him back off. "I don't need a doctor; I just need you to let me go!" With a wince, she straightened up, one hand still pressed to where he had jettisoned her bag into her stomach. "Please just let me go," she begged quietly. "Please."

He thought about it – for about half a second. "No."

Her whole body sagged back against the door and he strode back into the kitchen, allowing a surge of frustration to wash over him as he heard the mumbled string of profanities she aimed at his absence. What did she expect? No self-respecting Alpha would have granted her freedom. Rogue or no, there was something not right about her and he intended on finding out what it was.

Dean hovered aimlessly in the kitchen for a long moment before rolling his eyes and blowing out another grunt of frustration. "You don't have to stay out there, you know," he called out to her. "You can refuse to talk to me in here, too." Her silence was as subtle as a thunderstorm. "Taylor," he summoned.

There was a delay before the rustle of her movements announced that she was reluctantly shuffling down the hall. Her footsteps slowed just before she reached the kitchen doorway and he paused to listen, sensing by the shift in her breathing that something had caught her attention.

"Back door's guarded, too," he announced after a moment, letting loose a broad smile when her teeth grinding together confirmed his suspicion. When she rounded the door a moment later he had replaced the grin with a more sober expression. "Take a seat," he commanded, gesturing to one of the empty chairs at his kitchen table.

Her narked stare slid from his face and settled onto the plate of cold steak and congealing gravy he had in his hand. When her stomach gave a loud grumble she quickly wrapped her arms around her midriff.

"When did you last eat a decent meal?" he asked.

"This morning," she replied.

"Where?"

"Seriously? You're like the Spanish Inquisition. You want the table number and the waitress' name too?"

"Where, as in, diner or dumpster," he clarified, sliding the plate into the microwave.

"Diner," she mumbled after a pause. "I'm not an animal, you know."

"Good. Well, I've only steak for one, but there's plenty of other food." To demonstrate, he opened the fridge and started rooting around. "I can make you an omelette," he announced, glancing over a selection of eggs, bacon and tomatoes. "I've some frozen lasagne too," he said, "or if you'd prefer I could grill a chicken fillet."

"You don't have to do that."

It was the first sentence that she'd uttered without resentment or aggravation hardening its tone and it surprised him how this softer voice suddenly affected him. "I know," he replied, turning away from the fridge to look at her. "But I'm hoping that you'll become more co-operative if your belly is full," he smiled.

Having a full belly did soften her, not enough to make her answer any of his questions, but enough to finally wilt the hostility she had been doggedly trying to maintain. "What if we make a deal?" Dean suggested lightly, leaning back into his chair in an attempt to appear relaxed and approachable as she swallowed the last mouthful of food.

"The only deal I'm interested in is the one where you let me leave right now," she answered, setting down her fork.

"And I don't notify your pack," he added on.

She flashed him a humourless smile in reply, but he pushed on with his proposal. "You answer some of my questions and I'll delay with informing your pack."

She shifted in her chair, distractedly repositioning the cutlery on the empty plate in front of her.

"Tell me why your senses are so weak." When, as was expected, she didn't answer, he carried on. "Did someone in your pack do this to you?" Sitting forward he shoved his own empty plate aside and sat his elbows on the table. "Were you not safe there? Is that why you turned rogue?" He watched as she discarded the cutlery and began picking at the cuff of her sleeve instead. "Did this happen to anyone else in your pack?"

She was getting better at ignoring him. A bored expression settled on her face as she picked at a loose thread and he decided to give up – for now, at least. "Would you like me to stop asking questions?" He saw it then, suddenly decoded the subtle quirk of her lips that followed every question. "I've just figured something out," he grinned, leaning towards her. "You do this thing with your mouth; when the answer is no, it kind of turns up at one side," he explained, pointing at her lips, "and when the answer is yes, you press your lips together."

Her eyes moved to widen and she quickly lifted her hand to hide her mouth. Dean laughed and sat back. "Too late, Taylor, I've worked it out."

"Good for you," she mumbled.

"So, as I can now read a yes or a no I'll have to start at the beginning again," he announced getting up from the table.

He began clearing the dishes and stacking them in the sink, chuckling to himself as she kept her traitorous lips smashed into her hand.

It was when he was putting the butter away that the calendar stuck to the fridge door caught his eye. Tonight was the first full moon of the cycle, the time when all wolves were slave to the magnetic call that compelled them to phase, but there was no way he was letting her out of his house to shift into her wolf and run free in the forest.

"Tonight's a full moon," he said, turning to face her.

She returned a blank stare.

"I'm not letting you leave this house," he expanded. "Sorry."

When puzzlement flicked across her face he gestured towards the twilit streets outside the window. "I can't allow you to phase, you'll have to stay . . ."

She got up from her chair, clearing her throat as she hurriedly began grabbing the last few items off the table. "It's fine," she muttered. "I understand. It won't be a problem."

Her almost careless attitude towards the epic battle of not phasing on the night of a full moon baffled him for a short moment, but it wasn't until he began to consider how he would feel about it if the roles were reversed that realisation hit him like a smack up-side his head. No way. How could he have not grasped it before now? Could she not? Was she unable to . . . ? "Taylor."

"What?" she said, opening cupboards to find a home for the salt and pepper.

"Why won't it be a problem?"

"Why won't what be a problem?"

"You not phasing."

"It just won't," she replied lightly. "I'll cope," she shrugged. "Where do these go?" she asked, holding up the condiments.

"Taylor," he said, not being fooled by her nonchalance for one second.

"What?" she replied, forcing out a laugh.

Dean grabbed the salt and pepper shakers from her hands and she darted away from him, backing against the counter and nervously tucking her hair behind her ear. "Leave it," she warned.

"You can't -?"

"I said leave it!"

"You can't phase?"

"Of course, I . . ." she began, and then as if suddenly exhausted of all the pretense, deflated with a sigh and shoved her hands into the pockets of her hoodie.

"Are you serious?" Dean dropped the shakers onto the counter and took a step towards her. "You can't phase?"

"No."

"How is that possible?"

"It just is."

"It just is?" he repeated flatly. "You're telling me you can't phase and that's your explanation?"

"I said leave it. You don't need to know why I can't phase."

"I beg to differ."

"It's none of your business!"

She moved to walk by him, but he quickly blocked her path, forcing her back against the counter. "It is my business.

And not because I'm an Alpha – because I'm a werewolf. Who did this to you?"

"Let it go," she ground out.

"How long have you been like this?"

She tried to move again, but he slammed a hand against the edge of the counter, trapping her in place. "How long have you been like this?"

"What does it matter? Just let it go. It's my problem, not yours."

"Why can't you just give me one damned answer? Can't you see that I'm trying to help you?"

"Look, why don't you do yourself a favour and get this into your head. You. Cannot. Help. Me."

She shoved against him but he didn't budge an inch. It was alarming how weak she was. "You know, you shouldn't be able to speak to me like that. Your wolf shouldn't allow it," he said calmly.

"Well, she's not around to slap my wrist."

"What the hell does that mean?"

"It means she's on vacation."

"What?"

"She's sunning herself on a beach somewhere; Hawaii, Outer Mongolia, maybe. I can't remember, she hasn't sent a postcard in weeks."

"Your – your wolf is gone?"

Realising that her biting sarcasm had actually given him some information she folded her arms and pressed a loose fist to her tightly closed lips.

"Your wolf is gone? Taylor – are, you're not . . ."

Her guilty eyes slid from his face and drifted over his shoulder to a point somewhere behind him.

"Your wolf is gone?" It wasn't possible. Lycans just didn't 'lose' their wolves. They didn't just up and leave. "Your wolf is gone?" he repeated.

"Stop saying it!" she yelled and then pressed her fist back in place. "Just leave it," she mumbled from behind her fingers. "Please."

"How can your wolf be gone? How? And – for how long, I mean, for what – weeks ?"

Dean grabbed her shoulders, wanting to shake an answer out of her but she shrugged his hands away and attempted to push her way by him again. "Stop with all the questions, will you?" she grunted agitatedly, elbowing him hard when he refused to move.

"Taylor."

"No! Leave me alone. I'm not telling you anything!"

"You're leaving me no choice but to find out who your pack is, you know," he snapped impatiently, shoving her back against the counter. "If you don't answer my questions I'll have no other option." In that second he was sorely tempted to follow through on his warning. It would only take minutes to run upstairs to his office and start making phone calls. Her pathetic attempts to push him away came to an abrupt stop.

"If you contact my Alpha," she threatened in a low, dangerous voice, narrowing her eyes as she stared up at him, "I'll harm one of your pack."

"And you know exactly what that would force me to do," he replied, just as quietly.

"Yes, I do."

Dean paused, leaning back in disbelief as she glared determinedly at him. "You'd rather die?"

"If that's what it takes."

This time, when she pushed by him, he didn't try to stop her.

FIFTEEN

Dean scrubbed his hands across his face, blew out a long, slow breath and then sat back in his office chair. Okay, he said to himself, ordering his thoughts as he laced his hands behind his head. She's a rogue, a rogue, who for some really screwed up reason, has lost, or, can't connect with her wolf. Whatever has her this way originated from her pack and she's terrified of them finding her. That's what I know. I think.

Glancing down at the phone on his desk he knew he could find out more, but his hands stayed firmly put behind his head.

He'd met rogues before, dealt with them in all kinds of situations, but this was the first time that he'd ever seen a rogue so completely and utterly terrified of being returned to their pack that they would choose to die before going back.

He knew her threat of harming one of his pack was an empty one – she didn't have the strength – but her determined words in the kitchen earlier had finally made him realize that her need to leave his territory was, as far as she was concerned, for her own survival.

It had taken a few moments before he'd been able to shake his head clear of her alarming revelations and follow her out of the kitchen. She'd found the living room and had curled up in a tight ball in the corner of his couch, her refusal to make eye contact with him lasting for nearly half an hour, along with her silence. Not that he'd asked her more questions, he'd decided to drop the interrogation because it had been making him uncomfortable to see how distressed she was becoming, but all his suggestions of how he could try to help were met with ardent head shakes until the moment when he'd offered her a place in his pack. Then she had finally spoken.

"No."

"Taylor, come on, think about it – if you join my pack you'd be under our protection. No-one would be -."

"I said no."

"Even just temporarily, it would -."

"No."

"Why?"

"It would only make things worse."

"Why?"

At that point she'd clammed up again.

In the end, more frustrated than he'd thought possible, he'd got up from his chair and suggested she get some sleep, offering to show her where one of the guest bedrooms was. She'd refused of course, insisting that sleeping on the couch would suit her better, and he'd just been about to remind her that the house was securely guarded and that there was no way she'd be able to sneak out during the night when she had looked up and pleaded with him for one final time that he not contact her pack.

He'd been about to shrug a reply to his genuine indecision when her cowered form in the corner of his couch made him realize something; she was maimed, maimed in a way that he would never have thought possible and he couldn't pretend to ignore it any longer.

Lycans were violently territorial and unfailingly savage about protecting their own packs, but an honour code still existed beneath the aggressive covetousness, a code that compelled them to defend any of their kin when they were threatened by another kind – and there was no way another Lycan had done this to her. As an Alpha, this rogue was his responsibility. And as a werewolf, this injured female was his responsibility, too.

"I won't contact your pack," he had decided aloud. "But that doesn't mean I'm going to stop trying to help you. You know I can't ignore what's been done to you."

But how was he going to help her? The question ran unending laps inside his head while he had grabbed sheets, a duvet and pillows and had made sure that she was settled for her stay on his couch, and it was only as he had mind-linked with the patrol and warned them to keep an extra close eye on his house that he had reluctantly admitted to himself that, despite what he had told her, he was going to have to find out who her pack was. But, he'd have to be careful about it. Werewolves were a secretive lot; if he was going to start poking around he'd have to do it discreetly, otherwise he'd end up in the problematic situation of defending a rogue who didn't want protection – and maybe even from her Alpha who, although had the right to claim her back, could very possibly be a part of the disgusting situation that had been forced upon her.

"Messy," he muttered, pushing himself forward on his chair and flipping open his laptop.

He clicked onto a link that, through several well-hidden links, would eventually lead him into the official Lycan Alliance website. "So, Taylor," he said quietly, waiting for the page to load, "who out there is looking for you?" And someone had to be looking for her. Whether it was the monster who had maimed her or concerned family and friends, there had to be someone tearing up the country trying to find her.

An hour later Dean sat back and frowned darkly at the screen. An unnerving suspicion was creeping inside him. Of the twenty odd rogues that had been reported missing across the country not one of them came close to matching Taylor – or whatever her real name was. The pack websites all shared the same information about the current rogues; recent sightings, descriptions, pictures, suggestions of where they would be heading next, but not one single tiny bit of information popped up about Taylor. It spoke volumes. Alphas always reported rogues, and what they didn't reveal in the initial posting always filtered through from other pack members in Lycan chat rooms; rumours, pleas for help, warnings and so on. It was like her whole pack had closed rank and was pretending she didn't exist. Surely someone out there cared for her and wanted her back, or even just needed to know that she was safe? The silence was frightening.

Clicking out of the last page he turned off the laptop. He'd been sure that he would have at least been able to find out who her pack was. Frustrated that he was still stuck on square one he shoved back his chair and stood up, rolling out his shoulders and stretching his arms.

What he needed now was a run. His head was practically buzzing with the constant stream of questions spinning around and a hammering run through the forest would clear it all away, give him some free head-space to think. But a run was off the agenda. There was no way he was leaving Taylor alone in the house. He could tell by her steady breathing that she had finally fallen asleep – her earlier forced, measured breaths not fooling him for one second – but even though the house was guarded he wasn't going to risk leaving her.

Ignoring the thoughts of how amazing the forest would smell after the earlier rain he switched off the light and quietly closed the office door, pausing briefly in the landing to listen to the even breathing that drifted up from the living room.

He couldn't help but grin as he crossed towards his bedroom. She was going to be pissed with herself in the morning when she realized that she'd fallen asleep instead of escaping. And no doubt, he warned himself, peeling off his t-shirt and throwing it onto his bed, it'll make her even more determined to get away.

Dean had just flicked on his bathroom light when his wolf gave a low warning growl. Awareness hit his senses, prickling his skin and instinctively stilling him on the spot. Another wolf was in his house.

For a short moment he held perfectly still, his head cocked towards the direction of the faint signal coming from somewhere downstairs. And then he moved.

Every outer door in the house had been locked, he assured himself, silently darting back out onto the landing – he had checked them all, twice. The windows had been shut too, so how in the hell did whoever it was get in?

The sense of the stranger began to grow stronger as he reached the top of the stairs and his feet automatically took over when he traced the trespasser to the living room.

How had they found Taylor so fast? How did they get past his patrols, his boundary, how in the hell had they got inside his own damn house without him or anyone else sensing it?

It was just as he reached the living room door, and was preparing to mind-link with Nick for back-up, when the scent of the strange wolf hit him.

It stopped him as abruptly as if he had hit a solid stone wall. Heat coursed through him, a tantalizing scent rushed through his nostrils and a violent possessiveness suddenly raged inside him. He had connected with his mate. She was here, in his house.

Dean flung the living room door open. And then stalled in the doorway, confused. His wolf was howling for joy, but there was no-one in the living room. He could feel her though, the magnetic pull that tugged at his insides was trying to drag him further into the room, but he ignored it as he stared wildly around. Where was she? He didn't understand. He could feel her, smell her, every cell in his body was reacting to her presence, but . . .

It was then that his frustrated wolf took over and snapped at him to pay attention.

Taylor.

The second his eyes landed on her sleeping form his wolf began howling again. Stumbling over to the couch he sank onto his knees.

What in the hell? Her wolf was clear to sense; its strength rolled off her in waves, and whoever she was, it was pretty damn clear that she was no half-breed. "Taylor," he whispered, his trembling hands hovering over her. He wanted to wake her. He wanted to tell her that the awful thing that had hidden her wolf was gone. He wanted her to open her eyes and see him, feel the rush of their first connection.

She stirred, and still sleeping, turned her face towards him. For the first time since he had met her he saw a genuine, non-sarcastic smile playing on her lips. "Taylor," he murmured again, feeling almost delirious and then suddenly, incredulous. "Shit." Clumsily rolling off his knees Dean sat heavily onto the floor.

He needed a minute. His stupefied mind was split in two; the male side wanting a time-out to rationalize and get practical, his wolf side begging him to move back closer to its mate, pleading with him to breathe in the warm vanilla scent from her skin, feel its softness under his lips, taste its smooth honeyed - .

Dean scooted further back on the floor and ignored a howling protest. Taylor did not need to wake up to him slobbering all over her like a puppy.

For a long moment he sat in a heap in the middle of the floor, his face alternating between a serious frown and what he reckoned was a dopey grin of bliss. Over the constant whining of his wolf begging to be back beside its mate he came to realize that his bonding to Taylor had solved everything.

Taylor was his now, she belonged to him, and his pack. She was no longer a rogue; she was an Alpha's mate. And he would protect her from whatever vile piece of scum had tried to take away her wolf.

He shuffled to the side of the couch again. It was time to wake her up. He couldn't wait to see her expression once she felt the return of her wolf. And when she felt their connection? That was going to be even better. Man, he was going to let her know that he'd never let her go, never, ever, let anyone harm her again.

Reaching out he rested one hand against the side of her face. "Taylor," he whispered, "wake up."

SIXTEEN

In the haziness of that just-woken moment the following morning, Nyah forgot where she was or what had happened. For a short, carefree moment, aware of the comfortable, warm bed she was curled up in, she basked in the sensation of waking from a good nights' sleep and the sense of peace that blanketed her. But then her mind stirred awake, reminding her of the spiralling disaster that her life had become. And yet surprisingly, for the first time since the day she had learned of

Simon's appalling intentions, the remembrance didn't prompt her to leap out of the bed with her forehead sliding into a tense frown and her shoulders tightening under the weight of her stress.

Remaining motionless inside the duvet cocoon she wondered why. Yes, she'd finally got a decent nights' sleep, yes, she was indescribably comfortable and yes, maybe the part of her brain that doled out the panic juice was still asleep, but it was something else that was making her shrug off the worries so carelessly. For some reason she felt different; braver, more capable, impressively positive and . . . safe. That was it. She felt safe.

The alien sensation prompted her to open her eyes and lift her head out from under the duvet. Ah – yes. Dean Carson's house. Dean Carson's living room. Dean Carson's couch. His *comfortable* couch. "Argh, the one you weren't supposed to have fallen asleep on," she muttered, shoving down the top of the duvet and squinting around the room. "Idiot," she groaned, squirming into an upright position. The small clock on the mantel made her scrunched eyes widen in surprise. Eleven-thirty? She'd slept that long? Wow. She couldn't remember the last time she'd done that.

Nyah yawned and then flopped back down onto the pillow. The upside to having such a great sleep was that her brain would be in top condition to come up with another escape plan. The down side was that Mr Alpha was no doubt already gunning to get started on a fresh round of his interrogation programme first thing.

She winced at the full glorious Technicolor memory of the previous days grilling. Dean Carson had certainly mastered the Alpha scowl, but his intense blue-eyed stare had had no effect on her – not even a teensy bit. With her wolf gone, his whole swelled-chest, laser-eyed, clenched-jaw 'answer-me-'cos-I'm-an-Alpha' pose had been in vain; the only thing he'd made her feel was more pissed at herself for getting caught in the first place. And now that she thought about, she started to get pissed all over again. Why did he have to be such a damn do-gooder? Why couldn't he just grow a pair, ignore a stupid Lycan Law and let her go? And what was with all the concern? Why did he give a crap about what had happened to her? And his ashy-blonde hair was annoying, too. He had this long piece that kept flopping down over his eyes. It was really distracting.

Nyah sucked in a sharp breath and sat up abruptly. Dean Carson's hair was not distracting. It was lame. And nothing else, she warned herself, kicking off the duvet.

The last of her clean clothes sat in the bottom of her bag and she pulled them out. The next town she hit she'd visit a launderette – which will be today, she told herself, pulling on her jeans and a t-shirt.

Before opening the living room door she combed her hair through with her fingers and scooped the flecks of sleep from the corners of her eyes. A mirror would be nice, she thought, trying to smooth back her hair as she opened the door.

Noises drifted towards her from the direction of the kitchen and as she made her way down the wide, sunny hallway she amused herself with the idea that maybe Mr Alpha had had a good night's sleep too, and was going to announce that she was free to go straight away – no, she corrected herself – free to go once she'd had a big breakfast. The smells hovering in the air made her stomach growl.

He fixed her with the strangest expression when she walked into the kitchen. It was weird enough to make her snatch a quick glance down, just to be sure that she had actually put some clothes on. "Is something wrong?" she asked as he continued to stare at her, a coffee pot in one hand and a waiting mug in the other.

"How did you sleep?" he answered.

"Um, fine," she replied, although it sounded more like a question. He was waiting for something, she realized, so she added on a 'thank you', again, sounding more like she had asked it than said it.

"Good." With a perfectly obvious, snap-yourself-out-of-it shake of his head he returned to filling his coffee cup.

"Um, could. . . could I take a shower?"

"Sure." He took a deep drink from the mug and when his eyes met hers over the rim the expectant look was back. "I left a pile of towels on the laundry hamper for you."

"Thanks."

"No problem."

Nyah backed out of the kitchen. She was totally missing something she decided, heading for the stairs. Why had he been staring at her so strangely? What had he been wanting her to say? Or was it that he wanted to say something? "Oh no . . ." She froze on the top step. He'd found out about her. He'd made phone calls, tracked her back to Blackwater Ridge, spoken to Simon. He knew – or at least, he thought he knew. Simon had probably spun him a fantastical tale. Or worse – maybe he'd done some voodoo juju on him over the phone and now Dean was just like Blake and Karen and Michael.

No. Nyah pulled in a calming breath. She refused to have a paranoia meltdown. If Dean had learned something he would've been triumphantly waving it in her face this morning. He would've had a t-shirt with a 'Ha! Guess what I found out?' stamped across it. His weird behaviour was something else. "And not your problem," she murmured, marching across the landing to the bathroom. "Try to spend at least the first hour of this day in a semi-normal state of mind," she ordered herself, closing the door, locking it and then shrugging off her jeans and t-shirt. "You've had a good night's sleep. Use it to your advantage and force your brain to behave," she told herself.

The hot fingers of back-massaging water that jetted from the shower head returned her to the state of relaxation she'd woken in. After experiencing the world's crappiest showers in the motels she'd frequented, Dean Carson's shower was five star indulgence. Powerful streams of water pummelled her scalp, shoulders and back, and only Mr Alpha might get the wrong idea, she forced herself not to moan aloud with the bliss.

Surrendering to the fact that all the hot showers and delicious meals in the world couldn't distract her from the reality of her situation, Nyah shook herself out of her blissful state. She needed to get her smarts on. Last night she'd been foolish to think that she was going to be able to just sneak out of Dean's house. He had been way ahead of her, and still was, no doubt, meaning she had to figure out a way to get past the men watching his house, avoid the patrols that were no doubt covering every inch of his territory and then slip past the boundary line – and all with the crappy abilities of a weak and useless human. Either that, she thought, applying a second generous blob of shampoo, or you've got to turn up the begging and whining to a level that'll annoy him so much he'll kick you off his territory himself.

Regardless of how she was going to achieve her freedom, it wasn't going to be any time soon, and the unwelcome thought sent a familiar ripple of fear running through her. Dean appeared to be a more modern Alpha than her father had been. Smartphones with cameras that could have her picture uploaded onto the Lycan Alliance website in two seconds flat were probably tucked into every pocket of his pack member, and a rogue being sheltered in the Alpha's house was hot gossip no matter who the pack. It wasn't a stretch to guess that a few members were already curious for a glimpse of her. If she so much as stuck her nose outside the front door Simon could have her location within seconds and then he'd . . .

Nyah turned off the water and squeezed out her hair. Maybe persistent, high-pitched, begging was going to be her best option.

Smelling way too masculine than she liked, Nyah dried off and dressed, grimacing as the scent of his shampoo, probably called 'Manly Musk' or 'Essence of Dude', kept wafting around her. Next time, although it was nearly all gone, she'd use her own shampoo. "Stop with the next time," she muttered crossly. "You need to get out of here."

Dean was nowhere to be seen when she came back down and wandered in to the kitchen. He had left out breakfast, however. The table was loaded with cereal, bread, fruit and yogurt, and a plate with bacon had been set out by the stove, a pan and spatula lined up alongside them for her convenience. Either he was the most decent Alpha in the whole world or . . . 'He's buttering you up', a warning voice sang. Nyah shrugged and turned on the stove anyway. Two good meals in a row; for someone who was being held against her will, it wasn't exactly hardship.

She had eaten and was just putting the last of her dishes in the dishwasher when he appeared in the doorway. Of course, he had startled her, and so embarrassingly badly that she had dropped a fistful of cutlery. When it had been gathered up, and he had finished apologising for not making more noise, he offered her the use of his washing machine. It was tempting to say no. She didn't want him thinking that all his niceness was going to be paid back with answers to his questions, but she wanted her clothes clean – especially if she was going to be stuck here for another few days. And judging by the sneaky peek she had taken out his kitchen window while her bacon had been cooking, she was going to have to come up with a supremely spectacular plan to get past all the men he continued to have posted around his house.

Preparing for the next round of interrogation as she stuffed her clothes into the washing machine a while later, Nyah sternly reminded herself about the value of keeping her mouth shut. She had toyed with the idea of making up a story, something awful, something that would make him want her off his territory fast, but nothing clever would come to her. He was too damn smart anyway, he'd call her bluff and catch her out. The best thing to do, she agreed with herself, watching the clothes rotating lazily, was to not say a single word. Well - at least not until she was ready to start begging to be let go again. And then she'd use a suitably annoying whinging tone. And watery, sad eyes. And maybe some tears. Yes, definitely tears. She bet he was the kind of guy that wouldn't know what to do with big, wet female tears.

Nyah pulled in a deep breath and rolled back her shoulders. Round one, coming up.

Dean was in the living room, his back turned to her as he knelt in front of the fireplace, energetically shovelling up the ash from last night's fire and tipping it into a small metal bucket. She hovered in the doorway, knowing damn well that he knew she was there, but ignoring her anyway. Or maybe not -

"You weren't cold in here last night, were you?" he asked, his head bent low as he jammed the shovel under the grate to scoop up the last of the ash.

"No, I was fine. . . thank you."

"Good."

That was it? No, what's your name? Where do you come from? Nyah wandered over to the couch and perched on the edge. Another long moment passed and she watched as he brushed away the last of the ash from the hearth. "So. . . no twenty questions this morning?" she asked eventually.

"Is there any point? If I ask are you going to answer?"

She didn't need to reply, he already knew the answer, and once a few silent seconds had passed he gave a short laugh. "Thought as much."

"Are you going to let me go?"

"No."

"Are you going to contact my pack?"

"No."

"You're not?"

"No."

"So, why do I have to stay here then, why won't you let me leave?"

He stood up. Dropping the shovel into the bucket he brushed his hands off each other and turned to face her. "Because you won't be safe beyond the boundary of my territory."

"But . . ."

"You have no senses that will protect you, Taylor; you may as well be human. I'm not letting you go when the risk of you getting hurt is so high."

"But . . ."

"But, nothing. You wandered onto my territory. I'm responsible for you until you return to your pack and as I'm not prepared to allow that to happen you have to stay here." He picked up the bucket, shrugged as if to say 'it happens, suck it up' and marched out of the room.

"Wait!" Nyah ran down the hall after him, following him out the back door that led into a wide, open grassy yard where he carried on walking towards a compost heap. "You're going to keep me here indefinitely?"

"Uh huh." He tipped the ash out and she was forced to hop aside as a light wind aimed a puff of it towards her face.

"But, I can't stay here."

"Why?"

"Because I just can't! I have to go. You have to let me go."

"The only thing I have to do," he said calmly, putting the bucket down and giving her an intent look, "is ensure your welfare. You're a werewolf. I'm an Alpha. You're on my territory, ergo, I am responsible for you."

"You don't have to be," she offered weakly, "I mean, you could just neglect your responsibilities for once and let me go."

He didn't bat an eyelid. A pitchfork was resting against one of the low fencing panels that surrounded the compost heap. He grabbed it and then forked the ash into the existing pile of clumpy brown sods. "I never neglect my responsibilities," he said.

"But you can't keep me here forever," she pushed, "and I'm pretty sure you don't want me around."

He stopped his recycling to give her a look that was eerily similar to the one he'd fired at her in the kitchen that morning. "I do want you around," he said, brushing the annoying lock of floppy hair off his forehead with his wrist. "And I *can* keep you here."

"No, you can't," she insisted.

He shrugged and put the fork back.

"Seriously!" she yelled after him as he walked back towards the house. "You can't! And it's kidnapping," she added loudly as she followed him up the steps, onto the back porch and into the house. "You're holding me against my will!"

"Right - and that's worse than what's already been done to you?" he answered suddenly, stopping abruptly in the hallway to wheel around and face her. "Keeping you safe here is worse than having your wolf knocked unconscious?"

"It's – your – when it's against my will, yes, it is!"

He made to walk away, but held back at the last second and turned to her again. "Tell me something – while you've been here – have I mistreated you in any way?"

"No," she answered.

"Have I starved you? Threatened you?"

"No."

"So what's so bad about being here that you'd rather go back out there where you've no way of protecting yourself against whatever it is you're running from?"

She opened her mouth, but he cut her off before she could even form the first word of her reply. "You can't answer that, can you? You know it's safe here, you know how dangerous it is out there, and yet - ."

"And yet I still want to leave," she snapped.

"Why?" he snapped back, taking a step towards her "Why in the hell would you want to do that?"

"I don't have to tell you."

"Yes, you do."

"No. I don't. You're not my Alpha."

"I'm the Alpha whose territory you strayed on to."

Nyah folded her arms in reply and he looked away with a sigh.

"Look, Taylor, if whoever did this to you is looking for you, they're going to find you," he warned darkly, his sombre eyes returning to her face. "Wouldn't you rather they found you here - where you're protected?"

"No, definitely not," she replied, the half-laugh, half-gasp choking her voice.

"Well, I do," he said simply. "I want whoever did this to come right up to my front door. I want them to stand there and have the gall to try and claim you back. I'll have my entire pack surround them, every single member will stand with me, we'll fight, and nothing will . . ."

His determined words faded out as horrific images of Simon wreaking havoc against Dean's pack leeched air and heat from her body simultaneously. From the little she had seen of Dean Carson's territory, he had a far bigger pack than Blackwater Ridge. She had heard children's laughter this morning – lots of children. Simon wouldn't care for the harm he'd cause, in fact, he'd probably have Dean's entire pack under the robot spell in moments. He'd have them rip each other to shreds to save himself the effort, and she'd have to stand there and watch as it happened.

Nyah blindly stepped backwards, seeking the support of something that would hold her up, her deafness vanishing abruptly as her shoulders bumped against the hard surface of a wall.

"No – I, Taylor, that's not – I didn't mean . . ." Dean was stammering, his face crumpling with regret. "I'd never put you in harm's way, never."

She shook her head, her palms pressing into the cold wall. "No," she found herself saying repeatedly. "He'll, no, no . . ."

"Taylor, I'd protect you, I'd never let anyone harm you."

"You - you want him coming here? You want what he did to me to be done to you - and the rest of your pack?" she choked out.

"No. Taylor, I –."

"Because that's exactly what will happen. For every hour you keep me here you're getting closer to hurting your pack."

"I won't let anything happen to my pack – or you."

"You wouldn't have a choice!"

"Dammit, of course I would," he said angrily, stepping towards her.

"You're no match for him. Nothing is."

"I'm no freshly turned pup," he said, a dangerous cut to his voice. "I can fight."

"Not against that," she said quietly. "You wouldn't ever be able to fight that."

"What do you mean, fight *that*?"

Nyah could only weakly shake her head. She was starting to feel sick. What had she allowed to happen here? She should have fought tooth and nail to get out of this house and off this pack territory. Instead she had enjoyed his food, slept late on his couch and relaxed under his hot shower. What had she done?

"Fight what?" he said again, anger beginning to shadow his eyes. "What do you mean?"

"No."

"Taylor." His warning tone made her want to cringe, but she gritted her teeth and shook her head again, swallowing against another wave of nausea.

"Tell me what you mean about fighting 'that'. Tell me."

He moved closer to where she was clinging to the wall, and as his lifted his hands to place them either side of her, she realised he wanted to trap her in place until she gave him an answer. Before his palms could make contact with the wall she ducked under his arm and bolted. It was pointless, however. Dean was fast - fast because his wolf wasn't turned off.

"Ow!" she cried, when his hands grabbed her arms, spun her sideways and shoved her back against the wall. "Get off me!" she shouted, pushing at him and then squirming so she could aim a kick at his shins. "Get off of me!"

"Tell me!" he shouted back, grabbing her wrists so she'd stop jack-hammering them into his chest. He jammed his wide thigh against hers, leaving her powerless to land another kick. "I'm not letting go until you tell me!"

She struggled for another short moment, frustration over her weakness quickly building and filling her eyes with tears.

"Tell me," he ordered again, pressing the length of his body against her. Despite how he had her pinned she insisted on squirming, her whole body wriggling ineffectually as she tried to shove him away. Her breath was getting tighter with each twist, but when she freed one foot and raked it down his shin he eventually lost patience with her. "What can I not fight?" he roared, so loudly, so angrily, and so like an Alpha that the damn finally burst.

"The thing that did this to me!" she sobbed, her whole body sagging pathetically enough to make him grab her tighter to keep her upright. "Voodoo, magic, dark forces – whatever the hell you want to call it! He'll come here with his Shaman and before you'll even be able to catch a whiff of him he'll have you turned into a robot, and then all your talk about protecting me will be gone out the window because he'll make you do whatever he wants! Making me stay here is the worst thing you can do – you have to let me go!"

"What are you saying - magic? Dark magic - what – I . . . ?" he struggled to say.

"Yes!" she yelled back, fisting her hand and thumping it against her chest. "He maimed me with his filthy magic! I reek of it! You think this is who I am - what I am? It's not! You have to understand – you can't fight him!"

Dean released her so suddenly that she lost her balance and staggered forwards.

When she steadied herself and straightened up he was staring at her with a horrified expression, his hands fisted by his side. Nyah swallowed hard, her breaths colliding in her throat as she took in his fierceness. Now you understand, she wanted to say. Now you'll let me go.

For a long moment he stood in complete silence. She held silent too, waiting for him to speak, waiting for him to finally tell her to leave his territory before the monster hunting her found her on his land, but then she realised that the savage stare he wore wasn't because of Simon's atrocious act. No, the hate-filled stare was aimed directly at her – on her.

"Dean?"

His eyes narrowed and then abruptly, he wheeled around and walked away, strode down the hall, snatched his keys off the key-rack and marched out the front door. He slammed it so hard behind him that Nyah flinched. There was an ominous snap as the lock was sharply turned.

Nyah slumped back against the wall, faltered for a short moment as she stared after him and then slid down onto the floor where she burst into tears.

SEVENTEEN

Four hours later Nyah was still alone in the house. It had taken a long time before she had been able to peel herself off the hallway floor, but once on her feet she had dragged herself upstairs, washed her puffy face and had then wandered back downstairs again where she had curled up on the couch. She had been so exhausted that even lying down hadn't felt restful enough and she wasn't sure if it was due to the emotion of what had happened or her wolf-less body fading further. All the benefits of her solid night of sleep had been wiped out and even though she had wished she could lose herself in the nothingness of unconsciousness, her mind had refused to shut down enough to even let her doze.

After a long while she remembered her laundry and heaving herself up off the couch she dragged herself through to the small utility off the kitchen where she had transferred her damp clothes from the machine to the tumble dryer and then once the dry cycle had run, throughout which time she had sat cross-legged on the floor staring blankly at the spinning drum, she had folded everything neatly and put it back into her bag. She had then sat at the kitchen table for another hour, staring out of the window that framed a pretty view of the distant mountains before a short wander ended with her sitting on the stairs, facing the firmly-locked front door.

For a short while she wondered about the possibility of leaving the house – and the whole damned state itself if she could manage it – but the shadow intermittently passing over the small pane of glass in the front door told her it would be pointless to try; the Alpha's house was still being securely patrolled. Knowing she didn't have the energy to try anyway, she stayed put on the stairs, the silence in the house settling around her in a strangely comforting way.

When Dean returned later that was where he found her – sitting on the third step from the bottom of the stairs, her chin resting in her upturned palms. She didn't move as he took in her odd position, a flicker of concern crossing his face as he ushered a woman into the hall ahead of him before shutting the door.

"Taylor, this is Ellie," he said.

There was a definite tightness in his voice, as if he was still mad at her and trying not to show it. Why, though? Why was he mad at her?

"Hello, Taylor." Ellie looked to be in her late thirties. She was average height, but had a slimness about her that said there was lean muscle hidden under her jeans and pale pink blouse. Her dark blonde hair was tied back in a sleek pony-tail and she smiled cheerfully even though her eyes slanted with pity.

Nyah found her gaze quickly returning to Dean's face as she got to her feet. He'd brought back-up?

"I'm going to bring you to Ellie's house," he said flatly, not moving from where he stood beside the front door. "I'm holding a pack meeting. You can stay with Ellie until I'm done."

"Okay," she replied, her voice coming out in a hoarse croak. She cleared it quietly and stepped down onto the hall floor.

Dean opened the door, but just as she moved past him and was about to step out onto the porch she stopped. Going outside was a bad idea; she'd be seen, maybe even photographed.

"Everyone's in the meeting hall." Dean came to stand in front of her, ducking his head so she would pull her stare away from the empty street and look at him instead. "There's no-one around to see you."

"And only a few of us know you're here," Ellie added reassuringly from somewhere behind her.

Dean held out his hand, as if expecting she would take it, but she ignored him, stepping out onto the porch instead where she immediately squinted in the bright sunshine, her drained eyes highly sensitive to the stark light.

Carter Plains was massive compared to Blackwater Ridge, and its wide, leafy streets, as Dean had assured her, were empty of its inhabitants. Houses were set in neat little groups, each with its own garden, and further ahead, although it was a strain to make her watering eyes focus, she was sure she could see what looked like a children's playground beside a playing field.

It was a short walk to Ellie's house. Neither Dean nor Ellie said a word, although Ellie's silence seemed to be more in solidarity with her situation as opposed to Dean's obvious rankled muteness.

His festering continued as Ellie welcomed her inside her home and brought her through to the kitchen where she pulled out a chair and invited her to sit at the chunky table in the centre of the floor. Dean slunk across the room to hover at the window and trying to ignore him, Nyah focused on the six chairs around the table, wondering if Ellie had a big family.

"Taylor?"

She reluctantly looked over to see him pointing out the window. "You see that hall?" She followed the direction of his finger to where a white-shingled building sat across the street. Woven baskets stuffed with flowers hung beneath arched windows that sat either side of the red painted door. "That's where I'll be," he said.

She didn't particularly care where he was going to be, but she mumbled an 'okay' and it seemed to satisfy him. When he left the kitchen and closed the door gently behind him she let out a slow breath. Why in the hell was he so mad at her? Her eyes drifted down as she brooded over the question and she suddenly registered her fisted hands bulging out the front pockets of her hoodie. Maybe it wasn't him who was angry — maybe it was her. And she was angry, she realized. He had pushed her to the edge and finally got an answer to some of his damned questions and then had totally freaked out when he had heard the truth. Good. Maybe now he'd understand that letting her go was the best thing to do. Sighing, she uncurled her fingers and slid them out of the pockets, wedging them between her knees instead.

A plate with a scone suddenly appeared in front of her. When she looked up, a butter dish, a pot of jam, and small bowl of cream were being set down also.

"You look like you could do with something sweet," Ellie said. "I've blackcurrant, too, if you'd prefer that."

"Um, no, this, this is fine. Thank you."

Ellie returned to moving around the kitchen as she waited for the kettle on top of the huge range to boil. Mugs joined the jam and butter on the table and then after a few moments, with a steaming tea pot in one hand, she sat down.

Nyah wasn't hungry, but not wanting to be rude she cut the scone in half before setting it back onto the plate as Ellie plonked the heavy tea pot onto the table and then took a few moments to butter her own scone before adding a generous dollop of jam. "I'll be deeply insulted if you don't even try it," she said after a moment.

Nyah picked a piece off the side and popped it in her mouth. Despite how she felt, it tasted good. "It's delicious," she said, breaking off another piece.

Ellie gave a smile and pointed towards one of the empty mugs. "Would you like tea?"

"Please," Nyah said.

A semi-easy silence hovered as Ellie poured out the tea while Nyah took another bite. "Do you have a big family?" she asked, accepting her mug and then reaching for the milk jug.

"Four children and a husband," Ellie replied proudly. "My eldest two, the twins, Elise and Eric, are in Alaska at the moment – a field trip for their environmental studies course. The younger two, Conor and Aaron are here, in Carter Plains."

"How old are they – Conor and Aaron?"

"Aaron is thirteen and Conor is sixteen."

Nyah decided to try the second half of her scone with a little butter. Now that she had begun to eat her stomach was begging for more.

"Do you have siblings?" Ellie asked.

Nyah shook her head. "No, I'm an only child. Has Aaron been through his first phase yet?"

Ellie had finished her scone and scooped up her mug. "No, he's due to any day now, though. Dean is watching him like a hawk; he even brought him over to the meeting." There was such affection in her voice towards her Alpha that Nyah felt a tug of loneliness for her father. He had been just as caring for the younger pack members when he had been Alpha. He had always said that being present for the first phase was a humbling experience. It also helped to create a strong bond between an Alpha and his newest Were. She doubted Simon was even aware of which members of her abandoned pack were due to phase.

Ellie slid the plate holding two more scones in Nyah's direction. "One is never enough," she winked.

Nyah took a second scone. "Thanks."

"Honey, you look exhausted," Ellie said in a sudden rush of honesty. "Really, you don't look well at all. Are you not sleeping? How is your appetite?"

"I slept well last night," Nyah tried to reassure her, "it's just that . . . earlier on, Dean and I . . ." She trailed off. Ellie didn't need to know what was going on in her Alpha's house.

"He's worried," Ellie said gently. "He's trying to do what's right. That's what the meeting is about."

"Oh no." Nyah dropped the scone back onto the plate and looked out the window towards the pretty white building. "They're having a meeting about me?"

"Wouldn't your pack?" Ellie asked, her gentleness easing the tension Nyah could feel straining across her forehead. "You're Dean's responsibility, and your being here is – well, it's not exactly a typical rogue scenario."

Nyah didn't answer. But she did wonder how much Dean had told Ellie. "Does everyone know – I mean, is the whole pack in there?"

"Mm hm."

"Everyone? Even the patrollers? They're in there, too?"

"No, no. The perimeters are being watched over," she said confidently, and then added on 'sorry' with a little smile.

When Nyah frowned at her apology Ellie gave a light laugh and put down her mug. "No-one gets past the perimeter," she explained meaningfully.

"I wasn't referring to me getting out," Nyah corrected, soberly. "I was referring to something getting in."

"Oh, honey." Ellie shook her head sadly. "You're safe here."

'I'm not safe anywhere' Nyah wanted to answer, but turned her attention to picking currants out of the scone instead.

"Dean won't let any harm come to you," she continued. Clearly, Ellie was on Team Dean. "He'll do whatever it takes to protect you, I promise."

"In that case he should just let me go."

"He'll never let you go now," Ellie answered, with such knowing that Nyah couldn't help but look back up at her.

"What do you mean 'now'?"

Ellie reached for the tea-pot. "Now that he knows more about you and what happened to you," she said quickly. "More tea?"

"No, no thanks – but don't you think that that's the very reason he should let me go? Can't he see I'm a risk to his pack?"

Ellie slowly filled her cup as she carefully worded her reply. "Dean considers you to be part of our pack -."

"I never agreed to that," Nyah cut in crossly. "I told him that I didn't want to join."

"But you're his responsibility, just like every other member."

Irritably, Nyah shoved her plate away. "Why can't he just get over this whole responsibility thing?"

Ellie laughed gently. "Dean only knows responsibility. Even as a boy he used to look out for his family and friends the way he does now. Before he turned ten years-old they had him picked as a future Alpha, you know."

And he was probably made Alpha on his eleventh birthday, Nyah thought. Mr Responsible.

"He was only twenty-one when he became Alpha," Ellie announced. "The youngest Alpha the Carter Plains pack has ever had." It was said with such pride that Nyah found her attention focusing on Ellie's smiling face.

She saw it then, the resemblance between Dean and Ellie; they were brother and sister. They shared the same hair colour, the same almond-shaped eyes, although Ellie's eyes were more a bluey-grey than Dean's. His were a pure blue, the kind of pale blue that an early morning sky sometimes displayed, the kind of blue that held a touch of warmth, except for when he was in Alpha mode, then they could freeze over into a sort of -.

"Taylor?"

"Sorry?" Nyah jerked upright in her chair. What in the hell was wrong with her? Dean's eyes were blue. Big deal. Get over it.

"I was just saying that he's been Alpha for five years now and that he's learned a lot in that time."

"Uh huh," Nyah mumbled.

"So, maybe give him the benefit of the doubt. Put your trust in him," Ellie suggested softly. "He'll do whatever he can for you."

Nyah returned to fidgeting with her scone. "Carter Plains is a big place," she said lightly, wanting to change the subject. "Did I see a playing field and a playground?"

Ellie described Carter Plains in detail, leaving Nyah to change her estimation of it being massive to being super massive. The pack was huge, too; one hundred and seventeen members Ellie told her, most of which she saw when the meeting broke and they swarmed from the hall before dispersing beyond the view of Ellie's wide kitchen window.

Dean was quick to return to the house where he and Ellie held a long whispered conversation in the hallway, throughout which time Nyah cursed her lack of werewolf hearing, before he led her back outside. The walk to his house was another silent one. She was determined to make him talk as soon as they were back inside his house, though. His reaction to what she had revealed earlier was bugging her. She couldn't figure out why he had stormed off.

"Taylor," he began as soon as they were inside and the front door was shut behind him. "You need to answer some of my questions."

She wanted to laugh just then – it was exactly what she had been about to say to him.

"What you told me sounds crazy," he admitted, "I'm not saying I don't believe you, because I do, but seriously, if you want me to help you I have to know more."

"I never said I wanted you to help me."

"Well, there's a lot of stuff you don't say, but I'm guessing that you don't want to be without your wolf for much longer."

"You can't fix that."

"I can try."

She snorted out a humourless laugh and looked away.

Choosing to ignore her he continued to push. "You have to tell me what happened. I've got all these tiny snippets of information and I need to try and put them together."

She folded her arms in reply and looked down at her feet, but he rattled on anyway.

"Someone in your pack did this to you; that's why you won't go back. And they used a Shaman, which means a Lycan has gotten themselves into something pretty dark and dangerous. Your whole pack must be involved somehow, either voluntarily or not, 'cos otherwise, someone out there would be making a hell of a lot of noise looking for you. I'm starting to think that your Alpha is dead, too, or else completely incapacitated. So . . . here's what I think; how about I try to contact -."

"How about you do nothing at all."

"Taylor . . ."

"No. I'm serious. There's nothing you can do."

"Yeah, you're right," he replied testily. "There is nothing I can do because I'm completely in the dark. My pack is asking questions that-."

"You told everyone about me?" she gasped.

"I told them that - ."

"You – you didn't tell them about the voodoo stuff, did you?"

"No, I told -."

"Did you tell them that my wolf is gone?"

"No. I didn't, only Nick knows, but –."

"What is wrong with you?" she yelled, stalking towards him. "Don't you know that every word you say can go right back to my pack? Do you want them coming here? Do you?"

"No, of course not. All I'm trying to do is help you!"

"You can't help me! No-one can!"

"Don't I even get to try?"

"Why do you want to? Why are you so hung up on helping me?"

"And why are you so hung up on not wanting to be helped?" he yelled back, leaning over her.

"Because," she faltered with frustration, "I don't . . . you'll only . . . because it's complicated, alright?"

"I don't care how damned complicated is," Dean replied, fixing her with such a determined stare that she backed away a little. "But if you don't start answering my questions I'll go find someone who will."

"Wow." Nyah gave a short, stunned laugh. "You really have a death-wish."

"Oh, that's rich coming from you," he replied with a snort, moving to tower over her again.

"Maybe so," she agreed, in a low voice, "but unlike you, my death-wish only affects me. Yours manages to include your entire pack."

Dean visibly paled and although her livid stare held his she could sense his whole body tightening as he loomed over her. Accusing an Alpha of neglecting his pack was definitely up there on the top ten list of 'How To Piss An Alpha Off'. Suddenly, she wanted to take the words back.

Dean remained still for a short moment and then moved away, a slow exhale loosening his shoulders. She was drawing a breath to say 'I'm sorry' when, to her surprise, a smile broke out on his face.

"I was wondering what strategy you'd come up with," he said calmly.

Her mouth formed the word 'what?' but no sound came out.

His grin grew wider. "Well, you've obviously figured out by now that you can't escape from my house – and even if you did, you wouldn't get very far – so I had put my money on insistent begging, maybe even some crying, but I'll be honest, insulting me in the hopes that I'd throw you off my territory hadn't crossed my mind. Nice try, though."

An odd croaky sound trickled from her open mouth as he brushed by her and disappeared into the kitchen. When she remembered how to work her lungs and mouth again she followed him through. "That was a genuine insult, not a fake one," she announced.

Dean chuckled. His head was hidden behind the open fridge door. "Do you like pasta?" he asked, emerging with a red pepper and a carton of mushrooms in one hand.

She stared at him, her expression demanding that he retaliate to her comment, but he smiled instead, held up the vegetables and repeated his question about whether she liked pasta or not.

Nyah rolled her eyes and shook her head. "And this is your tactic, isn't it?" she realized. "Being nice so that I'll give in and answer your questions."

"My being nice isn't a game, Taylor. It's for real."

He chose that moment to push back the loose lock of hair that was hanging over one eye and all the fight she had burning inside her went out. "Fine," she sighed, taking the pepper and mushrooms from his hand. "I'll chop, you make the pasta."

There was a surprisingly long stretch of comfortable silence as they prepared their meal. Dean had made her sit at the table once the vegetables had been chopped and she watched him as he moved about the kitchen, his attention totally caught up in what he was doing. It seemed that he enjoyed cooking. He kept dipping a teaspoon into the sauce, his face setting into an intense frown as he considered the flavour before adding extra pinches of herbs, and on one occasion, a sprinkle of brown sugar.

He had a towel flung over his shoulder and every now and then he'd whip it down to wipe off his fingers or a tiny drop of escaped sauce that had landed on the work-top. The wayward piece of hair was attended to regularly, too, making her look away and even sit on her hands at one stage.

For some insane reason a memory of the unbearable meals she had been forced to swallow with Simon came into her mind. She was trapped in Carter Plains just as she had been in Blackwater Ridge, but yet . . .

"It's all ready," Dean announced, jerking her back to awareness.

"Why did you get so mad at me when I told you about the voodoo stuff earlier?" The question blurted from her mouth so unexpectedly that she winced.

Dean turned around to look at her. "I wasn't mad at you," he replied softly. But then he sighed and gave his own wince. "Okay – well, maybe I was at first – but only for a short while. I got mad at whoever it was that did this to you then. And still am now, I'd like to point out." He scooped her plate up from the counter and carried it over to where she sat, placing it down in front of her. "I'm not going to ask you any more questions, Taylor. It just ends up in a screaming match."

She nodded in complete agreement, but his back was turned to her as he crossed back to the stove to get his own plate.

"And believe it or not, I really don't enjoy it," he added.

"Me neither," she admitted quietly.

He sat down opposite her and picked up his fork, twirling it in his fingers as he marshalled his words. "Look – I'm responsible -."

"No." Nyah held up her hands. "Please don't give me another one of your 'I'm a responsible Alpha' speeches again. Now that you know what this is all about you should be catapulting me off your territory to protect your pack. That's where your responsibilities lie, with them, not with me."

"You're wrong," he said quietly, the nameless look settling on his face again.

"And you're stubborn," she sighed.

"Pot, kettle, black," he smirked.

Allowing her smile to spread she shook her head and picked up her fork.

"No more questions, no more arguments, okay?" he said.

"Okay."

"But you need to understand one thing; I'm not letting you go, so eventually, whoever wants you is going to find you, and the more I know, the better I'll be able to protect you *and* my pack when the time comes."

"Whatever you say," she said.

"I mean it," he pushed. "I'm serious about his, Taylor."

"I know you are."

"So . . . you're staying," he reiterated. "And you're going to tell me the truth about everything."

Nyah nodded once and Dean lowered his fork.

"Really? You're agreeing with me?"

"Yes, I'm agreeing with you."

"You're going to stay? And you're going to let me help you?"

Nyah looked up to meet his eyes. "Yes," she lied.

EIGHTEEN

Taylor moved into the guest bedroom for her second night in his house. It was the room across the landing, the one right opposite his, which was why he had decided to stay in his office until he knew she was asleep. He wasn't entirely sure why it felt so awkward. Or maybe he did; she was half-dressed, in a bed, in his house and she was his mate. And she'd had a helpless look in her chocolaty brown eyes all evening that had made him want to pull her into his arms and hug her or something. Yeah, 'or something' he snorted at himself. The magnetic pull that had vanished when her wolf had the previous night was back – not in full force – but enough to drive him nuts. And it was hell.

Wolves shared a mind-blowing moment when they connected with their mates – wolves plural, not singular. Finding your mate and then having the connection abruptly severed as you basked in the event was malicious. In that glorious moment, just when he'd been about to wake her, enough energy flowing between them to power a small nation, it was as if some sick bastard had gone and yanked out the plug. Just like that her wolf had vanished. It had been so abrupt that he'd snatched his hands off her face, leapt to his feet and staggered back. She'd grumbled in her sleep and rolled over, turning her back to him as he'd stared at her in shock. It had gutted him.

Even thinking about it now, as he rolled his head in a slow circle, the taut muscles in his neck cracking in protest, it still hurt. He'd spent the whole of last night convincing himself that as soon as she clapped eyes on him that morning she'd connect with him, but when she'd come in to the kitchen and looked at him like he was fit for nothing but a mental institute, he'd been devastated. And then when she'd told him the truth about how she'd had Black Magic worked on her he'd lost it. All he could think was that she'd fooled him, made him feel something that wasn't real, tricked him into believing that she was his mate. So he had walked away. He'd ripped into the forest and torn sods out of the earth as he'd pounded his anger out on the forest floor. Mad wasn't the word for how he had felt. He'd literally been seeing red. And making the decision that he wanted her gone hadn't been difficult.

With his mind made up he had gone back to the house, but just as he'd reached the front door he'd heard her crying in the hallway. Immediately, his wolf had reacted; it yipped and howled to get back into the house to comfort her and when he'd realized that that was what he had wanted to do, too, he'd understood that their connection was real. And with every hour that had passed today the initial draw he had felt towards her had begun to re-appear. It wasn't anything as powerful as when he'd first experienced it, but enough to start distracting him and generally making him feel like a love-sick puppy.

When she wasn't dodging his questions or flinging some sarcastic glare at him she had this way of fixing her eyes on him that made him struggle with his train of thought. It was an intent look, as if what he was saying was the most important thing that she'd ever heard and she didn't want to miss a word of it. And a couple of times, while they'd been talking at the table after dinner, she'd done this thing with her hair that was now seared into his brain for the rest of his life; she'd gathered it up at the back of her neck, twisted it into a knot, and then with her two hands laced together she'd held it against the back of her head while listening to something he'd been rabbiting on about. When she'd taken her hands away the knot had uncurled and her hair had tumbled down like something out of a shampoo commercial. The innocent sexiness of it had nearly knocked him off his chair. The second time she'd done it he'd actually had to get up from the table.

Something else was stuck in his mind, too. She hadn't meant it when she'd said she'd stay and let him help her.

He understood why, and he wasn't angry with her for lying to him, but it was frustrating to know that if she had felt their connection even the idea of leaving him would kill her. It also meant he couldn't let his guard down with her; she'd still try to get away from him. And the only way to prevent her from doing that was to get her wolf back.

It was motivation enough to make him jerk his chair closer into the desk and flip open his laptop. As soon as the search engine popped up he typed 'Black Magic' in and then groaned at the number of hits it produced. Settling into his chair he clicked on the first website and began to read.

The more Dean read, the more he began to balk. Clicking between sites he patiently followed links, soon realising that the expression 'in over your head' was clutching its stomach with laughter as it watched his pathetic attempts to fathom the stuff he was reading. Wincing at the graphic images of disembowelled animals he returned to the search engine home page and typed in 'Shaman'.

Although equally as confusing as the Black Magic sites, the information about Shamans was easier to read. Their religion was earth-based, so if Taylor was right about a Shaman working that spell on her, he must have performed it under duress. It wasn't in their nature to harm any living thing and this knowledge lit the first spark of hope. Perhaps he could find another Shaman to undo what had been done. Every spell had a loophole – all he needed was to find a willing Shaman.

"But where," he murmured, vaguely tempted to type in shamansforhire.com just in case. Dean sat back and considered his options. He'd have to be discreet in his search. And where would he even start? "Chat rooms," he said aloud, and reached towards the keyboard again. It was then that Taylor's wolf resurfaced.

Immediately, invisible hands grabbed hold of him in an attempt to pull him from the chair and drag him into where she slept. He tried to ignore the draw, but when his wolf joined in with the urgent pleas he was forced to get up from the chair. Dean crossed the room, shut the door, turned the key and then returned to his chair. It didn't help. Closing his eyes, he pulled in a few deep breaths and told his wolf to shut the hell up. He wasn't going to go near her. He couldn't. He couldn't trust himself not to wake her, and how freaked out would she be if she woke up to him hovering over her with big puppy dog eyes.

Not surprisingly, his wolf got angry. It wanted to be with its mate – simple as.

Dean dug his nails into the arm of his chair and kept his feet firmly planted on the floor. No, he repeated to his snarling wolf. Forget it. Just make do with sensing her from here. But his wolf wasn't going to take no for an answer. A flash of heat raced through him and his spine jerked, flinging him forward as it began to form its werewolf shape.

"Fine!" he whispered. Throwing himself off the chair he strode back towards the door, snapped the key around and yanked it open. "One minute," he warned his wolf. "You get one minute and that's it. Right?"

His hand shook as he turned the handle of her door and eased it open. Forcing himself to stay in the doorway he squinted into the darkness and then, as his eyes adjusted, he made out her shape in the bed. She was on her side, facing the window, one arm out over the duvet but loosely clutching the edge of it to her chest, her hair forming a depthless black shape where it spread out on her pillow. As if her wolf was aware of its mate's proximity, she sighed in her sleep.

"Forty seconds," he reminded his keening inner-self.

Her scent teased his nostrils and against his better judgement he drew in a deep lungful of her, regretting it the second he realized that he had left the doorway and was now standing at the end of her bed, his hands taking a death grip on the iron bed-end.

It was intoxicating to have the connection restored. He would have given his soul to have her wake up at that second and bond with him, but she continued to stay sleeping, her breaths steady and even.

"I wish I knew your real name," he whispered desperately. "I wish you'd at least tell me that."

She stirred and murmured something, prompting him to back away from the bed towards the door, but at the last second he paused. Had she . . . ? "What's your name?" he breathed, hardly daring to believe what he was suddenly thinking.

"Nyah," came the reply, almost instantly.

Don't, he ordered himself. Don't ask anything else. It's not right, it's abusing her trust, it's wrong on every damn level. "Who is your pack?"

She gave a little groan and rolled onto her back.

"Who is your pack, Nyah, tell me."

"Blackwater Ridge," she murmured and then sighed deeply. The sense of her wolf began to flicker.

Stop, he ordered himself. It's a blatant betrayal. She'll never forgive you. But her wolf was fading further and the part of him that wanted revenge for what had been done to her elbowed its way forward. There's no time to hold a mental debate about this, it snapped. Ask the damned question! "Who hurt you?"

She shifted restlessly and murmured a frightened 'no'.

"Nyah, you're safe. It's me, Dean. Tell me who hurt you."

With her wolf signal sputtering like a dying candle she kicked out under the duvet and whimpered softly.

"Tell me, Nyah, who hurt you?" He was at the side of her bed now, bending over her. She rolled away from him, curling into a tight ball, her head all but disappearing under the duvet. With a final wavering flicker her wolf vanished. He'd heard her reply though, muffled as it was, the single word was clear to hear: 'Alpha'.

Ignoring his wolf's yowling misery he left her room and returned to his office. Nyah, Blackwater Ridge, Alpha; pieces were falling into place with a loud thunk in his head. If he wasn't mistaken, Harper Morgan, the deceased Alpha of Blackwater Ridge had a daughter called Nyah. Could that be right? Taylor – no, Nyah – was Harper Morgan's daughter? He'd met Harper Morgan about a year ago. They'd spent a long afternoon together, along with the Alpha from the Carverback pack, shooting the breeze over a few beers and a vast fish-stuffed lake.

Dazed, Dean sank into his chair. Harper Morgan had been replaced by Alan Stenson, and then Alan had died – suddenly; a rogue attack, as far as he could remember. The current Alpha was . . . was – the name wasn't coming to him – Shaun, Stephen, something with an 's'.

The abrupt shrill of his phone flooded him with infuriation when it knocked him off his train of thought. Snatching it up he barked his greeting. "Dean Carson."

"Hello, Alpha Carson. This is Simon Northfell, Alpha of the Blackwater Ridge pack."

Simon Northfell had to loudly repeat 'hello?' a number of times before Dean could wrench words out of his blocked throat. "Alpha Northfell," he coughed, "sorry 'bout that, something seems to be interfering with the signal. Can you hear me okay?"

"Loud and clear," Northfell replied.

"Good, good. So, how can I help you?"

"Unpleasant business, I'm afraid."

"How so?"

"I'm trying to find one of my pack."

Dean closed his eyes and dug his knuckles into his forehead. "Someone turn rogue?"

There was a disappointed sigh. "Yes, unfortunately."

"Sorry to hear that."

"Yes. Have you had any rogues on your territory in the last three weeks or so?"

"Had a Taylor here, but -."

"No, no," Northfell corrected him. "Mine's a female."

"Oh."

"A little firecracker, too."

"What's her name?" Dean squeezed his closed eyes tighter. Sweat was already swamping his brow and it was a struggle to keep his voice loose.

"Nyah Morgan."

Even hearing Northfell say her name made him want to reach down the phone and rip his head off. "Harper Morgan's daughter?" he said with forced lightness.

"Indeed."

"An Alpha's daughter turned rogue. There's a first." Northfell didn't reply. "I'll let you know if I hear anything. Have you talked to Alpha Nickleson yet? He's further north than we are, but if -."

"I will be calling him next."

"Great. Okay. Well, as I said, I'll let you know if I see or hear anything."

"Thank you, Alpha Carson."

"No problem at all, Alpha Northfell."

"Shit," Dean exhaled when the phone was snugly back on its cradle. His mouth had gone dry and a sticky sweat had begun to soak through the back of his t-shirt. Standing up he pulled the t-shirt away from his back and tried to fan cool air under it as he began to pace the floor.

Simon Northfell. He'd heard rumblings from other Alphas about his sudden elevation into the Alpha position at Blackwater Ridge, and while no-one liked to disrespect an Alpha the general unspoken opinion of him wasn't kind. What in the hell was going on in Blackwater Ridge? Taylor – Nyah, he corrected himself – had said something about all her pack being robots. Was that what he'd done? Spelled them to obey him? No wonder there was a radio silence about her absence.

"Shit," he murmured again, stalling his pacing to stare in the direction of where Nyah slept. Should she know Northfell had called? Should he tell her?

No, he decided, turning away. She'd do something stupid and desperate if she did. He needed to deal with this on his own. Or at least, he and Nick did. There was no-one else he would trust with his precious mate's welfare.

It only took a second for Nick to respond to the mind-link as Dean left the office and crossed the landing once more. 'I'll be right over,' Nick replied.

Dean eased Nyah's bedroom door open an inch. She was still curled up under the covers, her body motionless in a deep sleep. He stared in at her, his gaze not moving until Nick's approach demanded that he leave her to go downstairs. He didn't know how he was going to get her wolf back. He didn't know what protecting her might bring him face-to-face with, and he didn't know where he was even going to start, but as he soundlessly closed her door and went downstairs to open the front door to Nick, he knew one thing for sure; Simon Northfell was going to pay for what he had done. With his life.

NINETEEN

". . . so wanting to prove them wrong, I went in." Dean paused his story, holding up the coffee pot to offer Nyah a top-up.

"Thanks," she said, pushing her cup towards him. They were sitting at his kitchen table, the pale evening light sliding closer to twilight as they dawdled over dinner – another relaxing dinner, she mused, his promise to stop the interrogation being rigidly kept. She was quietly impressed. And relieved.

It was her fifth day in Carter Plains. The elusive Escape Plan/Opportunity hadn't presented itself to her yet, but she was quietly confident that any day now it would. Dean was continuing to be super cautious about leaving her alone though, making her wonder if he'd actually believed her lie about staying, and it looked like his freak-out over the voodoo revelation had been the one and only time he was ever going to leave her by herself. Nick had been drafted in as her official babysitter and in his absence, Kyle, Dean's Delta, took over. It was annoying, but she had to admit, both Nick and Kyle were nice guys, Nick especially, he had a wicked sense of humour that had her looking forward to Dean's nightly runs when he would take over watching her. However hard she watched in return though, she could find no sliver of a moment when patrols around the house were at a minimum or attention wasn't subtly trained on her every move.

You're not trying hard enough, a little voice reminded her. It was the voice of Narky Nyah, the Nyah who wanted her gone from Carter Plains before Simon could come and do his worst. Narky Nyah was right, of course, she knew damn well that every day she stayed in Dean's house was a day closer to trouble, and her snipped comments were becoming more frequent and less easy to ignore. Narky Nyah had her number; she knew that Naïve Nyah's desperation to leave was starting to wane.

Dean slid her cup back towards her. Meal times, she realized, were fast becoming another favourite time, too. Dean had busy days; he spent hours in his office with his Alpha duties, meaning it was only when they sat down to eat together that they got to talk. And boy, did they talk – about everything that wasn't her screwed up life, of course – but everything else was fair game, like the story he was telling her now, the story about when he was younger and his friends had dared him to have his palm read by a fortune teller at a fair. Real fortune tellers had a gift that enabled them to see the truth supernatural beings could hide and she knew that the outcome of his childhood dare wasn't going to be a good one, so blocking out the thought of how she was going to miss their natterings, she picked up her cup and focused on him.

"I had no idea that she was the real thing," he continued, now filling his own cup. "I was so sure that she was just going to feed me some nonsense about marriage, kids and travel – you know, the usual stuff."

Nyah nodded, watching as his face softened with a growing smile. He looked up at her and she found herself smiling back.

"She told me to sit opposite her," he grinned, resting his forearms on the table, "and then she asked for my hands, so -" He gestured towards her hands which were occupied with cradling the coffee cup, but intrigued by his story she quickly put down the cup and slid her hands, palm up, across the table towards him.

"I let her take hold of them," he carried on, sliding one hand under each of hers. "At first, she just held them loosely –

225

like this." He demonstrated the gentle hold that the fortune teller had used that day and although still caught up in the story Nyah registered the heat from his palms and how her own smaller hands nestled so comfortably inside of his.

"But then she obviously got a sense of something, because she -." He began to laugh then, and she joined him, giggling as his grip increased and he mimicked the shocked expression that the unsuspecting fortune teller had worn. "Her face," he started to say, but laughter had taken hold of both of them, and although he wanted to carry on with the story and she wanted to hear it, they were both infected by the hilarity and found they couldn't stop.

It was then that Nyah felt it. Something happened deep inside her. Something clicked, snapped or switched on. Something changed. Suddenly, she could feel her wolf, feel a trace of her presence uncurl from whatever fathomless place she had been hidden in. Before she could react something even more incredibly powerful hit her.

Dean still had a hold of her hands and a river of heat burst from where his skin touched hers, surging up her arms, spreading out across her chest and swelling through her entire body. Tiny invisible chains began to form, their links snapping together as they whipped unseen from somewhere inside of her towards Dean, binding him to her, locking him to her. And then his scent hit her – the most delicious, enchanting aroma that she had ever experienced swirled inside her head, taking her breath away.

It had taken milliseconds. Dean was still laughing, she was too; the connection had happened so fast that her brain hadn't even cottoned-on to what was exploding inside her body.

Nyah had always quietly assumed that Tanya's supermarket encounter with Alan had been greatly embellished. But now she knew better. Tanya's description wasn't anyway near what she had felt because no words could describe what connecting with your mate felt like.

Mate.

The single word slammed through her brain and she fell suddenly silent. So did Dean. His laugh stopped abruptly. He didn't move. He froze, in entirety. She even heard his breathing stop. He could feel it, too.

Suddenly, she wanted to be closer to him. She wanted to shove the table and chairs aside and fling herself against him. She wanted him to wrap his arms around her and draw her closely against him. She wanted to be close enough to him to dissolve into his skin. And she wanted to kiss him. Badly. Her heart was hammering madly in her ears as she stared, transfixed at his handsome face. His brilliant blue eyes were burning into her, his full lips slightly parted as he continued to remain perfectly still. She belonged to him, he belonged to her, and the need to be touching him was hurting.

"Taylor. . ."

The spell broke.

Snatching away her hands she shoved back her chair and jumped up.

It was gone, the overwhelming passion had gone. He was just Dean again; Dean, the Alpha who wouldn't let her go – the Alpha who had worked some magic on her – just like Simon.

"What – what did you do to me?" she choked out, backing away towards the wall. "What did you do to me!"

"Taylor -." Dean stood up, moving towards her carefully, an expression of pain tightening his face. "What you felt – it was – we're. . ."

"You're just like him!" she screamed. "You did something to me, you made me feel something! You're twisted, just like him!"

"No, Taylor, no!"

She staggered away from his outstretched hand. "Don't you touch me!" she yelled. "Keep your filthy, poisonous hands away from me!"

"I would never hurt you, Taylor," he said gently, not moving any closer. "What you felt was not magic, it was real, it was – it was . . . don't you see?" he pleaded with her. "We're mates, we belong together, what you felt was our connection."

"No." Nyah shook her head furiously. "You did something to me, when you touched me, when you held my hands, you did something."

"You were laughing," he tried to explain. "You were happy, and it made your wolf surface, I could feel her, and then we connected. Our wolves connected – we're mates, Taylor."

"No."

"Yes."

She bolted. Dashing from the kitchen she flew into the hall and took the stairs two at a time. Bursting through her bedroom door she grabbed her bag and quickly shoved the few loose clothes lying on the chair into it.

"What are you doing?" Dean rushed to her side and tried to grab the bag from her, but she ducked aside and shot back out the door again, her feet stumbling dangerously on the stairs as she charged down.

There was no-one on the front porch when she flung open the door, or at least, no-one tried to stop her when she sprung off the top step and landed neatly on the path. She knew she had no chance of outrunning anyone, but that wasn't going to stop her from trying.

She hadn't even made it off the lawn when a large, strong arm encircled her and lifted her clean off her feet.

"I'm not letting you leave," Dean barked at her. "You're my mate, and I won't let you go!"

"Put me down!" Nyah squirmed and kicked, but he hefted her into a tighter grip and wheeled back towards the house. "Let me go!" she screamed.

"Never."

With her back pressed tightly to his chest she struggled in vain as he kicked the front door shut behind him. "I'll put you down," he said, "but if you try to run off again I'll drag you back every time."

Without releasing his hold he lowered her until her feet were on the floor. "Don't try to run," he warned her again. He let go.

Seconds later she was off the ground again, twisting ineffectually in his grasp, her heels landing hard against him, but not causing any pain. He didn't reply to her protests and screams of abuse, he simply held her against him until she fell still.

When he set her back down she tried again. It was pointless, the sober part of her brain knew that, but the panicked part kept telling her to run, run, run.

"Stop," he said patiently, as she strained for the handle of the door again. He carried her further into the hall, away from the door that led to her freedom and it bolstered her strength. A sharp kick to his shin tore a hiss from his mouth and his retaliatory squeeze made her cry out. "Stop fighting me!" he yelled.

"Let me go!" she screamed back, even louder. "Let me go!"

"No, I'm not letting you leave!"

"Put me down, let me go!"

No, stop – stop fighting me, stop – Nyah!"

This time when she stilled and he put her down she didn't try to run.

"You – you know my name," she panted, turning to face him, swallowing hard as she backed away from him towards the stairs. Her heels hit the riser of the bottom step and she stopped, one hand blindly grabbing for the banister. "How do you know my name?"

"You told me," Dean sighed, a heavy, defeated sigh that visibly deflated him.

"No I didn't," she replied quietly.

"Yes, you did," he corrected her. "You don't remember because you were asleep."

Nyah felt her knees weaken and she sank onto the stairs, one hand still gripping the banister above her head.

"The first night you were here your wolf surfaced," he confessed.

"What?"

Dean lowered himself onto his hunkers before her and she instinctively leaned back away from him.

"It's happened a few times – when you've been sleeping. And I felt her earlier, too – when we were talking. I think it happens when you're relaxed, or happy, maybe."

Nyah stared disbelievingly at him even though she knew he was telling the truth. Her wolf had surfaced at dinner, she had felt it, she couldn't deny it, but yet . . .

"The first time it happened," he said, "was when I felt our connection. I've known that we're mates since your first night here."

"No, we're not," she insisted. "We are not mates."

"You felt it," he said.

"No – I felt . . . it wasn't that. It can't be."

"I saw the way you looked at me."

Nyah squeezed her eyes shut. "It's not real. It can't be, and I don't feel it now, so . . ."

"It was the same for me at first, but now it's there all the time. It's not something magic that I did to you; it's real, Nyah."

"Stop saying my. . ." she shook her head and flashed her eyes open to fling an accusatory stare at him. "How did you find out what my name is?"

"You told me," he repeated gently.

"In my sleep," she confirmed angrily. "You've been interrogating me while I've been sleeping – ever heard of the word manipulation?"

"It's not how you think. It didn't happen that way."

"Yeah? I just happened to be thrashing about in the bed yelling out my name – was that it?"

"No."

He was remaining irritatingly calm as he continued to hunker before her. His hands were loosely clasped together, but every now and then one hand would free itself and reach for her. And every time it did she reeled away from it.

"On your second night here your wolf surfaced again. I tried to ignore it, but my wolf was so desperate to be close to you that I nearly phased. I went into your room, I went no further than the end of your bed, but when I was standing there, feeling totally frustrated, I said that I wished I knew what your name was. I was talking out loud, not actually asking you, but you heard and . . . you told me."

And there was no way he had just left it at that single question either, she guessed. "What else did you ask me?"

"Your pack name."

"Did I tell you?"

He nodded once.

She couldn't work her mouth to ask him what else he had found out, but the hang-dog look he was wearing made it pretty obvious.

"I couldn't let it go," he admitted softly, pre-empting the next question. "I had to ask."

Nyah closed her eyes. "I can't believe you did that," she breathed.

The magnitude of his actions swelled hotly inside her, but when she opened her eyes to tell him that he was nothing but a stupid, interfering idiot he looked so miserable that the words of anger died on her tongue. His face was sagging with remorse and when he reached out to her again she found she couldn't yank her hand away.

"I'm not going to say I'm sorry, because I'm not," he said. "You're my mate, and I will do whatever it takes to protect you." He slowly slid his hand over hers and when she didn't pull away he let out a relieved breath.

"Just please tell me that you didn't call him, or anyone else from my pack," she pleaded, looking up to meet his remorseful eyes. "If he finds out I'm here. . ."

His contrite expression suddenly morphed back into his more familiar Alpha one, the 'I'm in control, so don't worry' one, and whatever fear she thought she had been feeling up to that point was nothing compared to what crawled into her at that moment.

"He rang here, looking for you."

Nyah's slick palm slid from the banister with a small squeak before it fell heavily into her lap.

"He has no idea you're here. I told him that the only rogue that had passed this way was a Taylor and he corrected me straight away, said his rogue was a female. He has no idea, Nyah, no idea at all that you're here."

"He'll find out," she croaked in reply.

"I'll be ready for him."

She shook her head. "No you won't. You'll never be ready for Simon Northfell."

"Nick and I have a plan, okay? We've doubled the patrols and I've been researching . . ."

His words faded as it all began to play out in her mind; what would happen once Simon Northfell came. First there would be confusion when communication with the patrols would suddenly cease. Then there would be anxious orders, and pack members, like Nick and Kyle, would tear into the forest. They would vanish within seconds and Dean would experience the violent silencing of the mind-link. He'd start shouting then, directing pack members into the safety of their homes – except they wouldn't be safe at all. And then Simon would arrive. He would materialize in the thick of the panic, his pinched face calmly smug. Dean would rush him. And with a flick of a wrist or perhaps a click of fingers Dean would be on the ground. Or maybe not. Maybe he would turn to face her, his eyes flat and dull, his limbs responding to Simon's orders as he grabbed for her.

"Nyah – Nyah!"

Dean's shake reeled her back. Her teeth clacked together loudly in her head, but it wasn't because of his touch, it was because of the cold. Ice water ran through her veins, her skin goose-bumped so severely that every inch of her stung and when she tried to speak her jaw remained tightly clamped, the muscles frozen stiff.

Dean whipped his jumper off, drew it over her head and then gently guiding her hands inside the arms, slid it down over her body. He scooped her up into his arms so fast that her head spun and grabbing onto the fabric of his t-shirt she buried her head into his chest.

Simon Northfell's face had fixed itself in her mind. He was sneering, his black eyes glistening with delight as she saw him wiping out Dean's pack. Images of Ellie and her children crumpling to the ground flashed before her and she squeezed her eyes tighter, willing the horrific images to stop. They refused, though. Simon's face continued to leer at her before it slowly morphed into Dean's face, and just like before, he was emotionless as he dragged her, screaming, towards Simon. Then Simon was wrenching her away, reminding her that they had pups to conceive, and Dean was watching her go, his face slack, his mind obliterated.

"Drink this, Nyah, here, drink this."

A waft of alcohol stung the insides of her nostrils and she felt the thin, cool rim of a glass being tipped against her lips. "Drink it," he ordered. She parted her lips and allowed the liquid to wash over her tongue and trickle down her throat. It was brandy. It scalded her throat, but the heat felt good inside her and she took another mouthful when he tipped the glass against her lips for the second time.

The fiery liquid eased the tremble in her limbs and as the heat spread throughout her the frightening images evaporated.

She was on the couch, Dean was beside her, holding her tightly in his arms, his lips pressed to the top of her head. "It's okay," he soothed, "it's okay, I won't let anything happen to you."

"You won't be able to stop him," she murmured against his chest, her voice having difficulty making its way through her tight throat. "You've no idea what he's capable of."

"Shh," Dean replied, pulling her even tighter into his body. "I'll protect you."

"No, you're not listening to me."

Nyah sat up, but didn't move away from him. She was feeling a sense of the overwhelming urge to be close to him again. It surprised her; her wolf had returned to its abyss of a prison so she shouldn't have been feeling anything, but it was there, nudging her gently, pestering her to stay physically close to him. She'd thought all along that her wolf was gone, but clearly, it wasn't. How that was she didn't understand, but there was comfort in knowing she was still deep within her. Somewhere.

Briefly closing her eyes to gather her distracted thoughts she pulled in a breath. "Listen to me. I've seen what he can do. He turned my pack members into robots with his voodoo magic. Their faces were blank, their minds were empty, he just . . . turned them off or something. And they did whatever he ordered."

Dean began shaking his head, but she carried on before he could argue with her or tell her that it wouldn't happen to him. "Dean, I've seen it. He can make people do whatever he wants.

Karen and Blake; they were wearing these necklaces and it made them do everything he ordered. They didn't even know who I was. If he put one of those necklaces on you you'd kill me if he ordered –."

"Don't you dare talk that way," he cut in angrily, tightening his already fierce grip on her. "I would never hurt you, never."

"You wouldn't have a choice," she replied, grabbing a fistful of his t-shirt. "If he -."

"No-one could ever make me hurt you. You're my mate. It would be completely impossible for -."

"But that's it, Dean! It's not impossible, not at all. What he did in Blackwater Ridge was like something you'd see in a horror movie – but it wasn't make-believe, it was real. Look what he did to me -!" Releasing one handful of his t-shirt she thumped her fist against her chest. "He bound my wolf! If he can do that he can do anything!"

His mouth opened to argue, but then fell shut again.

"You know I'm right," she said softly. "I know you want to protect me, but you have to understand that you're no match for him. No-one is."

Dean released one of her arms to run the backs of his fingers down the side of her face. His gentle touch sent a shiver of warmth through her, making her want to close her eyes and curl against him again.

"Simon may never come here," he said. "He may never find you."

"He will. He needs me."

"He needs you?"

Nyah let her self-reprimand out with a heavy sigh. Would she ever learn to keep her damned mouth shut?"

"He needs you for what?" Dean asked slowly, his tone covering the 'and you'd better tell me' warning that went with his question.

"You promised me that you'd ask no more questions," she reminded him, releasing his t-shirt.

"Nyah . . ."

"No. You already know too much."

"Too much? That's a joke, right?"

Nyah slid away from him, burying her face in her hands as she sagged back into the couch. He was quick to take her wrists and gently pull her hands away.

"What does he need you for? What's he planning on doing? Is this why he buried your wolf?"

"No more questions!" she wailed, snatching back her hands and moving to push herself off the couch.

"Whoa." Dean beat her to it and before she could stand up he was kneeling on the floor in front of her, the front of his thighs pushing against her knees and his hands slamming against the back of the couch so she was trapped between his arms. "All promises are off," he said sharply. "Enough of this drip-feeding me information. You're going to tell me exactly what's going on."

"No I'm not," she replied, looking him square in the eyes. "You have no idea how much danger I've already put you in. If I tell you any more you're only going to be in deeper."

"And what about you? You're in more danger than anyone else right now. How am I supposed to help you if I don't know the truth?"

"You don't need to know everything."

"I do!"

"No, you don't. There's nothing you can do about any of it anyway, so just let it go."

She squirmed forwards, but he put one hand on her shoulder and held her back. "That bastard has done the worst thing imaginable to you, and you think I should let it go? You're my mate, Nyah. I will never let it go, not until he's shredded into pieces at my feet!"

A knock on the front door brought their erupting argument to a pause.

"That's Nick," Dean muttered. "Dammit – he's here for the new walkie-talkies."

Nyah folded her arms and sat back. Perfect timing, Nick, she thought gratefully. Dean frowned at her and then sighed.

"Look after Nick," she said. "Go on."

"This conversation is not over," he warned her, getting to his feet and backing out of the room. "So stay there – do not move," he ordered with a pointing finger.

As he hurried upstairs, calling out to Nick and telling him to come on in, Nyah pulled up her legs and let her forehead drop heavily onto her knees.

Someone's having a laugh, she decided; The Fates, The Powers That Be, whoever it was that nudged the world and its inhabitants about like little chess pieces on a board. Not content with throwing her life into a frightening and complicated mess, they had now decided, just to spice things up a little, to add her mate into the mix.

If Simon so much as got a whiff of the fact that Dean was her mate he'd kill him. And do it with her watching, too – just to teach her a lesson. The thought of it made her shiver hard and she huddled tighter. Now, more than ever, she had to get out of Carter Plains. She was only barely skimming the surface of their mate connection, whereas Dean was in deep, and if he was right about how it had been getting stronger for him, wasn't there a chance that it would happen to her too? How hard would it be to leave then? Naïve Nyah tentatively raised her hand to ask a question: if being happy was making her wolf re-surface wasn't it possible that in a few weeks she may be fully restored? Yes, Narky Nyah snipped in reply. And what damn good would that do? Simon would still come calling and

Dean would still die. Stop being selfish. Get out of here before your connection prevents you.

How, though? How in the hell was she going to get out of here? If Dean was being Mr Super-Watchful up to now, tonight's revelations would push him into overdrive.

"Dean, you got the new walkie-talkies?"

Nyah lifted her head and twisted around on the couch to see Nick standing in the doorway of the living room. He frowned at her, threw a quick glance around the room and then gave an awkward laugh. "Sorry, Taylor, I thought you were Dean."

She smiled at his reddening face.

"It's – I got his scent. You're wearing his clothes," he explained, pointing towards the dark blue jumper that was swamping her frame. "Sorry, didn't mean to disturb you."

He backed out of the room just as Dean came down the stairs. They spoke for a few short moments in the hall and then Nick was gone again. When Dean came back into living room Nyah was on her feet.

"Do we have to talk about this tonight?" she pleaded.

"I knew you'd do this," he sighed, trailing his fingers through his hair. "Just like I know that you won't talk about it tomorrow either."

She shrugged and wrapped her arms around herself. "I'm tired. And I don't want to end up having another yelling match with you."

Dean came to where she stood and unwrapped her arms, clutching her hands against his chest with one hand while tilting her chin up with the other so that she would look him in the eye. "I will protect you, Nyah. I need you to understand that."

Like I need you to understand how much Simon will hurt you, she wanted to say in return. Instead, she nodded. He leaned towards her then and gently pressed a kiss to her forehead.

Five minutes ago she would have flung her arms around him and brought his mouth to her own, dragged him over to the couch and allowed the need she had felt for him to overpower her. But five minutes ago their pending separation was something hovering way off in the distance. Five minutes ago she didn't have her Escape Plan.

TWENTY

It was Nick who had unwittingly handed the Escape Plan to Nyah on a plate. He had mistaken her for Dean simply because she was wearing his scent-covered jumper and it had only taken a second before Nick's innocent comment had taken root in her brain and flowered into an idea that had potential to work. Now, two days later she had it all planned. She knew exactly what she had to do and how to do it – but, she was stalling.

Because that stupid mate connection is growing, Narky narked. And she was right. Two days had passed since that fateful dinner and already she could feel the magnetic pull that was drawing her to Dean growing stronger. When he was upstairs in his office he was too far away. When he was sitting opposite her at the table he was too far away. When he was standing right beside her he was too far away.

Get used to him being far away, muttered Narky. Shut up, Naïve snapped.

Nyah rolled over in her bed to check the time. It was eleven-fifteen. Dean had gone out to run and Nick was downstairs in the living room watching television. She had left him to watch his favourite cop show and every now and then the sound of gun-shots and dramatic music would sound out. She would have watched it with him, but not long after dinner another bout of exhaustion had pressed down on her, and pretending that she was fine and didn't want to just slide onto the floor and die, she had pushed herself to keep going so as not to worry Dean. He had begun to notice her spells of tiredness, but she had brushed them off as nothing more than stress and worry catching up with her. As soon as he had left the house she had stretched and yawned, announcing to Nick that she had a book to read and was off to bed. Nick barely noticed the early hour as he had flung himself onto the couch and snagged the remote. "Sweet dreams," he had waved as she'd said goodnight.

Eleven-nineteen, the clock said when she checked it again. Groaning, she pummelled the pillow and then flipped onto her back, angry with her involuntary impatience for Dean to get back. It was one of many involuntary emotions she was developing, emotions that had her firmly ensconced in Carter Plains when she should have been three states away. Sighing, she flung one arm over her eyes and allowed Narky and Naïve to argue it out.

Something woke her a while later. She came out of a dreamless sleep, the sensation of a presence in her room too strong to ignore, and lifting her heavy head off the pillow she turned over in the bed.

A figure stood by the side of her bed. It was shadowed by darkness, but she didn't need to see the face to know who it was – Cassius Ochre. Nyah screamed.

Scrambling out of the bed she threw her back against the wall, her eyes darting into every shadowy corner of the room when she saw that he had vanished.

Nick burst through the door a second later. "What is it?" he yelled, flicking on the light. "What's wrong?"

"I, I – Cassius Ochre . . ." Seeing her trembling finger pointing towards the empty space at the side of her bed restored some common sense. "I was dreaming," she said, her hand falling heavily to her side. "I'm sorry, I must have been – I was only dreaming."

"Nightmaring," Nick corrected. "You okay?"

Nyah blew out a shaky breath and relaxed. "Yeah. I'm okay, sorry for freaking you out."

"It's fine." He still took a good look around the room, though, she noted, as she gingerly sat back onto the edge of the bed.

"That was some scream," he grinned. "I think you may have woken the dead with that one. What exactly did you dream?"

"That the Shaman was here."

"Oh, right." Nick nodded as if to say 'enough said'. "He's not though," he said quickly, purposefully looking around again. "I'd sense it if there was someone here."

She gave a tight smile in agreement.

"Wouldn't I?" he said suddenly. "I mean, you don't think it was some satanic mumbo-jumbo thing, was it?"

"I hope not," she replied with a painful swallow. "Although, I mean, he's a Shaman, he can do some pretty powerful . . ."

"Nah." Nick shook his head and drew himself up. "You were dreaming. It was nothing more. There's no -."

The sound of the front door being nearly wrenched off its hinges made them both jump. It was followed by a sprinting pound up the stairs and then Dean rushed into the room. "You okay?" he panted. "Is everything okay? What happened?"

He hurried to where she sat on the far side of the bed, kneeling on the floor in front of her where he grabbed hold of her shoulders and frantically searched her for signs of an injury.

"You told him?" she frowned at Nick. "It was just a dream!"

"You screamed, I linked," Nick explained matter-of-factly. "I wasn't going to wait until I got up here to tell my Alpha what it was you were screaming at."

"Damn right," Dean muttered, exhaling loudly once satisfied that she wasn't hurt. "You sure you're okay?"

Nyah pulled her scowl off Nick to aim it at Dean, but when her eyes landed on him she noticed what he was wearing – or wasn't, to be exact. In his dash to rescue her he had only put on his tracksuit pants after phasing back. Not his t-shirt.

"You okay?" he asked again, mistaking her enthralled muteness for upset. "You got a real fright, didn't you?"

"Uh huh," she replied, jamming her hands between her knees so they wouldn't reach out and lay themselves on his smooth, muscled, bare-skinned . . .

"You're shivering – here." He grabbed the comforter from the end of the bed and swept it around her back and over her shoulders. "Come here." He got up from his knees to sit beside her, drawing her into his side so he could keep her warm.

"I'm fine." She ducked out from under his arm and stood up, clutching the comforter to her chest. "I'm okay, really."

"Nyah . . ."

"Really," she insisted with a laugh that was too high-pitched to be anything but normal. "I'm alright. You should go finish your run."

"I'm not going anywhere," Dean stated, twisting around to look at where Nick was still standing. "Go on home, Nick, I'll see you tomorrow, and thanks."

"No problem, Alpha Carson," Nick replied, giving Nyah a goodnight nod before he ducked out of the room.

Dean turned back to face Nyah. "Are you sure you're okay?"

"Mm hmm."

Frowning, he stood up and came to where she was standing by the wall nervously tugging at the comforter which wasn't doing a great job at covering up her bare skin. The vest top and shorts she wore were hardly scandalous, but she suddenly felt incredibly self-conscious.

"What did you dream about?" he asked, resting his hands on her shoulders. As usual, his touch sent a million volts of electricity charging through her.

"It was nothing."

"Nyah, it was hardly nothing when it had you screaming."

She sighed and dragged her eyes away from his worried face. "I dreamt that the Shaman was here, that's all. It was nothing, just a dream."

"But it frightened you."

"Yeah, I guess it did."

She could feel his eyes on her – and not in the 'I'm concerned' way, more in the way that her eyes had been on him a second ago, the way that they had suddenly been fixated with the tones of his skin, the flecks in his eyes, the cupid's bow of his upper lip. She felt him move, but too nervous to look back at him she continued to let her eyes skate around the room.

His hand came to rest on the side of her face and it took everything she had not to close her eyes and lean into him.

"Do you think it was more than a dream?" he asked quietly.

"What?"

"Do you think it was some sort of magic spell or something? I mean – do you think it's possible he's actually located you?"

Suddenly, she had no hesitation in looking directly at him. "Nick said that too. Is that what you think? "

"Wrong thing to say," he chastised himself quietly, his free hand taking hold of the other side of her face. "Sorry. That was stupid of me."

"Is it what you think, though? Do you -."

"No. It's not what I think at all. It's just that you seem so freaked out I thought that maybe you did."

"I'm not that freaked out."

"Yeah, you are. Look at you. You're stuck to the wall trying to hide yourself under this thing." Releasing her face he lifted up a loose edge of the comforter and waved it at her. "Freaking out."

"No, I'm not freaking out, I'm, it's . . ."

His scowling frown eased, but only because something clued him in. Maybe it was her jack-hammering heart, maybe it was her scalding hot cheeks or maybe it was the fact that as he moved a fraction closer to her she quite obviously braced herself.

"You feel it," he said. "You can feel our bond."

"Um, I feel a bit warm or um, I think I'm just . . ."

"You can feel it," he said, a smile creasing his eyes. "And your heart's not racing with fright, is it?"

"Yes it is," she replied quickly, wrenching the wrap tighter against her chest as if it would block out the thumping he could so clearly hear.

"I don't think so."

"Yeah . . .well . . ." She had to shut her eyes then. She couldn't allow them to meet with his and start off a chain reaction that she'd end up regretting. She'd never leave Carter Plains if Dean Carson kissed her. Never.

"Yeah well, what?" he smiled wickedly, ever so slowly pressing the length of his body against her while lowering his head to brush his lips against the side of her ear.

"Okay! Fine!" she wailed, squirming to free her hands so that she could shove him back a little. "So I feel something! But you can't blame me! I mean, you're all . . ." waving an irritated hand at his naked chest didn't knock her brain into gear. "Half naked and stuff," she offered, pathetically.

Her equally pathetic shove didn't do much to deter him either. He was back to where he had been and just to let her know she wasn't going to wriggle away from him he planted his hands on the wall either side of her head.

"Why are you fighting it?" he asked. "Don't you believe that we're mates?"

"I do," she answered, her eyes back to being shut again. "I know we are, but . . ."

His lips were skimming her ear again, and then dropping a feather-light trail of kisses down the slope of her neck. It made her dizzy, made her bones liquefy, made her weak-kneed, made her feel all the other metaphors that she'd ever read or heard about.

"You smell of the forest," her lust-drunk lips blurted out. "I can smell pine on your skin."

He lifted his head from where it was buried in the curve of her neck and shoulder to look at her. Passion had swollen his pupils so widely that there was only the tiniest ring of blue visible in his eyes.

"It was raining," he explained, in a choked, husky voice. "Everything was damp."

"Uh huh," she mumbled, her attention now caught by the drop-dead perfection of his bare chest. Naïve, who didn't care about what touching his bare skin could result in, raised her hand and rested a single fingertip against his skin. Narky, who very much cared about what touching of any kind could result in, wanted to slap her hand away and run from the room – but for some reason she was paralysed.

Dean closed his eyes as her single fingertip began to trail down his chest. One fingertip wasn't enough, though, the other nine wanted in on the action too, and they were quick to spread out across the hard slopes of his chest.

She hadn't been lying when she had said that she could smell the forest from him, and now that she was touching him it seemed to raise traces of other scents from his skin. Every aroma that existed between the earth of the forest floor and the sky above the tree tops drifted towards her. Being able to define the scents again was incredible and she rested her forehead against him as she drew in a deep fill of the wonder.

"Nyah," he breathed, before cupping her face in his hands again and tilting her head right back. His lips were on hers before she could even open her eyes and the bone-liquefying sensation intensified ten-fold as he began to kiss her.

Whether it was right or wrong, or fair or unjust, or nothing but a future torturous memory she didn't care. Flinging her arms around his neck she pulled him to her, allowing the want to dissolve into his body to swell right through her. His hands released her face, but only for the short moment that it took them to clamp around her waist and lift her up so that she could wrap her legs over his hips. Crowded against each other they deepened the kiss, their lips almost frantic as their mouths moved together.

"You're mine," he murmured breaking the kiss to press her back against the wall and wind his hand deep into her hair. His lips moved to say something else, but she didn't give him the chance to speak, instead she slanted her lips against his again, turning his words into a muffled groan.

It was Dean who eventually called a time-out. "Whoa," he exhaled, resting his forehead against hers. "We need to slow down a second."

"Yeah," she panted, as Narky found her tongue and began screaming a silent torrent of abuse. "We definitely need to slow down."

"Don't get me wrong," he said, clearing his hoarse throat, "it's not that I'm hating a single thing about what we're doing, but . . . I'd rather, I mean . . . I think it would be better if we waited until, well . . . your wolf is back . . ."

"You're right," she murmured, tilting her head so that she could trace the edge of his ear with the tip of her tongue. "We should wait."

"Yes, we should," he chuckled lifting her clear off his hips and setting her feet onto the floor again.

It was easier to think when they weren't pressed together and an immediate swell of regret rose inside her, joined by a snarl of 'it's too late to be sorry now!' from Narky.

"But that doesn't mean I'm going to say goodnight." Dean's smiling voice interrupted the soundless rant and she looked up at him. Before she could ask what he meant, he whipped her back up off the floor into his arms, carried her across the room, out the door, across the landing and straight into his own room.

"You're sleeping in my bed from now on," he announced, flinging back the covers with one hand and then lowering her onto the bed.

"I, um," she began, watching as he rounded the bed and got in on the other side.

"You might have another nightmare," he pointed out, sliding her across the wide space between them and drawing her snugly into his chest as he lay down. "And if you do I'll be right here beside you when you wake up," he said, drawing the duvet over them both.

"Oh no," she breathed. "You do think it was more than a dream." She squirmed to sit up, but he held her tight, clutching her to him with enough desperation to confirm her suspicion.

"I'm being cautious," he said calmly, "I read some stuff on the net yesterday and I don't want to take any chances."

"What did you read?"

"We'll talk about it in the morning," he replied, flipping onto his side to face her and rest one hand on her face. "It's probably nothing anyway, there's so much -."

"What did you read?"

Dean sighed quietly and gave her a long, thoughtful look before replying. "It's possible – vaguely – possible," he emphasized, "that a locating spell could be performed to find you. And . . . " He paused and winced, searching for the gentlest words to finish the sentence. "Now that your wolf has re-surfaced it may have just given him a tiny bit more of a chance."

"But she only surfaced for a few seconds," Nyah reminded him. "It wasn't like I lit up the place like the fourth of July or anything."

"I know," he agreed, "but I'm very protective of my beautiful, precious mate," he smiled, "and to be honest, I just want to have you in my arms all night."

"So you're using my fear to get your wicked way."

"Guilty," he replied, kissing her softly on the mouth.

Conscious of their earlier agreement Nyah didn't grumble when the kiss lasted for just a few moments. Appealing as it was to lose herself in the deliciousness of Dean's touch she knew that what she so suddenly wanted to forget wasn't going to be ignored; Simon was coming. There was no doubt in her mind at all. Dean could use comforting words such as 'vaguely' and 'tiny bit more of a chance' but she knew in her heart and soul that Simon had finally caught up with her and the first person he would cut down to claim her back was Dean.

Pressing herself further into his warm, solid body Nyah forced herself to stay calm. "Tell me about where you run at night," she asked sleepily. "What's your territory like? What kind of scents are there?"

Dean began to recall his run and she lay quietly beside him, wishing she had some way to record the memory of the moment; the soft rumble of his voice, the heat from his body, the way it felt so natural to be curled against him. Maybe it was wrong to savour it; maybe to protect them both she should slide from his hold and announce that she'd prefer to sleep on her own. Or maybe this perfect moment would keep her together in the dark days to come.

Stay where you are and enjoy every second of this, Narky ordered from somewhere at the back of her mind. Commit it to memory as good as you can, 'cos first thing tomorrow morning, girl, you are . . . Out. Of. Here.

Twenty-One

Nyah woke before Dean, aware that a goofy smile was etched onto her face, and in absolutely no hurry to peel herself away from his body as sleep slowly released its hold on her. If Dean was right about her wolf surfacing when she was happy and relaxed, she must have sprouted fur and howled at the moon last night. They'd talked for hours, Dean refusing to allow her slide an inch away from him – not that she'd wanted to.

Smiling, she allowed herself a long, admiring look at her mate. He was on the flat of his back, one arm acting as her pillow and the other resting on his chest where his hand lay protectively on top of hers.

For a long moment she listened to the steady rhythm of his sleeping breaths, her fingertips feeling the drumming of his heart from where they lay on his warm skin. He was so peaceful; not a single worry line marked an inch of his face and there was a ghost of a smile softening his mouth. Happiness drained from her body. She was about to change all of that for him.

Nyah slowly untangled her legs from his and then eased away from his hold. He stirred and stretched out a sleepy hand towards her.

"Sleep on," she whispered, propping herself up on one elbow to press the softest kiss on his mouth. "I'm going to make breakfast."

He murmured a drowsy request that she hurry back to his bed and she replied with another light kiss – the last, she warned herself, her throat tightening as she smoothed back a tousled lock of hair from his forehead.

With a final look, she slid away from him, slipped out of the warm bed and then left his room.

Dean knew as soon as he peeled his eyes open that he had slept way longer than he should have. Cooking bacon, fresh toast and brewing coffee teased his nostrils as he sat up, lazily stretching out his back before sliding his hands through his hair.

Swinging his legs over the side of the bed he grabbed the pair of jeans slung over the foot of his bed and pulled them on. With a grin, he decided to pass on the t-shirt.

It was gone ten-fifteen when he glanced at the grandfather clock in the hallway as he padded down the stairs. He had slept way too late. Why hadn't Nyah woken him sooner?

Dean inched into the kitchen with an apologetic grimace on his face, fully expecting Nyah to reply with a black scowl. What he didn't expect to see was an empty kitchen.

The toast had popped, bacon was sitting quietly on the pan and the pot of coffee sat cooling on the counter. "Nyah?" Dean stood completely still, focusing on the silence of the house that he was waiting to be broken by her reply. "Nyah?" he repeated, louder this time, when his first call wasn't answered. Frowning, he ducked into the utility room – it was empty. Then he crossed the hallway and took a quick glance around the living room. Again, it was empty. Returning to the hallway he turned to look at both the back and front door. They were closed. "Nyah? Nyah – where are you?"

An invisible fist of fear punched him hard in the gut. Nyah wasn't here. The house was too still, too silent. She was gone.

Darting back into the kitchen he forced himself to make a focused study. It was the strangest thing; breakfast had been made in entirety; toast, bacon, coffee – even the table had been laid he noted, slowly scanning the neat setting. When his eyes landed on the folded sheet of paper propped against the milk jug a wave of stinging realization shot through him.

For an agonizingly painful moment he was trapped in place. He knew what was written in that note. He knew what its innocent, simple shape meant for him. He knew that the very first word was going to be 'sorry' and that reading beyond that would be pointless. Part of him wanted to stay paralysed in that moment – the before moment – the moment where, although he already knew the awful truth, there was a tiny chance that she wasn't gone. Another part of him wanted to snatch the note up and read the words, because maybe it said something that didn't mean she was gone, something like 'Gone to borrow milk from Ellie. Be back soon!'

And then there was the final part of him, the part that suddenly jerked him into action, the part that yelled at him for wasting precious time. With one stride he was at the table, the note in his hand.

'Dean. Please understand why I had to leave. For what it's worth, I will miss you. Nyah.'

"Nick!" He roared silently, balling the paper and flinging it across the room. He slammed his fisted hands against his head and mashed his eyes tightly shut. This wasn't happening, it couldn't be. Nyah couldn't be gone.

Lashing out he smashed one foot against the nearest chair and sent it soaring across the room where it exploded against the wall, fragments of wood raining onto the floor with a dull clatter.

His wolf reared up then, sensing the absence of its mate, anguish building as Dean grasped how helpless the situation was. Nyah could have gone North, South, East or West. He had no way of knowing. Hell, she could be hiding upstairs and he wouldn't be able to trace her scent.

Leaning heavily onto the table he stared forlornly at the place settings, breaths rushing angrily through his nose. She had planned it so well; telling him to sleep on, making the entire breakfast so that the sounds and scents wouldn't raise suspicion, slipping out of the house without – wait. His head shot up. How in the hell did she get out of the house?

When he flung open the front door Kyle was alert and attentive. Nick was sprinting up the path just as Dean grabbed Kyle by the arm and dragged him into the house.

"What's wrong?" Nick called out, running behind the startled figure of Kyle who was being launched aggressively into the kitchen. Kyle steadied himself on the back of one of the kitchen chairs and looked around in complete terror.

"Alpha Carson!" Nick said sharply. "What's wrong?"

"Nyah is gone," Dean ground out through gritted teeth, his stare nailed to Kyle, "and I want to know how."

Kyle's mouth opened and closed, but no noise came out.

"She's gone?" Nick faltered. "But how . . . ?"

Kyle shook his head, his Adam's apple bobbing up and down as he convulsively swallowed. "I don't know how she . . ." he choked out. "I never heard her leaving, I swear."

"Well she did," Dean snarled. "And I want to know how in the hell you didn't hear her!"

"I, I don't know!" Kyle was supporting himself on the back of the chair, his whole body shrinking away from the fury of his Alpha. "I swear Alpha Carson, I never heard her. I would have stopped her if I had, I would have!"

"How long is she gone?" Nick asked, hoping that the calmness he was forcing into his voice would ease the blind rage burning through his Alpha.

"I have no idea," Dean answered. He threw his hands back up into his hair and turned to face the stove. "She made breakfast and sometime during then . . . she left."

"I heard her making breakfast," Kyle was quick to confirm. "I heard her. I could even hear her talking to you."

"I wasn't up," Dean corrected him sharply as he spun back to face him. "I was asleep."

Kyle frowned. "But — I, I heard her talking to you. She, she said something about eggs with your bacon and . . ."

"I was in bed the whole time," Dean assured him, "so if she was talking to someone it wasn't me."

Kyle chanced a confused look at Nick.

"Did you hear Alpha Carson reply?" Nick asked.

Kyle shook his head.

"You sure?" he pushed.

"I'm sure," Kyle confirmed, sounding a little more confident. "It was only her voice I heard – but . . ."

"But what?" Dean asked.

"You – you were up."

"I wasn't."

"But . . . you brought out the trash."

Dean drew in a rough breath. "I didn't," he said slowly, his voice steadily rising. "I woke up less than ten minutes ago."

Kyle wasn't going to be contradicted. "Alpha Carson," he began. "I'm not mistaken."

"Neither am I," Dean replied sharply.

Nick threw out his arms to create a barrier as Dean took a threatening step towards his Delta. "Hang on a second," he said calmly. "Kyle, what made you think that Alpha Carson put the trash out?"

"I got his scent," Kyle answered. "I heard the back door opening and I came down off the porch to go round the back, but as I got halfway round the side of the house I got Alpha Carson's scent so I turned back."

Kyle abandoned the supporting chair to stand tall and face Dean again. "I'm not mistaken, Alpha Carson," he said evenly. "It was just gone nine-thirty when you went out the back door this morning."

"Well, then, I was sleepwalking, Kyle," Dean snapped. "'Cos I have no memory of being out there!"

"It wasn't you," Nick said quietly. "It was Nyah."

"What?" Dean and Kyle said together, rounding on Nick.

"Nyah took out the trash," Nick repeated. "That's how she got away."

Dean and Nick shared a short, disbelieving stare before they dashed out of the kitchen and down the hallway. Dean threw open the back door and made a bee-line for the trash can as Nick stood on the top step of the back porch and scanned the spread of the yard.

"I can get your scent," Nick said, his seeking coming to an abrupt stop at a point near the far end of the grassy space. "There." He lifted his hand and pointed towards something unseen. "By the riverbank."

Dropping the barely-used bag that Nyah had taken from the kitchen back into the trash can, Dean sprinted after Nick as he ran towards the river.

When they reached the muddy strip of land a moment later Dean's legs weakened and he dropped to his hunkers. Discarded by the side of the river were one of his sweatshirts and a pair of his jeans.

Nick stared down at the abandoned clothes. "Crap," he muttered. "That's how she did it. She used your scent to slip away."

Shocked into muteness, Dean stared forlornly at the small pile. Suddenly, he was able to visualize her escape, it played out like a movie in his mind; Nyah pulling on his clothes while the bacon sizzled on the pan, softly talking to someone who wasn't there so that the someone who was there would hear her and not suspect anything. Nyah taking the trash out, hoping that his scent-covered clothes would prevent Kyle from coming round back and seeing her, Nyah tearing across the grass towards the river, shucking off his clothes, slipping quietly into the water, letting it drag her down-stream towards the - . "No!" Dean yelled, springing to his feet and kicking out at the sweatshirt. "You fool, Carson! You stupid, stupid fool!"

"What? What is it?" Nick exclaimed, ducking to avoid the air-borne sweatshirt.

"I told her exactly how to escape!" Dean yelled, "I am such a stupid, damned, fool!"

He thrust out a finger towards the west of their territory. "She's taken the river to the bridge and she's hopped a freight train – one of the freight trains that I told her all about last night when she asked me where I liked to run. The trains that run every half hour, the trains that run both North and South, the trains that are taking her somewhere that I have no clue of! She didn't even know there was a damned river here until I told her!" He kicked out again, sending the jeans flying clean across the river. They landed with a soft flutter on the opposite bank. "Yeah, that's right, there's a river at the back of the house, Nyah," Dean mimicked himself bitterly, "A river that runs under a bridge about four miles west of here, the bridge that the freight trains cross. And because the bridge is so old the trains go real slow, so slow in fact, that you could easily hop on board and sit back while you're carried hundreds of miles in damn knows which direction far, far away from your mate!"

Nick silently followed Dean's desolate stare towards the rickety wooden bridge, barely visible in the far-off distance where it spanned the wide river.

"I can't believe she's done this," Dean said, all his anger deflating with a ragged sigh. "I promised her I'd keep her safe. Why didn't she believe me?"

"She did believe you," Nick replied. "But I reckon she's so scared that nothing you could have said or done was going to keep her here."

Dean's fist strayed towards his chest, distractedly kneading it as his wolf howled mournfully inside. The baying made him want to phase and find uninhabited land where he could grieve the loss of his mate in solitude, but the dominant nature of his Alpha pushed through and told him to take action. "I'll link and gather the patrols here," he announced, dropping his hand. "When they arrive tell them to sweep both sides of the river in both directions."

"Yes, Alpha," Nick answered, straightening to attention.

"I'm going to head for the bridge."

"And I'll start looking here; see if I can pick up a trail," Nick said determinedly.

"A trail?" Dean gave a short, humour-free laugh. "We're not going to find anything, Nick," he conceded, turning to jog towards the bridge. "We've absolutely no way of tracking her, and Nyah knows it."

Twenty-Two

Two days after Nyah had disappeared Dean finally stopped sending out patrols along both directions of the riverbank. He knew that searching for her was pointless and yet finding his mate was as basic a need as breathing. He had scoured the train tracks, too, over one hundred and fifty miles in each direction, hoping with every mile that he raced over he would find something – anything – just the tiniest thing that would give him a clue as to which direction she had gone in. But he had found nothing. Likewise when he had extended his search to the neighbouring belt of towns that lay further along the tracks; if he had thought that catching her feeble scent in vast expanses of grassy fields was hard, a three day hunt for it amongst thousands of equally feeble-scented humans was impossible. He would never give up, though. If it took until his dying day he would keep on searching.

Swinging his pick-up onto the dusty road that led to Carter Plains Dean glanced down at the map spread out on the passenger seat beside him. Five towns had been circled in red pen and first thing tomorrow morning he was going to be back on the road and heading straight for them. Nick and Kyle were capable of managing the pack in his absence so a quick overnight stop to check in and swap clothes out of his bag was all he needed.

Once he reached the outskirts of his territory he mind-linked with Nick, telling him to meet him at the pack house. Nick could catch him up on what had been happening while he ate, then he wanted to shower, re-pack and try to get a few hours' sleep. He hadn't had a decent night since Nyah had gone; his dreams were full of violence and anxiety, the fear of Northfell finding her before him playing havoc with his mind.

Nick appeared just as he parked the pick-up outside the pack house. Grabbing his bag and map he opened the driver's door and climbed out, Nick not needing to ask how the search had gone.

"Alpha Nickelson reported two rogues skirting the edges of his territory this morning," Nick told him as they walked towards the house. "One was a female, he said."

Dean shook his head. "Whatever mistakes Nyah made when she stumbled onto my territory won't be made again. She's too smart for that. She's going to stay smack bang in the heart of human territory where she knows I won't be able to trace her."

Nick agreed with a sigh as Dean unlocked his front door. Stale air hung in the hallway as they stepped inside.

"House has only been empty for three days," Dean grunted, sniffing against the unfamiliar scent of his vacant home.

"Yeah." Nick wrinkled his nose in agreement. "Weird isn't it? I'll open some windows." He went straight through to the kitchen while Dean dropped his bag at the foot of the stairs.

"How's Aaron doing?" Dean called out as he shrugged off his jacket. "Any sign of his first phase yet?"

Nick didn't reply.

"Nick," he repeated, draping the jacket over the banister. "How's Aaron?"

Stepping into the kitchen Dean saw what had Nick so silent. A stranger was standing against the far wall of the kitchen, his hands casually resting inside the pockets of his crumpled coat, his weather-beaten face calm as his stare slid from Nick to Dean.

"What the . . ." Dean began. "How the hell did you get in here?"

"My name is Cassius Ochre," the man replied in a gravelly voice.

"I don't give a shit who you are — what the hell are you doing -."

"Dean," Nick interrupted sharply. "It's Cassius Ochre — Northfell's Shaman."

"You son of a bitch." Dean moved to launch himself across the room, but before he had even covered two feet of floor space he found himself being flung backwards. With a heavy thud he landed hard against the fridge. A dull clattering smash sounded from inside.

Dean's hand strayed to where the back of his head had cracked against the door. "Son of a bitch," he muttered again.

Nick had assumed an attacking posture, but seeing the effortless response of the Shaman he faltered and stayed put, stretching out a helping hand as Dean clambered to his feet.

"I mean neither of you any harm," Cassius announced softly, sliding his hand back into his pocket. "And we have little time, so please, let's not waste it with pointless aggression."

"What do you want?" Dean snarled. "And where's Northfell? Is he here, too?"

"Simon Northfell is not here," Cassius replied. "Not yet, anyway."

"So what are you doing here, then?" Nick asked, glancing quickly at Dean who was still clutching the back of his head.

"I need to see Nyah," Cassius said. "Where is -."

"Screw you," Dean spat. "Get the hell out of my house."

Understanding that Dean was not prepared to listen, Cassius turned his attention to Nick. "Where is Nyah?"

"Not anywhere you're going to touch her," Nick snorted.

Cassius sighed and murmured a low comment about over-protective Lycans. "Mr Carson," he said patiently, moving away from the wall towards the table. "I want to help, Nyah. I want to undo some of the damage I have caused before it's too late. Please allow me; it would be better for all concerned if you do."

"How did you get into my house?" Dean yelled, ignoring his statement.

"The same way Simon Northfell will get in," Cassius snapped, growing impatient at being disregarded. "I walked right through the heart of your territory, Mr Carson, right past your patrols, your women and children – and not one member of your pack knew I was there. When Simon Northfell comes here for Nyah it will be the exact same, except that he will not leave them unharmed as I did. Now, if you want to avoid that I would advise you rein in your anger and share a civil conversation with me."

Dean pressed his lips into a tight line.

"Thank-you," Cassius replied. "Now where is Nyah?"

"She's gone," Dean answered simply. "And don't waste your foul breath asking me where because thanks to your handiwork I've no way of tracking her."

Cassius gave a grunt of agitation. "I waited too long," he chastised himself.

"Too long for what?" Dean demanded to know.

"To come here," he replied. "I located her on Monday night, but – I waited, I didn't want to raise suspicion by leaving."

"Raise suspicion with Northfell?"

"Yes, Simon Northfell." Cassius leaned against the back of one of the dining chairs and looked down, his copper-skinned face sliding into a dark frown.

"He doesn't know you're here," Nick guessed.

Cassius shook his head. "Let's hope not."

Watching Cassius stare distractedly at where his hands gripped the back of the chair Dean realized that he had been right; that was no dream Nyah had had. Cassius had worked a locator spell to find her.

"I take it this means you're not on Northfell's team anymore, then?" Dean asked.

Cassius gave a short, wry laugh. "Anymore?" he said looking up. "I was never on his team."

"So what you did to Nyah was of your own free will?"

"No, absolutely not," Cassius answered, disgust twisting his mouth. "Harming her was the singular most appalling act I have ever committed."

"So why did you do it?"

Cassius leaned across the table towards Dean. "I had no choice. I was forced into it. I didn't want any dealings with that vile man, but he refused to take no for an answer."

"Really," Dean snorted, his eyes flicking sceptically over Cassius as they met nose-to-nose over the centre of the table. "Explain how a man with your abilities was unable to say no."

"Northfell took my daughter," Cassius answered. "That's how I was unable to say no."

Dean backed off. Cassius retreated too, but he released his grip on the chair with an aggressive shove as he straightened up. "When he first approached me I turned him away," he began to explain quietly, "said I wanted nothing to do with him, but then a day later Louisa went missing and he appeared on my doorstep again, advising me that if I wished for her safe return I had to do what he wanted. And what Simon Northfell wants," Cassius said darkly, "Simon Northfell gets."

Dean stepped back from the table, his anger waning as he grasped the predicament of Cassius's situation. "I'm sorry," he said calmly. "I shouldn't have judged you."

"I deserve to be judged," Cassius replied honestly, shoving his hands back into his pockets. "And I will be for what I've done."

"You didn't have much choice," Nick offered begrudgingly.

Cassius shrugged as if to say that didn't matter. "I could have handled it differently. I tried – I did try to protect her – but I failed."

"Yeah, you failed alright," Nick muttered, turning away from the table to lean against the kitchen counter. He folded his arms tightly and stared down at his feet.

"I failed her and her father," Cassius added, almost as if he was muttering to himself.

"You knew Harper Morgan?" Dean asked.

"Yes, I knew him well."

"How?"

"Harper came to me many years ago when his wife Lori was dying. She had been bitten by a vampire during a battle over territory, but by the time he had found me the venom had taken her past the point where I could have helped. I did what I could for her in her last days. Nyah was just a young child at the time and Lori fought so hard to stay alive, but . . ." Cassius trailed off with a rumbling sigh that rolled into a wet cough. Fumbling in the pocket of his mac for a tissue he held it to his mouth until the racking had subsided. "Harper kept our friendship as a secret," he continued hoarsely, a short moment later, "he didn't want word of our alliance being broadcast, but Northfell found out somehow; obviously he filed it away for future reference."

"Self-serving bastard," Nick muttered to his feet.

"That's an understatement," Cassius replied wearily, shoving the tissue back into his pocket.

Dean began to pace a steady tread on the kitchen floor. Cassius' connection with Harper was an interesting sidebar, but he didn't care to hear about past events. He was stuck in the now. "There must be something you can do to help Nyah," he said. "Surely you have some way of helping her."

"If she had been here, yes, I could have helped."

"What were you going to do?"

"Return her wolf," Cassius answered. "It might have given her a chance against Northfell."

"So why can't you do it now?"

"I cannot perform the spell without her present." He gestured towards an aged satchel propped against the wall in the corner of the room where he had been standing moments before. "If I release her wolf's corpus essence without her being physically present to absorb it, it will simply drift unanchored."

"Her corpus what?" Dean replied, his stare drawn to the bulging satchel. Something of Nyah's was in there?

"Her corpus -." Cassius broke off to wave away his explanation. "It doesn't matter. The fact is that I needed her here. Now I have no choice but to restore it for Northfell tomorrow."

"Wait – you're – how come you can restore it for him?" Dean stammered. "You can't – not – why him?"

Cassius sighed agitatedly and threw another dismissive wave in Dean's direction. "It's too complicated to explain. My hands are tied, that's all you need to understand." Tugging the sides of his open coat together he drew himself up. "I'm sorry, Mr Carson, I am, but there's nothing I can do to help now." He cleared his throat with a determined finality before glancing between Dean and Nick. "I must leave. I've taken a huge risk by coming here and I can't delay any longer."

"No." Dean darted around the side of the table and stepped in front of Cassius as he moved to pick up his satchel. "You're not going anywhere until you help. And don't give me any of that 'too complicated to explain' bullshit. You're going to tell me exactly what's going on – even if it means explaining it to me like I'm six years old – so sit."

"Mr Carson," Cassius warned.

"No," Dean snapped in reply. "You owe this to Nyah and her father – stay and fix this."

Cassius held up his hands in refusal, but before he could fully draw breath to protest again Nick spoke up.

"Why can't you find out where she is now – like you did before?" he demanded. "If you did one of your spells to find her here, why can't you do it again?"

"She's fading too fast," Cassius explained. "I tried a locator spell before I left Blackwater Ridge yesterday, but it didn't work."

"Fading?" Nick repeated.

"Yes." Cassius paused to turn his pitied look back onto Dean. "How bad was it before she left?"

"How bad was what?"

Cassius regarded Dean warily as he stared up at him from under his lined brow. "Being without her wolf is killing her," he explained in a tone of 'didn't you know?' "The spell I cast was meant to be lifted within a week – it's been nearly a month now. If Nyah is still alive it won't be for much longer."

Dean sucked in a tight breath and wheeled around, his hands fisting tightly into his hair as he struggled to control his panic.

"Okay," Nick cut in resolutely, pushing himself away from the counter. "So do something to fix that. Work your voodoo magic and get her strong again."

"It doesn't work that way," Cassius answered as Dean kept his back turned to them, his eyes mashed shut, his hands trembling as he continued to keep a rigid grip on his fistfuls of hair.

"Well what way does it work?" Nick asked louder, approaching him. "You don't just turn up here to say sorry and then refuse to do anything about it – you said you wanted to make amends, so bloody well make them!"

Cassius remained silent.

"Come on!" Nick yelled. "Do something! You're a Shaman – a medicine man. Find a way to help her!"

"What can I do?" Cassius yelled back. "What can I do that won't risk my daughter's life? You think I wanted to do this to Nyah? Do you think this is how I wanted to honour my friendship with Harper Morgan?"

"Nyah is dying!" Dean roared, spinning back around. "And you're the only person who can help her. Give her back her wolf – now!"

"I can't," Cassius ground out. "I have nothing here to bind the corpus essence to her. Northfell took some of her blood, but it's in Blackwater Ridge, with him. Without that I have no other way."

"Why does he have her blood?" Nick asked, his face twisting with revulsion. "Why would he want . . .?"

Dean suddenly yanked out one of the kitchen chairs. "Sit," he ordered Cassius, gesturing sharply towards it. "And tell me what in the hell is going on."

Cassius threw a surrendering glance at the clock sitting on the mantel above the stove and then sat with a weary sigh.

"Start at the beginning," Dean commanded, "the very beginning. Don't leave anything out."

Cassius spoke, Dean and Nick listened, and for a long while there was only the sound of Cassius' throaty voice rumbling in the kitchen, neither of them able to interrupt him as he laid the bare facts out before them.

"Demons," Dean choked out eventually. "He wants to engineer some kind of . . . werewolf demon pups?"

"He's immersed himself in the blackest of magic," Cassius confirmed. "And it's taken him to a dark place. Originally, I was to summon the spirits of his ancestors and extract some of their essence for Northfell to absorb. But now he's moved onto better things; he wants demon blood. What he's planning to create is unnatural, an abhorrence."

"And he wants Nyah to carry them."

"Yes. And the chances of her living past the birth are -."

"Enough." Dean had dropped into a seat not long after Cassius had begun talking, but now he hastily stood up and returned to walking lengths of the kitchen floor. "I won't allow that to happen, so we're not discussing it. Just tell me what his next move is."

"As soon as Nyah escaped he demanded that I return her wolf, but returning her wolf cannot be done without locating her first. And locating her cannot be done when she is without her wolf."

"But you found her -," Nick began.

Cassius cut him off by raising a single finger. "Using some of the blood that Northfell took to summon the demon he needs. I only managed to get enough to work the spell the one time – and even then I barely managed to pinpoint her to here."

"And Northfell had no idea you could do that," Dean commented.

"He didn't," Cassius confirmed, "but he's learning; he's found another way. He can locate her himself, but only once I've restored her wolf. And as that particular spell is currently beyond his capabilities my plan was to restore it for her here and give her the opportunity to stay running from him. Then, tomorrow night, I can work the spell again, but as her wolf will already have been restored, the spell -."

"It won't work," Dean finished for him. "But he'll still be able to locate her."

"Wait," Nick cut in. "Either way, Northfell still gets to find her."

"Yes, but she'd have had a head start," Cassius said, "And Northfell agreed to return Louisa once I worked the spell." He turned to look at Dean. "Please understand, Mr Carson; Louisa's life is at stake. I will not stop Northfell from locating Nyah."

"I know, I know," Dean assured him hurriedly.

"And even though I cannot believe a word that spews from his mouth," Cassius continued, "I have to hope that he will return my daughter to me, unharmed, tomorrow evening."

"Is there any way you can delay him?" Dean pushed, "any way at all? I've been searching for Nyah, and I will find her, I know I will, but I need more time."

"No," Cassius shook his head slowly. "He's hell-bent on having her location by tomorrow evening at the latest – the spell is linked with the waning moon cycle."

"Dammit!" Dean spat.

Nick got up from his chair. "Dean . . ." he began, but then trailed off. He had nothing to suggest, nothing that would offer comfort.

"This can't be happening," Dean stated, panic rearing inside him again. "This just cannot be happening."

"Dean," Nick said again.

"No." Dean shrugged off Nick's conciliatory grasp. His wolf was snarling inside, fear urging it to overwhelm Dean and phase so it could return to searching for its mate. "I can't lose her."

"We'll find her," Nick soothed.

"How?" Dean rounded on him. "How? It's like looking for a needle in a haystack! She could be anywhere. Even if we knew which damned direction she was in it would help – but we've no clue, Nick. We have nothing!"

Nick watched helplessly as Dean scrubbed his hands over his face and began pacing again.

"I can't lose her," Dean repeated desperately. "I can't. The pain I feel right now is unbearable — and that's knowing she's alive — if she . . . if she was gone, it would . . . "

"Mr Carson," Cassius said suddenly. "You and Nyah - are you, is she . . .?"

"My mate," Dean stated forlornly. "Yes, Nyah is my mate."

"How is that possible?" Cassius rose to his feet. "How can that be? Her wolf is gone — removed. How did you connect with her?"

Dean's panic faltered. Cassius had a sudden look of hopefulness on his face. "Her wolf surfaced when she was here. I felt our connection, she -."

"Her wolf surfaced? You felt it? You actually sensed her wolf?"

"Yes, when she was asleep, twice, but then it happened again, and she felt it too, that was when our mate connection was established."

"It worked," Cassius exclaimed, surprise suddenly brightening his face as he looked delightedly between Dean and Nick "I thought it had failed, I thought I hadn't –."

"What worked?" Nick butted in. "What did you do?"

"I altered the original spell," Cassius answered, his gesturing hands alive with a renewed vigour. "Northfell wanted her wolf removed; I felt that if I could somehow bury it deep inside of her instead it would give her a chance. I didn't think it had worked – yes, the corpus essence that I transferred from her into the vessel was weak, but I assumed that was because of what I had done."

Dean's mouth worked to speak, but he couldn't order the sudden rush of questions he wanted to blurt out.

"This changes things," Cassius announced. "This certainly changes things."

"How? What can you do?" Nick asked urgently.

Cassius ignored Nick to focus intently on Dean who was still struggling to speak. "Did you mark her?"

Dean's stammering breaths ceased and he drew himself up. "That's none of your business," he growled.

"I understand the delicacy of my question, Mr Carson," Cassius acknowledged, "but now is not the time for delicacy."

"No," Dean answered flatly. "I did not mark her."

Cassius' delight dimmed for a short moment. "It would have been better if you had," he said after a moment, "but not to worry – the fact that your mate connection has been forged is enough."

"Enough to what?" Dean asked with hesitant hope.

"Restore her wolf and locate her," Cassius replied, already darting into the corner of the room to snatch up his satchel. "I'll need some of your blood," he announced unbuckling the chunky brass buckles, "and if you have any of Nyah's personal effects that would help also."

"There's a t-shirt, a hairbrush, a toothbrush, a -," Dean began to list.

"Hairbrush," Cassius said quickly. "Perfect. And I'll take some of your hair, too."

Dean made to dash from the kitchen, but Cassius called out to him, slowing his charge from the room. "Mr Carson," he said gravely, bringing Dean to a stop in the doorway. "You know that all I'm giving you is a head start? Tomorrow night Simon will know where she is, too. And he'll search until he finds her. You do understand the danger that you're putting yourself in?"

"All I care about is Nyah," Dean answered.

"I appreciate that," Cassius said, "but Simon won't tolerate another hitch in his plan. He won't hesitate to kill you if he thinks you're trying to stop him."

"Not if I kill him first," Dean replied simply.

Cassius placed his satchel onto the table with a remorseful sigh. "I've told you what he's capable of," he warned. "You won't be able to fight him."

"Well, then we'll die trying," Nick replied for Dean, stepping in beside him in solidarity.

Cassius sad gaze moved between them both, before he shook his head and looked down. "I hope for all our sakes that it won't come to that."

TWENTY-THREE

"Nick – are you in shock?"

Dean threw a curious glance at Nick's taut expression profiled against the rain-streaked window in the grey light of the pick-up cab. They had been driving for nearly two hours and Nick had barely uttered a word.

"I think I must be," he finally muttered, blinking his eyes hard as if trying to smack himself out of his stupor.

"Over what part?" Dean asked, his short disbelieving laugh revealing his own incredulous state.

"Shit, I'm not sure," Nick replied dryly. "Maybe the part where we watched a trail of powdered hair, shaman spit and a bunch of other weird stuff trace itself across a map and settle onto a town called Mosse. Or maybe the part where a shaman inked voodoo tatts on our chests so that Northfell can't use hex necklaces on us – take your pick."

Dean agreed with another humourless laugh. Rain was hammering against the windshield; it made driving in the already smothering darkness a difficult task and they had countless miles to go before they would be anywhere near Nyah.

"What about you?" Nick asked. "You haven't exactly been Mr Chatty Pants either. You not freaked out by any of what just happened?"

"I'm still stuck in the horror of hearing that Northfell wants to mate with Nyah so she can carry his engineered pups for him – and how he's decided to use demon blood for an extra evil-fuelled boost. Shaman spit and voodoo inkings are really not an issue for me right now." Dean glanced at the dash display again. Time was time moving way faster than the miles he was racing to cover.

"Cassius wasn't exaggerating when he warned that Northfell's totally off the reservation," Nick sighed.

"No, he certainly wasn't."

There was a shared silence, the steady whoosh of the wiper blades battling to fling the sheets of rain off the windshield all that filled the sombre air.

"You think we're going to be able to do this?" Nick asked eventually.

Dean stared straight ahead for a long moment before replying. "I know that now would be a good time to give a rousing Alpha speech, but, to be honest, Nick, I don't know. I think the best way to handle this is one step at a time. First off, I just want to find Nyah. Cassius' warning about the dangers of her wolf re-emerging has me worried. I know it's going to kick off soon for her; it's been three hours since he did that spell, and what if she's in the middle of a public place when it happens? What if she starts phasing in a crowd or hits the deck in a -."

"Dean," Nick interrupted, "don't do that, don't go there – you'll drive yourself insane. Look -." Nick gestured towards the clock. "It's gone one in the morning; chances are she's tucked up in bed. It's the best place she could be."

"But what if she isn't?"

"She'll deal with it. She'll take herself somewhere safe."

"Yeah, you're right," Dean yielded after a moment.

Nick reached forwards to grab a map off the dashboard. "So how are we doing for time?"

"We've nineteen hours and seventeen minutes before Cassius hits Northfell's deadline of eight o'clock tomorrow night – if Cassius can stall until then."

"And Mosse is . . ."

"At least another eighteen hours away."

"Okay . . ." Nick replied, folding the map up and shoving it back onto the dash. "No stopping then."

"No," Dean confirmed. "I'll drive for another four hours then you can take over while I try and get some sleep."

"It's a damn pity the flight was fully booked," Nick commented, settling back into his seat and closing his eyes.

"Yeah, but any kind of a delay would have got us into trouble. And we would have had to hire a car at the other end. Way too complicated," Dean reminded him. "It's simpler this way. And I need simple right now."

Nick grunted in reply. "Gotta agree with you there."

When the screeching audience, grating jingles and smarmy one-liners of the game show host became too much to bear Nyah grabbed the remote and flicked herself into a silent dimness.

She hadn't even been paying attention – except for the part where Mary-Lou from Missouri won a microwave and became so hysterical that even Scott Powerhouse, game show host extraordinaire, allowed his super-professional expression to slide into one of panicked horror. All Nyah wanted the television to do was drown out the silence that reminded her of where she was, as opposed to where she wanted to be.

Remaining completely motionless on the bed she glanced around the room. The One-Eyed Cat was easily the worst motel she had stayed in. Depressing didn't even come close to describing the place, but the coma-inducing exhaustion that had crept upon her two days ago had reduced her to such a wreck that if the first place offering accommodation on the outskirts of Mosse had been a morgue she would have taken it.

Get up, she told herself. It's gone one o'clock in the morning. You need to sleep. But her body refused to move. Even her fingers remained curled around the nauseatingly sticky remote.

Maybe I should just continue to lie here, she thought. It would be easy. I could just give in, let the tiredness win and let death follow. With a groan she forced herself to roll onto one side and then wiped the fingers that had been infected by the emote off her jeans. "Shut up with the death wish," she ordered. If she was going to die it wasn't going to be in some pox-ridden hell-hole of a motel room. It was going to be on a forest floor, on a bed of dry pine needles, a warm afternoon sun filtering down through the branches and a gentle chorus of bird-song drifting around her. "Many, many years from now," she muttered, groaning as she heaved herself upright.

Rummaging in her bag she pulled out the t-shirt she liked to sleep in. There was still a faint scent of Dean's fabric softener wrapped around its fibres, and even though she knew that it would physically hurt she breathed it in and allowed herself a short moment of pretending.

Returning to reality, she swallowed back the hard lump swelling inside her throat and stood up. The room spun, but that was nothing new. She waited until the floor and ceiling had settled back to where they belonged and then using the cardboard-thin walls for support she crossed through to the mildewed bathroom.

With one hand supporting her weight over the sink she brushed her teeth, wondering in a remarkably matter-of-fact kind of way about how many days she had left to live. Yesterday she would have guessed four, maybe five. Today she reckoned less; three days, maybe two, and it was tempting to imagine the comfort of surrendering to the approaching end. Once she faded completely there would be no more pain. The emptiness she felt – the emptiness that had swelled and consumed her with every mile that the train had taken her from Carter Plains – would be gone. There would be nothing. Complete nothingness. It would be nice.

"Stop!" she hissed at herself, throwing a nasty glare at her exhausted reflection in the stained mirror above the sink. "You made a decision; you have to stick to it. You are not going to allow yourself to die."

In the box car of the freight train, a stomach-churning stench of over-ripe melons eventually driving her to leap out after seven long hours, she had held a long and serious debate with herself - her most honest yet. She was dying, the fact could not be ignored any longer, and although checking out would mean an end to most of her problems and pissing Simon off big-time, it also terminated the tiny, tiny piece of hope that she and Dean might end up together someday. Life was too precious, Dean was too precious, and she couldn't let either of them slip away willingly. The problem was deciding who she would allow to restore her wolf and therefore, her life; Dean or Simon.

Staying with Dean would fix her within weeks; maybe even less if he marked her. But Simon would still find her, and Dean would probably end up dead.

If she returned to Blackwater Ridge however, Simon would restore her wolf, too. She would have to make him agree to a deal; stop controlling everyone in turn for her co-operation, and if he wanted her carrying his pups badly enough he would have to agree to it. Wouldn't he?

Neither of her options promised her a future of lemon drops and picket fences. Both guaranteed misery, because whatever way she looked at it she would most likely end up being claimed back by Simon. All that the decision really boiled down to was whether she wanted Dean to live or die. And that was easy to decide.

So, this was her last night as a rogue. Tomorrow morning she was going to take her final journey back home to

Blackwater Ridge. It was going to be so good to see her pack again; Karen, Blake, Michael – all of them. And she would contact Tanya first thing, too. The baby must have been born by now – was it a boy or a girl? And what had Tanya named it? Allowing herself to think about her friends after shoving all thoughts of them into the back of her mind for so long was a relief, and being back amongst them was one of only two comforts that she could hold on to. The second was her memories of Dean, but thoughts of him would be kept in a deep place, a place she would not allow herself to go to very often. It would be easier that way, easier for everyone if she embraced her 'calling' with Simon and put aside her feelings for Dean.

Scooping a handful of water from the tap she leaned forward to splash it on her face. Of course, thinking that she could put aside her feelings for Dean was easy enough when her wolf wasn't around to argue. When her wolf was back their mate connection would re-surface, too, and according to what she had heard, the first few weeks of rejecting or ignoring a mate was hell on earth. Reaching out, she blindly grabbed for the sandpaper towel. She'd just have to suck it up.

That was when it hit.

The most unmerciful pain exploded inside her body doubling her over so acutely that she cracked her head against the side of the sink before crumpling onto the chipped tiled floor.

Nyah screamed and curled into a ball. Her whole body was on fire with the pain and she cried out, suddenly afraid that this was the end, this was death. But as another wave of searing pain ripped through her, she quickly realized that what was happening was connected to Cassius Ochre as a yawning chasm opened within her and her wolf began to emerge. She buckled and twisted as it clawed its way up from whatever abyss it had been hurled into and a lucid part of her screaming mind told her to lock herself inside so that her emerging wolf would not be able to wreak havoc in the town. It was with gargantuan effort that she managed to grasp the shower curtain and yank down the pole so that she could wedge it against the door and the edge of the shower tray to keep the bathroom door jammed shut.

Blinded with agonizing pain she writhed in agony, praying for her consciousness to slip away, but as she twisted and thrashed on the hard floor her mind remained clear and alert. If Cassius had restored her wolf it meant Simon was coming. She would have fared better if she had been able to willingly return to him; now he would come and say or do who knew what as punishment. Curling into a tight ball, her breaths rushing in burning streams through her nostrils she could feel her mouth filling with blood as her teeth bit down into her tongue. Maybe worrying about what Simon was going to do was pointless; if this pain kept up she'd be dead before he found her. Another spasm snapped her onto the flat of her back, her body arching dangerously as she felt her consciousness waver. The room began to dim before her and she squeezed her eyes shut, hoping that darkness would suck her into oblivion, but when another searing rush of agony flung her eyes wide open again she knew that she wasn't going to be that lucky.

Countless hours of torture passed before the tormenting pain began to wane, only to be replaced by a base sense of savagery. Her wolf was enraged and the violence of it shuddered through her as it struggled to phase. Whatever pain that she thought she had felt before then was eclipsed by the torture of her body mutating at bone snapping speed one moment and then unbearable slowness the next, her wolf's want for carnage so completely overwhelming that she slashed and ripped at the tiled walls, her claws gouging chunks of tile away as she fought to break free of the small room.

During the moments when her strength had waned enough to phase her back to human form, she lay panting and weak on the floor, her fingernails torn and bloody, every muscle and bone in her body screaming with pain. She knew only by the changing light that morphed inside her small cage that deep night had faded into early morning. The greying light of dawn had dulled the bathroom ceiling when she had been in human form, but by the time her wolf had phased numerous times more, smashed itself continually against the confining walls before collapsing and transforming her back, a softer, declining light heralded evening time.

Dean and Nick were forty-six miles outside of Mosse when Dean sensed the first faint awareness of Nyah's wolf. It tipped the bare edges of his consciousness, its signal weak and worryingly distorted. At the thirty mile mark it was strong enough for him to know that Nyah was in distress.

"Intense," he struggled to explain to Nick. "It's coming in waves. Right now I can sense violence, fury . . . but a few minutes ago it was a sort of . . . confused exhaustion."

"Cassius said it would be hard for her," Nick reminded him and then nodded towards the clock that read five-twenty pm on the dash. "You think he's been able to hold Northfell off? There's still two hours and forty minutes before the deadline."

"I hope so," Dean replied tightly. "But Blackwater Ridge is only three hours from here – if he wasn't able to stall him, Northfell could already be ahead of us." Dean grunted in frustration and agitatedly scratched at his head. "What in the hell was Nyah thinking coming so close to Blackwater Ridge? I thought she was smarter than -." He broke off with a wince as another wave of her distress rolled over him. "It's getting worse," he muttered, flooring the pick-up. "Hold on, Nyah, hold on, baby."

"It's just the disorientation," Nick offered, calmly. "Take it easy or we'll get pulled over for speeding."

"It feels more than disorientation to me," Dean replied, darting out of the lane to overtake a string of cars as he sped along the wide, flat road that led to Mosse. "It's fear. Something has her panicking. And nothing or no-one is going to make me stop this car until I get to her."

Nyah's distorted signal was so clear that, by the time they entered Mosse, Dean had no problem in finding the motel she was hiding out in. 'The One-Eyed Cat' was sitting right on the edge of the town and he swung into the parking lot, his tyres spitting out dust and gravel as he skidded to a stop outside the stretch of uniform units.

Dean scanned the empty lot as they jumped from the truck. "I think we beat him to it."

It was as Nyah lay twisted amongst shreds of shower curtain and what had once been her clothes that she felt his presence swell around her. Immediately her wolf's aggression calmed. Opening her eyes she blinked away the last of the dizziness and then drawing in a few steadying breaths she rolled onto her side and dragged herself up into a sitting position. No way – no way! How had he found her? How in the hell had he found her so fast? Her bloodied hands grappled frantically with the pole blocking the door, but she had jammed it in good and hard. It wouldn't budge.

"No, no, no," she whispered, scooting back and then slamming her two bare feet against it. "Come on!" she spat, pounding her heels harder, "move!" With one final, desperate shove the pole popped away.

Scrambling to her feet she flung open the door and dashed back into the bedroom, hastily snatching clothes from her bag.

"Hurry, hurry," she hissed at herself, jamming her feet into her boots as she yanked up her jeans and fumbled with the buttons. He was getting closer. His energy was starting to curl itself around her like a soft, warm blanket, and boy, if ever she wanted to allow herself to be wrapped up in something it was that.

Seizing whatever clothes were closest she flung a sweater over her head and then shoved the rest into her bag, swung it over her shoulder and then stopped dead. Front door or bathroom window – front door or bathroom window?

Neither! her wolf replied, *our mate is here, stay!* "Bathroom window," she decided and spun around.

The front door burst open.

"Nyah!"

She froze in place, her back turned to him, her face wincing with the awful pleasure that the sound of his warm voice brought.

"Nyah, it's okay, I'm here." His hands were on her, turning her towards him and cupping her face. "I found you," he breathed. "I thought I wouldn't make it on time, I thought -."

"You shouldn't be here!"

The relief on his face froze as she shoved him back and stepped away. "Why did you come? You shouldn't have come – you shouldn't have!"

"Nyah . . ."

"No. You have to leave; you have to go right now!"

"We're ahead of Northfell," Dean replied calmly, reaching out to touch her again. "It's okay, Nyah, I have you now, you're safe."

"It's not me! It's – dammit! Why did you have to come!"

"Nyah -." He grabbed for her again, quickly drawing her into his arms. "You're coming back with me, I'm -."

"No, I'm not!" she yelled, jerking free. "I'm not going anywhere with you, I'm going back to Blackwater Ridge!"

"You're what?"

She hadn't even realized that Nick had come into the room until he choked out an 'Are you nuts?' as Dean began yelling at her.

"Have you any idea what he's planning to do?" he shouted. "He's going to -."

"I know what he wants!" she snapped back. "And I know exactly what he'll do if he finds you –."

"Dean!" Nick's frantic shout halted her words. "Northfell's here!"

Immediately, Dean grabbed her and shoved her behind his back as Nick began to back away from the door.

"Through the bathroom," Dean whispered, jerking his thumb towards the ravaged room behind them, "quick!"

But Nyah didn't move. It was pointless.

The handle of the front door began to rotate, and in perfect horror-movie style, time slackened into slow-motion as the door was pushed ajar. Dean was nudging against her, trying to make her move, but she stayed in place as three figures appeared in the widening doorway; Simon Northfell, Michael and Blake.

Simon stepped into the room, took a moment to glance around, sniffed once and then settled his cold, black stare upon her. "Hello, my darling Nyah."

Her mouth refused to work and when her eyes darted nervously over his shoulder to where Michael and Blake flanked him her heart dropped when she saw their expressionless eyes. Elbowing her way past Dean she stepped forwards. "I'm coming with you," she said.

Simon raised a single eyebrow.

"Over my dead body," snarled Dean.

"Be careful what you wish for," Simon warned lightly, still watching her.

"I'll come right now," Nyah insisted, "we'll leave straight away."

"What are you doing?" Dean hissed, snatching her back towards him and clutching her tightly to his chest.

"Let me go!" she demanded, "I want to go back home!"

Simon took a few casual steps further into the room. "Miss Morgan has requested that you release her, pup. As her Alpha I would advise you to do so."

"Why? So you can put your filthy hands on her? She's my -." Dean grunted in pain as Nyah drove her elbow into his belly and the second his hands loosened she darted away from him. Simon was quick to wrap one bony hand around her arm and yank her to his side.

"Boys," he sighed wearily at Michael and Blake. "Could you please?"

Nyah squeezed her eyes shut. There were a few moments of scuffling, grunting and snarling before a surrendering silence fell and she cautiously opened her eyes. Dean and Nick were both in a tight hold.

"I swear, Northfell, if you so much as lay one finger on her I'll kill you, you evil son of a bitch!" Dean roared, struggling ineffectually against Michael.

Simon rested a hand against his chest. "Why, now I feel bad. You know who I am and I have no earthly idea who you are."

"Dean Carson."

"Ah." The utterance hung in the air and Nyah closed her eyes again.

"Alpha Carson of Carter Plains."

"That's right," Dean spat. "Remember that name; it belongs to the wolf that's going to end your pathetic life."

"It's a pleasure, etc., etc.," Simon's smiling voice replied mildly. With her eyes still mashed shut Nyah sensed Simon turning towards her. "Any particular reason as to why this whelp is behaving in such a threatening manner?"

"He knew my father," she answered, opening her eyes, but keeping her stare stuck to the tatty carpet.

"I'm her mate," Dean ground out.

"No!" Her head whipped up and she shook it frantically at Simon. "No, he's not. He's lying."

Simon's eyes narrowed and then slowly tracked from Nyah's face back onto Dean's.

"Nyah is my mate," Dean stated again.

"No, I'm not," she insisted in reply, shaking her head at Dean, her eyes begging him to stop.

"Someone here is telling porky pies," Simon replied. He contemplated the anxious silence for a short minute and then suddenly grabbed her, jerking her head to one side and roughly yanking her hair back. "Hm," he smirked, running two fingers down the unbroken skin of her neck. "You haven't been marked. It still doesn't tell me which one of you is lying, but I'm glad to see that you haven't been infected by that whelp."

Nyah pressed her hand against her neck when Simon released her. It felt like a million worms had wriggled under her skin. "He knew my father," she said again, "he feels a duty towards him. That's all this is, nothing more. He's not my mate." Even as she said the words she could hear her wolf howling pitifully.

"Whether he is or not is of little matter," Simon decided. "But you did lie to me, Carson. You had my rogue and you denied it."

"I – that was me – I told him my name was -." Nyah began.

"Was I talking to you?" Simon snapped, making her flinch away from him.

"Northfell," Dean warned. "I swear, if you -." Michael drove his knee into Dean's kidneys, the force of his hit buckling Dean's legs. Nyah swallowed back a scream.

"Blah blah, I'll break your neck, blah blah, I'll eat your innards," Simon sang, waving his hands theatrically. "Blah blah blah - enough." He clicked his fingers. "Boys, take care of this. Nyah – with me."

Nyah allowed him to walk her towards the door, but she craned her neck to take one final look over her shoulder at Dean. "Please don't hurt them," she begged Simon as the door was wrenched open. "Alpha Northfell, please. Don't hurt them. I was coming back to you, I was, they just got here when -."

"Shut up, Nyah, you whimpering little brat," he hissed, "I'm not even five minutes in your presence and I'm already sick of your whining voice."

"Nyah!" Dean yelled and she whipped her head back towards him in time to see Michael and Blake suddenly swing Dean and Nick to one side. In perfect harmony they were smacked into the wall and braced in place by a single arm. Stepping back, Michael and Blake each raised a foot and then in one clean, synchronized flash of movement drove their feet into Dean and Nick's knees.

Nyah choked on her own weak scream as the sound of smashing bone was drowned out by two roars of pain.

Yanking her out of the room, Simon bundled her into his waiting car. "That's what happens when you lie, Nyah," he said lightly, sliding into the seat beside her. "You would do well to remember that."

The sickening sounds of Dean and Nick's punishment continued to swim around her as she huddled against the car door, and her only hope that neither of them was dead was that Blake and Michael were quick to return to the car. They climbed into the front seats and without a word Michael started the engine and drove away.

Twenty-Four

When Dean came to, he was face down on the floor, sticky blood congealing in a pool under his cheek. "Nyah," he mumbled and then regretted it the second that his ragged breath sent him into a spasm of agonizing coughs. Northfell's henchmen had really worked him over. Gingerly lifting his head he carefully turned it to one side. Nick was motionless on the floor a couple of feet away from him.

"Nick," he grunted, before spitting out a glob of blood. "Nick, come on, buddy, wake up."

Readying himself for pain he slowly pushed his weight onto his hands and then pushed himself back onto his knees. He stopped halfway when the shattered bones, although already knitting back into a solid piece again, screamed against the action.

"Dammit." Rolling onto his ass instead Dean let out a groan. He hurt in places where he didn't even think nerves existed and when he looked down at his right arm he was pretty sure it was going to have to be re-broken; the bone had set, but at a strange angle judging by the way that his arm stuck out.

He glanced over at Nick again. "Nick, wake up," he called, scooting towards him. "Come on, buddy, open your eyes."

Nick groaned and racked out a string of coughs.

"You okay?" Dean asked, grabbing the broken chair that lay over Nick's legs.

"Shit – no, dammit . . . shit." Nick had fallen in an awkward heap against the wall and allowed Dean to pull him away so he could roll onto his back. "I think every bone I have is broken," he groaned.

"Can you sit up?"

"In a year maybe," he wheezed, taking Dean's hand and dragging himself up. "Shit," he moaned again.

"Think you can walk?" Dean rasped.

"Hell no," Nick coughed. "I can just about breathe." He groaned again and tentatively flexed his right arm out. "Sons of bitches, I'm going to enjoy kicking their asses," he muttered.

"Think I'm going to need you to re-break my arm," Dean announced, displaying the oddly shaped limb.

Nick snorted. "I mock your screwed-up arm. I have a dislocated shoulder."

"Ouch," Dean winced, seeing the awkward position of Nick's left shoulder. "Okay. So who goes first?"

"Let's just try standing up," Nick suggested.

Using the wall, the bed and the smashed up chair they both heaved themselves upright.

"You know, they left us in a twisted heap on purpose," Nick panted. "They knew our bones would knit together all screwed-up, make it harder for us to follow."

"Only being stone-cold dead will stop me from following," Dean answered and then held out his crooked arm. "I can't phase until this is fixed, so come on."

When Nick let out a loud yelp a few minutes later Dean rolled his eyes. "Don't be such a baby," he joked through a dry cough. "You've had worse than this done to you in the past."

"That curly-headed mutant is going to get such a beating," Nick growled out in reply, massaging his freshly-set shoulder.

"We're not going to hand out any beatings, Nick," he replied. "They're Nyah's pack mates, remember? It's Northfell who did this, not them."

Nick sank onto the bed and began rubbing his knee caps. "Are you going to be able to drive?"

For the first time since he had come to Dean glanced towards the window. "Yeah, I should be – whoa."

"What?" Nick spun round to follow his stare. "What time is it?" he asked, echoing Dean's exact thought as he saw the inky blackness outside.

"Ten-fifteen . . . we've been out cold nearly five hours. We need to get going right now."

Hobbling and wincing they left the smashed-up motel room and limped across the lot. Dean awkwardly climbed back into the driver's seat of his pick-up, wincing as he stretched to pull his seat-belt across.

"Did you see the hex necklaces?" Nick asked as he strained to pull across his own seat-belt.

"Yep," Dean replied, starting the engine. "Next time we're having our asses handed to us on a plate forget about fighting back and focus on ripping them off instead."

"Cassius said he's got every pack member wearing them," Nick replied. "It's gonna be some job."

"The second the hex isn't touching the person they're free, though" Dean reminded him. "So as soon as the necklace is off we've got to let them know who we are and what's been happening."

"Hi there," Nick began sarcastically as they skidded out onto the road. "My name's Nick. Your Alpha's planning on spawning demon babies with your ex Alpha's daughter and you've been his butt monkey for the last month. Don't worry if you can't remember anything – it's probably better if you don't. Now – any idea where your Alpha might hang out when he wants to summon demons?"

Cloying humidity hung thickly in the air of Blackwater Ridge when Dean and Nick slid soundlessly from the truck less than three hours later. They had parked on a narrow track set way back from the edges of the forest surrounding the territory, and as they moved along the path the first acrid waft of Lycan urine announced their location.

'We're here,' Dean pointed out silently. 'Stay low and quiet.'

'And alive,' Nick added dryly.

Blackwater Ridge had a small pack, but with every creeping mile that carried Dean and Nick further into the territory it became obvious that patrols were not in place.

'He left the place unguarded?' Nick asked as they hunkered low in the last of the dwindling trees.

Dean scanned the simple settlement set out in the clearing ahead of them. There wasn't a soul to be seen. 'Maybe there's no-one left to guard it,' he suggested, staring at the deserted and completely neglected street. Lawns were overgrown, loose trash cluttered paths and flower-beds, and when he peered further along the un-lit street he had to blink a couple of times to be sure that what he was looking at were two burned-out houses.

'Whew,' Nick's disbelief whistled in his mind. 'What the hell has been going on here?'

'Hell being the operative word,' Dean replied darkly.

A movement to their left urged them to duck lower and a familiar face came into view.

'That curly-headed son of a bitch is mine,' Nick growled. 'I owe him a knee-cap crushing.'

The figure was walking a slow, mechanical lap of what Dean reckoned was the pack house. If the pack house was under watch it made sense that Northfell was in there. And Nyah. But he couldn't sense her – or any other wolves – it was eerie.

'Around the back," Dean decided, jerking his head towards the rear of the building. 'Next time he comes round we'll take him, okay?'

As soon as the patroller vanished Dean and Nick slipped from between the trees and scurried across the overgrown lawn, darting around the back of the house to take cover behind a bank of dense shrubs. They waited in silence, watching the side of the house intently until Blake rounded the corner again, his long steps unwavering in speed as he lapped the house.

Dean moved first. Flinging one arm around Blake's neck and clamping a hand over his mouth, he drove a knee into his back and hauled him backwards. Nick had the hex necklace ripped from his neck before he made contact with the ground.

Immediately, the glazed, robotic appearance vanished, but clearly stunned, it took a moment before Blake became aware of his surroundings and began to sit up. "What the -."

Dean slammed his hand over Blake's mouth again, swiftly cutting off his voice as he gave his head a warning shake and when Blake gave a wide-eyed nod to confirm he understood, Dean lifted his hand away. "My name is Dean Carson," he said in a low, urgent whisper. "I'm the Alpha of the Carter Plains pack. This –," he gestured towards Nick who was hunkered beside him, "- is my Beta, Nick Fisher. We're here for Nyah Morgan. Do you know who she is? Do you know what's been going on here?"

Blake nodded vigorously and turned his alarmed stare onto the house.

"What's your name?" Dean whispered.

"Blake Creedon," he replied, his eyes darting back to Dean. "What – what the hell did he do to me?"

Nick was still holding the necklace. He held it up and grimaced. "He's been controlling you with these," he explained. "Your Alpha's involved with some pretty screwed-up shit, you know."

Blake scrambled to his feet and Dean and Nick followed. "He's in there," he swallowed, gesturing towards the house. "He's been making us . . ." he began, then trailed off to lean forwards with his hands on his knees. "Oh man," he said quietly. "The things I've . . ." his guilty eyes slid upwards to land on Dean's face. "Michael's wearing one of those things, too," he said in a low whisper. "We need to get it off him."

"Where is Michael?" Dean asked.

"In the house." Blake threw another wary glance at the pack house and straightened up again. "Simon's in there with Nyah – wait -." He paused, his pale face creasing as memories began to re-load. "Nyah's back – she, she was gone – she got away. He found her again?"

Dean nodded tightly. "Nyah's my mate. I'm taking her back. And then I'm going to rip your Alpha asunder."

"Right," was all Blake could breathe in reply.

"Can you get Michael to come out here?" Nick asked, staring at the dark windows of the house. "Are there any more of your pack in there?"

Blake dragged his sleeve over his mouth and drew in a jagged breath. "It's just Michael in there, the others are all in their houses – but one word from Simon and they'll all be here. We have to be careful."

"Are they all as strong as you two were?" Dean asked.

Blake frowned and then remembrance slackened his mouth. "Oh, man, I'm sorry . . . I, oh. . ." his horrified eyes drifted down towards Nick's legs.

"Forget about it," Nick grunted. "Just try and get Michael out here."

Blake nodded. "Okay," he swallowed.

313

Dean and Nick remained behind the cover of the bushes while Blake stepped back out and walked towards the back door of the house. He kept his movements slow and even as he opened the door and stepped inside. A moment later, he returned, another recognisable figure appearing at his back as they emerged from the dim house.

Blake pointed towards the bushes where Dean and Nick were crouching low. Michael strode towards them and Blake stepped in behind him, grabbing him quickly while Dean and Nick rushed forwards.

Michael's initial confusion was stronger than Blake's had been. He writhed on the grass as they struggled to hold him down, Blake repeatedly pleading with him to be quiet. When lucidity returned he finally stilled and then unsteadily got to his feet.

Dean explained the situation in bullet points. By the time he had done Michael's expression was aghast, his eyes drifting out of focus as his mind abruptly replayed the forgotten weeks of Simon's control.

When he turned to Blake for confirmation all Blake could do was give him a tight nod. "No," Michael trembled, "I, I didn't, did I?"

Blake nodded again.

"But I – I couldn't have. I mean – Leanne and Eddie – I didn't, they. . ." There was a pause and then Michael spun round, clutching his middle as he leaned over and threw up.

Dean and Nick shared a concerned look. What in the hell had Simon made them do?

They waited in silence until Michael had spat the last of his horror away. Wiping the back of his hand over his mouth he turned to face them again. "Northfell's inside," he stated evenly. "In what used to be the dining room. Nyah's in there with him. We need to hurry, he's already started."

"Wait," Blake grabbed Michael's arm as he began to push by him. "We can't just march in there. Once Simon sees we're not under his control he'll get the others here – we'll be completely outnumbered."

"Maybe we should try to get the necklaces off the others first," Nick suggested. "We could do with more numbers on our side."

"We don't have time for that," Dean said, already moving to stand beside Michael. "And you don't know what kind of trouble that could stir. A surprise attack against Northfell would work better."

"But Northfell is – he's . . ." Blake threw an irritated hand towards the house. "That's not just some rabid werewolf in there," he warned desperately. "This guy is way off the grid and you're not going to get within ten feet of him. Rushing in there is not the way to do this."

"Nyah is in there," Dean reminded him in a harsh whisper. "I can't stand out here and argue battle tactics when I know she's in danger." Turning to Michael he jerked his head aggressively towards the house. "Come on."

"Wait – hold on." Michael grabbed Dean's shoulder. "Blake's right. We have to smart about this. We should split up; Dean – you and I will go in. Blake and Nick – you two go and rip some hexes off. At least if we get into trouble we know there'll be back-up coming, right?"

Dean considered Michael's suggestion with a tetchy sigh and another anxious glance at the pack house.

"We need more numbers," Michael pressed. "Northfell's a lunatic. And look, I had no idea that Blake was any different when he brought me out here – it should be easy enough for them to get those things off."

Dean exhaled. "Okay, then. But, Nick -." He pointed a cautioning finger at him. "Be careful."

"Yes, Alpha Carson," he winked and then turned to Blake. "Ready?"

With Blake leading the way they crept off and Michael motioned at Dean to follow him towards the house. "I hope you're ready for this," he said opening the back door. "There's some nasty shit going on in here."

Nasty shit didn't come close to describing what was happening in the pack house. Once upon a time, the building had probably been a beautiful, characterful place. Now it was swamped in darkness. The walls were daubed with strange symbols and pentagrams and as Dean passed one of the markings the rusty tang of fresh blood confirmed his suspicions about what the viscous liquid that formed the shapes was. Bloody carcasses littered the floor; chickens, rabbits, a fox and numerous ravens lay scattered about, their lifeless, glassy eyes making Dean shudder with revulsion. Deeper into the house the scent of blood grew stronger and he pressed his mouth tightly shut, darting a quick glance at Michael's pained expression when the scent of Lycan blood became too obvious to ignore.

Michael came to a stop outside a set of double doors.

"Here?" Dean mouthed.

Michael nodded and reached out for the handle. "She's unconscious," he muttered in his ear. "He has her tied to a chair."

Dean motioned for him to open the door.

Ever so slowly Michael eased the handle down and carefully tipped the door open, but before Dean could peer over his shoulder to look inside the door was wrenched from Michaels hand and slammed back against the wall.

"You persistent whelp!" Simon's voice hissed from the murky shadows.

The room stank. Dean almost gagged as the foulest stench of rot and death barrelled into him, but he swallowed it back and made to shove past Michael. The moment he crossed the threshold of the dark, sweaty room he crashed into an invisible wall.

"Sorry," Simon's voice sneered just before he materialized from a gloomy corner. "You're not invited. This is a private party for the bride and groom."

He saw her then. She was sitting on a chair in the centre of the room, her arms hanging over the back of the chair, her wrists and feet bound with rope. "Nyah!" he yelled.

She didn't react to his cry. Her head sagged low against her chest, her long black hair hanging in a still curtain and blocking his view of her face as he shoved against the invisible barrier, desperate to help her.

"Invitees only," Simon reminded him as the door began to slowly swing shut. "Although -." The door froze and Dean found himself staggering forward as the barrier suddenly evaporated. "Perhaps you should watch."

A macabre clutter of trinkets hung around Simon's neck, amongst them a werewolf fang and an assortment of tiny bones that Dean pointedly yanked his stare away from. The hollow clinking sound that they made as Simon strode towards him sent another shiver of revulsion rattling down his spine.

"Please — do come in," Simon offered pleasantly before making a sharp beckoning gesture with his left hand. A force suddenly catapulted Dean right into the centre of the room where he crashed to his hands and knees only feet away from Nyah. Behind him, Michael's sudden shout of pain was cut short by the door slamming shut.

"No more interruptions," Simon ordered, and then, with a feather-light stroke, brushed his fingers across Dean's back just as he was turning to attack. Dean's entire body went limp in response to the touch and he twisted sideways, crumpling back onto the floor, his head cracking painfully off the hard wooden surface as he collapsed onto his back.

Simon lifted his foot and rested the tip of his boot against Dean's cheek, pushing his head forcefully so as to turn it towards where Nyah was slung to the chair. "Best seat in the house," he pointed out. "Considerate of me, no?"

From his prone position Dean could see a thin strip of Nyah's face. Her eyes were shut, blood was smeared on her cheek, and as his eyes frantically raced over her slumped body for signs of injuries he realised that the jeans and sweater she had been dressed in earlier had been replaced. Rage burned through him as he took in the pale blue dress she now wore. The very thought that Northfell had been touching her made his breath rush through his gritted teeth, and when his eyes landed on the thick rope binding her bruised feet the force of his enraged breaths sent spittle flying onto his chin.

It was as he stared at the knotted rope that he saw the markings on the floor. Nyah's chair was in the centre of a pentagram.

Close beside it, a short distance from his paralysed feet, his eyes widened as he saw another pentagram daubed onto the wooden floor – a body lay in a rumpled heap in its centre. It wasn't hard to see that considerable amounts of fluid had been used to draw the pentagrams, and the lingering scent of Lycan blood that hung thickly in the air around him told him what he suddenly did not want to know. Slowly but surely, Dean was beginning to grasp the horror of what Michael and Blake had been forced to do.

His growing revulsion was interrupted by Simon's booted feet walking by, the heel of one foot purposefully grinding the immobile fingers of Dean's right hand into the floor. Pain flashed through him, but the cry died in his throat, a hissing breath the only sound his useless body could make. With the angry tide of breaths continuing to tear in and out of his nose he followed Simon's movements around the room and from his skewed viewpoint on the floor he spotted two items set beside the outer ring of the pentagram opposite Nyah; an ornate knife with a curved blade and an unassuming metal chalice.

"Time for the guest of honour," Simon announced, lifting a book from a table. He cleared his throat reverently before lowering his head to read.

The guttural-sounding words were meaningless to Dean as he stared around frantically. He couldn't let this happen – this was the part where Northfell summoned a demon! Begging his legs to obey his order to move he glanced down desperately at his limp limbs, the veins in his face bulging hotly as he strained to incite a tiny movement from any part of his body. Nyah's as good as dead! he yelled at his pathetic body – Move! Get up!

A suffocating stench of sulphur suddenly overrode the stink of Lycan blood and Dean's struggle against the paralysing spell came to a halt. A watery green fog had begun to swirl up from underneath the still body and from somewhere deep below something else began to rise too, the vibrations of its approach thundering ominously beneath him as his head began to rattle against the floor. Despite his juddering vision he could clearly see that the snaking light inside the pentagram had intensified enough to completely envelope the crumpled figure, and when the ground grew still again he watched in dread as the figure suddenly stirred and then drew itself up in an elegant, fluid motion.

"Yes?"

The voice that came from the throat of the red-haired girl was eerily distorted as she turned to face Simon. It sounded as if the single, nettled word she had uttered was comprised of two voices, her own, natural voice and that of what Dean could only guess was the demon possessing her body.

"Yannek." Simon tipped his head half-heartedly. "Welcome."

The girl lifted her nose towards Simon and pointedly sniffed at the air. "You stink of dog," she stated flatly. When her eyes drifted from Simon's face towards Dean he would have winced if his face would have let him. The girl's eyes had rolled into the back of her head and all that stared out at him were two opaque globes of milky whiteness. The pale stare slid by him and settled on Nyah. "I hate dogs."

"Yannek," Simon began, "I -."

"Where am I?" Yannek demanded. "Where have I been summoned to?"

Before Simon could answer, Yannek stepped to the very edge of the pentagram and squinted out into the darkness. Simon took a discreet step back.

"Topside," it grinned. "The Kingpin's petri dish. How nice."

"Yes," Simon replied testily. "Yannek, I -."

"I was busy down there, you know," it cut him off again, pointing down at whatever place it had been sucked from. "Flaying isn't a job I like to rush."

Simon faltered briefly. He had moved further along the edge of the pentagram and Dean could now clearly see his face, eerily lit by the green light oozing inside the circle. "I apologise."

"Apology accepted." Yannek performed a bow and then registering the body it possessed grinned maniacally. "Nice meat-suit." It spent a long moment suggestively running its hands over the slim curves before turning its attention back to Simon. "Enlighten me as to why I have been brought here."

"I require some of your blood," Simon replied, indicating the knife and chalice sitting by his feet.

"Don't you all," Yannek sighed. "And what do I get in return?"

"What do you desire?"

"What do you desire?" Yannek mimicked Simon's voice perfectly. "What do you think I want?" it asked, returning to its double-toned voice.

When Simon didn't answer Yannek leaned towards him. "I want out to play."

"Don't you all," Simon replied, with his own mimicking sigh.

Dean's stare flicked back to Yannek's face – or whosever face it was that the demon was distorting into an enraged frown – was Simon actually trying to piss the demon off?

"Give me what I want and I will release you from this demon trap," Simon announced.

"I'm not sure I can trust you," Yannek sulked.

Simon spread out his hands and shrugged. "Your insecurity," he warned. "Not mine."

Yannek rolled back the shoulders of the body it possessed and then flicked back a length of the deep russet hair. "I get to keep this meat-suit," it bargained. "And –," a pair of cold blind eyes landed on Dean. "A puppy to have as my very own."

Simon gave a short laugh. "As you wish."

"And that one, too." Yannek jerked a thumb towards Nyah.

"No." The smile was quick to slide from Simon's face. "That one is mine."

"Aw, pwease," Yannek pleaded in a baby voice. "It's so pwetty. And I want."

Simon ignored him and bent down to pick up the knife and chalice.

"Free me first," Yannek ordered, dropping the tasteless baby sounds.

"No," Simon replied flatly. "Your blood first."

Yannek folded its arms.

"Blood first," Simon repeated. "If you refuse I'll send you back."

"And replace me with whom?" Yannek sneered. "You won't find my power in any -."

"Silicus, Malfreze, Azerkaan," Simon began to reel off. "My eggs are not all in the one basket, Yannek."

"Maybe not," it replied, "but you called me first."

"Because you're weaker than the others," Simon retorted. "You're easy to rip from whatever hell dimension you skulk around in."

Yannek fell silent and Simon dropped to his hunkers, the knife and chalice still in his hands. "Step back."

The demon stilled as it considered it options. 'Don't trust him!' Dean wanted to yell out, desperate to prevent any part of what Simon was planning from happening. How could the demon be so stupid? Couldn't it tell that Simon was not going to give it anything it wanted?

Simon lifted his head and fixed an impatient stare at Yannek. "Would you prefer to return to your oh-so-important-flaying?" he asked.

Reluctantly, it stepped back and Simon slid the knife and chalice over the outer lines. "I don't need a lot," he said, standing upright again. "A few teaspoons should do."

"And then you release me," Yannek said, the gravelly depths of its true demon voice suddenly louder than the light tone of its host.

"Yes," Simon sighed, wearily. "I will free you of this demon trap."

"Don't cross me, dog," Yannek warned, quickly striding to the edge of the bloody line. "I'll mark you if you do, and any of my kin who are free on this plane will hunt you down."

Simon spread out his hands as if entirely innocent of any deceiving thoughts. "Why wouldn't I set you free? What do I care if one more of your kind is loose?"

Yannek frowned and circled a finger in Simon's direction. "What do you want my blood for?"

"None of your business," Simon replied, but Yannek had the chalice and the knife on its side of the line and reminding Simon of the fact, bent down and lifted them off the floor. "It is my business." It traced the tip of the blade around the inner surface of the cup and the resulting squeal that grated out made Simon wince. He didn't answer Yannek however.

Dean threw another glance at Nyah. She hadn't moved once; he was finding it difficult to tell if she was even breathing. He wondered at that moment where the hell Nick, Blake and the others had got to. Someone needed to burst into the room and prevent Simon from getting Yannek's blood, or worse still, allowing him to set the thing free.

When Dean looked back towards the demon it had placed the chalice back on the floor and was threateningly resting one foot upon its rim.

" . . . do you care?" Simon was replying impatiently. "Do I ask you what you intend to do out here? No – because it's none of my business."

"That's your choice," Yannek retorted. "But I'm a precious little thing when it comes to donating blood. I have standards." The bare foot resting on the rim of the cup pushed down. Immediately the edge of the cup began to buckle.

Simon sucked in an agitated breath. "Alright," he snapped. "I need to ingest your blood, as does she," he revealed, jerking his head in Nyah's direction.

"Why?" Yannek asked.

"None of your -."

The cup buckled further.

"A new breed of Lycans!" Simon spat out, his hands jerking out as the cup grated against the floor.

Yannek lifted the foot away and leisurely bent over to pluck the cup back up. "You're a fool," it sneered, "welcoming such chaos. Have you any idea how mutated those whelps will be?"

Simon barked a single, loud laugh. Then he threw back his head and flung his arms out by his side. "I welcome chaos!" he declared. "A brave, chaotic, new world!"

"And I shall be here to enjoy it," Yannek realized. Wedging the chalice under one arm it grasped the blade in one palm, curled its fingers tightly around it and then slowly and purposefully drew the blade straight between the clenched fingers. Black drops of molasses-like liquid oozed free. They snaked over the pale, porcelain skin, worming their way to the edge where they gathered in a heavy drooping glob before snapping free and falling into the chalice.

The steady drip sent a fresh wave of horror through Dean. Simon wanted Nyah to drink that? Frustration ripped through him as his body continued to lay in a pathetic stupor while his mind screamed and thrashed. There was complete silence in the hallway outside the doors. Nick and Blake should have been back by now, and why wasn't Michael doing something? His eyes dragged themselves away from the dripping blood. Nyah was still motionless. Was it a spell? It had to be – Northfell had her this way on purpose, otherwise she'd be screaming blue murder.

Simon clapping his hands together with glee snapped Dean's attention back. Thick black blood was still dribbling into the chalice. "Thank-you," he said waving at Yannek to stop, his trembling hands desperate to take possession of the chalice.

"One last drop," Yannek said, making a show of watching a heavy glob slide from the fist and land with a sickening plop. "All done." Lowering the chalice to the floor, Yannek nudged it towards the edge of his confine.

"Further," Simon ordered, his fingers straining to grasp the neck of the chalice.

"Release me first," Yannek demanded, halting the chalice just at the edge of the scarlet mark.

"I can't," Simon replied quickly. "Not while your spilled blood is in the circle with you. Pass me the knife and chalice and then wipe off that hand."

Dean watched incredulously as the demon obeyed. Simon snatched up the chalice and knife as soon as they were within reach while Yannek hurriedly smeared the bloodied palm across the sweater of the body it possessed.

"Now what?" Yannek asked excitedly.

"Now I keep my side of the deal," Simon replied smoothly.

Setting the knife onto the ground, but keeping the chalice in a tight grip he picked up the book that he had read from earlier.

Yannek rubbed its hands together in anticipation.

Simon began to read aloud and Dean found himself wishing that he could laugh. When the words Simon spoke began to register with the demon it let out a scream of rage. "Release me!" it bellowed. "You said you would release me!"

Simon continued to call out the words and once again the ground began to tremble and the snaking fog began to form a twisting column around Yannek. Simon snapped the book shut and threw it aside.

"We made a deal!" Yannek shrieked, flinging itself against the boundary of the circle.

"Yes," Simon agreed, turning his back to Yannek as he held the cup up as if in offering to some god. "I said I would release you – I just didn't say where, exactly." He began to laugh and Yannek went demented. It thrashed and kicked at the invisible wall, red hair whipping from side to side as it hammered frantically at the impenetrable shield.

As if oblivious to the commotion Simon lowered the cup to his lips and took a deep pull of the black liquid. Dean knew that if he wasn't paralysed at that moment he would have gagged as Simon swallowed and then licked his lips. All that was missing was an approving smack of his lips. Simon turned his bloodied smile onto Nyah. "Your turn," he sang.

Dean's desperate breaths rushed through his nostrils, his eyes bulging feverishly as Simon began to walk towards her. No – she couldn't drink that stuff, she couldn't. His wolf snarled and writhed, furious as to why it couldn't phase and protect its mate. Nyah! he screamed inside. Don't drink it! Don't, baby – wake up! Nyah, wake up!

Simon ran a hand over the top of her head, trailing it down towards the back of her neck where he roughly grabbed a fistful of her hair and wrenched her head up.

It lolled heavily to one side and Simon changed the pressure of his grip, jerking it under control.

Nyah! Dean roared. Nyah!

"Drink," Simon crooned, bringing the edge of the cup to her lip. "It's a wedding day gift from me to you."

It happened in a short, frenzied moment. Nyah's eyes suddenly flashed wide open – "And here's mine to you," she spat before throwing herself back into the chair. Nyah raised her knees and slammed her bound feet hard into Simon's belly. The chalice flew from his hand, flipping over in mid-air, the thick blood hanging for a split second before slapping onto his forehead. The force of Nyah's kick shunted him backwards and he stumbled, the blood momentarily blinding him as he staggered near the edge of Yannek's pentagram. The hysterical bellows of rage came to a sudden stop as Yannek saw what was happening and it threw itself towards the edge of the pentagram again, its white gaze fixed on Simon's lurching body as he swayed dangerously close.

"You bitch!" he snarled, wiping the glutinous mess from his eyes. "You stupid little bitch!"

The heel of his boot landed on the outer ring of the pentagram and Yannek stretched its two hands forward, fingers wriggling in anticipation of one final, tiny step. Simon teetered on the brink, cursing as he tried to open his eyes.

Dean wanted to look at Nyah. He wanted his eyes to tear themselves away from what was unfolding so that he could reassure himself that she was unhurt and that none of the foul blood had touched her lips – but he couldn't. His unblinking eyes remained glued to Yannek, the whirling green fog now clearly trying to drag the demon into whatever place Simon had commanded.

"I'm sorry," Yannek cried, in a pitch-perfect replica of Nyah's voice. "I, I didn't mean to," it cried out.

Simon roared, lurching blindly towards the voice with his hands outstretched. "I'll kill you for this!" he began, "I'll cut your -."

Yannek's shriek of victory sliced through the air. Wrapping its hands around Simon's neck it wrenched him inside the circle, grabbing him into a choke-hold as it ripped the protective talisman clean off his neck.

"Who's the fool now!" it cackled malevolently, holding the thrashing Simon with ease.

Dean's vision vibrated violently as the greedy mist enveloped the two figures. There was one final roar of victory from Yannek and then the light flared and spat, forcing Dean to mash his eyes shut, his last glimpse showing him Nyah quickly turning her head to one side in order to protect her eyes from the searing light.

The end came so abruptly it was as if someone had simply flipped a switch. The room fell completely silent in one staggering soundless explosion, blackness flooding every corner as the searing light extinguished.

When Dean cautiously opened his eyes the red-headed girl's body had returned to a motionless crumpled heap.

Yannek had gone back to whatever hell dimension it had come from. And it had taken Simon with it.

TWENTY-FIVE

Nyah bounded down the porch steps of Dean's house as a familiar silver car pulled up on the street outside.

Squealing with delight she hopped up and down on the path until the passenger door opened and Karen emerged. Before she was even fully upright Nyah had her arms flung around her. "I thought you'd never get here!" she cried, squeezing Karen tightly.

"We're early," Karen laughed, her reply muffled by Nyah's hug. "Blake was hammering on my hotel door at four o'clock this morning."

"Still took you two hours to get ready, though," Blake grumbled, climbing out from the driver's side of the car.

Nyah released Karen to run around the bonnet to meet Blake. He pulled her up into his arms and swung her around. "It's good to see you smiling," he said into her ear as he set her down.

"Nyah, meet Tom," Karen said, pushing him forwards. "I know you've already kind of met, but, you know, here he is – officially."

"Hi, Tom. It's nice to meet you – officially." Nyah took his hand with a beaming smile just as Dean appeared from the house.

"Welcome to Carter Plains," he called out, hurrying across the lawn to greet them. He stuck his hand out to Blake. "Great to see you again, Blake."

"You too, Alpha Carson, you too," Blake grinned, but then not satisfied with a mere handshake yanked Dean into a hearty bear hug. "Wow, this is a nice place," Blake said releasing Dean and nodding in approval as he looked around.

"Spacious," Tom agreed, gesturing towards the mountain range in the distance. "All that part of this territory?"

"Uh huh," Dean smiled, drawing Nyah into his side. "I'll show you later."

"Blake?" Nyah threw a sad glance towards the now empty car. "You couldn't contact him?" she asked quietly.

Blake's smile faded and he shook his head. "No. I haven't heard from him since he left. He just . . ." he shrugged and trailed off with a sigh. "He needs time alone."

"Poor Michael," Nyah murmured. "I hope he's going to be okay."

"He's taken it bad," Blake admitted. "What Northfell made him do – what he made us both do – he feels responsible."

"He's gone somewhere up north," Karen said to Nyah, giving Blake's arm a sympathetic squeeze. "Canada, we think. He'll be okay. He just needs time to deal with it all."

Nyah nodded and Dean slid his arms around her waist, pulling her back against his chest. "Michael's seems like a tough guy," he said softly. "Give him time. He'll be back when he's ready."

Nyah forced out a smile.

"Come on, girl," Blake grinned, chucking her under the chin. "Show me round this place. The size of it is making me dizzy."

"The smell of barbequing meat is making you dizzy," Karen corrected. "Cos, you know, you haven't eaten in like, two hours or something."

"Are the others far behind you?" Nyah asked, wondering how long it would be before she got to see the remaining members of her pack.

"A couple of hours, probably," Blake guessed.

"They're normal, you see," Karen pointed out. "They didn't feel that getting up at stupid o'clock this morning was entirely necessary."

"Hey," Blake argued. "I sacrificed the breakfast buffet to get us on the road early."

"I think you may have already mentioned that," Tom said lightly, "five times."

"Six," Karen sniffed. "But hey -," spreading out her arms she smiled at Nyah. "It was worth it."

"Agreed," Blake said, and then unconsciously rubbed a hand over his stomach.

"Food's this way," Dean laughed, nodding towards the playing field set further behind them.

"If you insist," Blake grinned.

"We have so much to catch up on," Karen whispered, linking her arm with Nyah as they walked towards the playing field. She threw an appreciative glance at Dean as he walked ahead with Tom and then winked at Nyah. "So much."

An area of the playing field had been set up for the visitors from Blackwater Ridge. Three barbeques were already sending out puffs of smoke and the cluster of picnic tables were groaning under the weight of food crammed onto them. All of the Carter Plains pack were milling around. The children were playing a loud game of chasing in a corner of the field while some of the men were throwing a ball around. Others sat in groups on the colourful rugs spread out on the grass while Ellie fussed about the tables with a few of the other women, rearranging plates and straightening glasses.

"This is . . . " Karen struggled to speak, as they approached the picnic area. "This looks amazing."

"We want everyone to feel welcomed," Nyah explained. "And when the rest of our pack get here later Dean's going to officially offer a place in Carter Plains to anyone who wants to join us."

Karen squeezed Nyah's hand and nodded, glancing around as kind welcoming faces began to approach them. "It's so nice here," she whispered, "I'm so happy for you, really, you deserve this so much."

"Oh no," Nyah cleared her throat and shook her head. "Don't start with all that. You'll have me crying in five minutes if you do."

"Sorry," Karen laughed gently. "You'd better introduce me to your new pack, then – it'll stop me getting all mushy and emotional."

With loaded plates they settled onto a rug under the shade of a massive sprawling oak tree a short while later.

"So -," Nyah said, sitting down tailor-style and balancing a plate of food on the skirt of her dress, "- tell me what happened after Dean and I left Blackwater a fortnight ago."

"Gosh," Karen swallowed a mouthful of burger. "It's two weeks already? Wow. That's hard to believe."

Nyah agreed with a nod as she took a bite out of her corn cob. "It feels less than that for me, too. Everything is still very . . . vivid."

"How are you doing?" Karen asked sincerely, putting down her burger and wiping off her fingers. "Have you been okay?"

Nyah nodded as she wiped her mouth and fingers, too. "I cried all the way back here," she admitted. "All two days of driving. Poor Dean, he didn't know what to do."

Karen remained silent, her attention fully focused on Nyah.

"Then once we got back I slept for the first few days, "Nyah continued. "And then I began feeling better – bit by bit, you know."

"Sure," Karen replied.

"I didn't want to talk about it at first, but Dean pointed out that I had gotten too used to keeping secrets so I forced myself to say everything that was in my head. There were lots more tears of course," she said with an embarrassed laugh, "but saying it all out loud seemed to lift this huge weight off me and I found that I'd room in my head for other stuff again. Normal stuff, nice stuff."

"Like how hot your mate is stuff?" Karen winked.

Nyah smiled and picked up her corn again. "Maybe," she said secretively.

"Those eyes," Karen said quietly, glancing over to where Dean and Tom were sitting at one of the picnic tables. "Seriously, Nyah. How do you not spend your entire day just wanting to gaze into them?"

Nyah pointed to her conveniently full mouth and smiled.

"And his hair," Karen added. "I have to say – very sexy." She took a bite of her burger and then still chewing jerked her head towards him again. "And he's got that whole Alpha vibe, too," she managed to say around a mouthful of food, "- very hot."

Nyah laughed and pressed her cool glass of soda against her burning cheeks. "Okay, you have to stop with admiring Dean now. I know how gorgeous he is. You're melting my face here."

Karen took another enormous bite of her burger and made noises of satisfaction which Nyah knew weren't because of the delicious food.

Rolling her eyes good humouredly she wiggled her finger at Karen's burger. "When you've finished stuffing your face I want you to tell me about Tom."

Karen chewed at break-neck speed and swallowed hard, washing down the food with a long drink of soda. "Tom," she began, wiping her mouth, "was ringing and ringing when I was zombiefied. And then because I didn't answer or call him back he got into a bit of a strop 'cos he thought I'd dumped him."

"Oh no," Nyah breathed. "That's awful."

"Yeah," Karen agreed sneaking a quick glance over to where he sat. "He feels really bad about it now – knowing that I was going through all of that while he was having a big sulk." Her soft expression was still in place when she returned her gaze to Nyah. "Of course, now he won't let me leave his side."

"I know that feeling," Nyah replied. "But to be honest, I'm quite happy to have Dean sticking to me like glue."

"Me too," Karen admitted with a grimace. "Who would have thought, eh? Although – does that mean he's not going to let you go to Colorado next month?"

"He's undecided," Nyah answered. "We've only talked about it once, though. And he knows how much I want to see Tanya. I don't think he'll say no outright, but there'll probably be a long, long string of conditions."

"But – is he not coming with you?"

"Yeah," Nyah laughed, "not that that matters – he's still being Mr Cautious about it."

"Did you give him the Big Brown Nyah Eyes treatment?"

"Not yet. That's for emergencies only. And I'm not sure if it works – hey," Nyah waved towards an approaching figure. "Here's Nick."

"Hello, ladies," Nick said warmly as he strolled up to where they sat. "I didn't think you guys would get here so early," he smiled at Karen, "sorry to have missed your arrival."

"That's okay," Karen replied. "Blake was an eager beaver this morning. He had us all up at the butt-crack of dawn."

"How are you doing?" he asked her gently, hunkering down by the edge of the rug. "How are things in Blackwater Ridge?"

Karen gave a half-hearted shrug. "Okay, sort of. Michael's gone."

"Yeah, I heard," he said.

"He needs some time to himself," Karen explained, even though Nick already knew, "and we're all trying to decide what we want, where we're going to go. We're all up in the air, I suppose."

Nick nodded in understanding. "Blake's been keeping Dean in the loop – he told me about your packs decision to separate."

"No-one wants to stay in Blackwater Ridge now," Karen admitted, "it's just not the same anymore."

Nyah rubbed her upper arms. She wasn't cold, but the memories of her last horrific time in Blackwater Ridge still made her skin prickle. The shock of seeing the frightening condition of the place that she had only known as home was still raw, and she stared unseeing into the distance as images of what she had witnessed flashed through her mind. Karen was so right when she said that it wasn't the same any more – it never would be.

"Sweetheart?" Dean's gentle touch pulled her back from the murky room where the demon had been summoned to the sunny afternoon on the open playing field in Carter Plains. "You okay?" he asked discreetly, hunkering beside her.

She smiled up at him and nodded. "Yeah, I'm okay."

"Nick!" Blake's greeting turned all their heads and Nick hopped up, enthusiastically clasping Blake's outstretched hand in his. "Hey, Blake," he beamed. "How are you? Great to have you here."

"Thanks for inviting us," he replied. "This is some place you guys have."

"Did you get a look around?" Nick asked.

"Not yet," Blake answered. "I didn't want to insult anyone by not eating first."

Nick flung an arm around Blake's shoulder and began to walk him away. "Well, how's about we run off some of those burgers with a grand tour, eh?"

"I'll be just over here," Dean murmured to Nyah, kissing her forehead before standing back up to wander back to Tom. Kyle had joined them, too, and he waved over at her.

"So – has everyone pretty much decided to leave Blackwater Ridge, then?" Nyah asked Karen. "Was it an immediate decision?"

"No," Karen shook her head and shifted into a new position on the rug. "A few hours after you left we held a pack meeting – not in the pack house, of course – we all sat on the grass outside Michael's house – which was weird, because it was the middle of the night – anyway, everyone agreed that

Michael should take the Alpha position, but he refused straight away. I've never seen him so adamant about something. It was just – no, straight out. It kind of threw everyone a bit. Michael said the position should be Blake's, but Blake said no, too. He said he wasn't Alpha material and then, well, it all got a bit gnarly for a while." Karen pulled a bit of bread from the last piece of her burger, her frown fixed to it as she rolled it between her fingers. "We all agreed that we wanted someone to pull us back together, lead us as a pack again – but no-one wanted to do it. And then Michael said he was leaving, said he didn't deserve to be part of a pack after what he'd done." Karen sighed and dropped the little ball of dough onto her plate. "Some people stayed quiet, Leanne and Eddie Stone's family especially, but others argued that it wasn't Michael's fault, it was Simon's; he was the one that made Michael do it." She shrugged and blew out another tight sigh. "It didn't make any difference though," she said looking back up. "Michael insisted that taking the lives of pack members was unforgivable. After that he just got up and went into the forest. He was gone for hours – he didn't appear until the following afternoon and, well, then he left."

Nyah pushed her plate off her knee and leaned forwards. "So the pack agreed to splinter?"

"Not at first. There was a lot of discussion about what we could do to stay together, but bit by bit we began to realize that it was already happening. Michael was gone, I'm going to the

Carverbacks to be with Tom, you're here in Carter Plains, Tanya and her kids are going to stay in Colorado with her sister, and . . ." Karen faltered, " there are those that didn't make it at all."

"I see what you mean," Nyah agreed quietly. "It kind of has happened already."

"I think Blake wants to stay here, too," Karen said discreetly, lowering her voice. "He likes Dean and he wants to be part of a big pack. You know Blake; he's always loved to be surrounded by lots of people. I think staying in Blackwater Ridge would kill him."

"And what about the place itself?" Nyah asked with a sort of hesitant curiosity. "What happened with my . . . the pack house?"

Karen stretched to one side and picked up a bowl of fruit pieces. "Well," she began, throwing a wary glance up at Nyah. "We agreed, like you suggested, that . . . . burning down the pack house was the best thing to do."

Nyah nodded once and subtly drew in a calming breath.

"Cassius Ochre came," Karen continued, hesitantly.

"He did?"

"Uh huh. He's actually a very gentle man. I think you'd like him."

Nyah shivered. "In time maybe, everything's still too fresh. I just see him as the man that worked that awful magic on me."

"I get that," Karen said and popped a strawberry into her mouth.

"But – he came anyway, and helped to . . ." Nyah broke off with a humourless laugh. "Clean up?" she offered weakly.

"Yeah, clean up," Karen said dryly. Sensing that Nyah was okay to talk about the annihilation of her old home she relaxed a little. "He did a lot of his magic mojo inside the house first and then he came out and sprinkled all this stuff around the perimeter before setting it alight. He said the place was full of negative energy. Once the charred wood cooled down he had it all brought into the forest and buried in blessed ground – all that's left now is a huge square of scorched grass."

Nyah pulled a face of disbelief.

"Yeah," Karen agreed, "I know burying the charcoaled wood sounds a bit weird, but he said that it would be best. To be honest, I don't want to know why."

"I hope it's buried deep," Nyah murmured as Karen searched amongst the bowl for more strawberries.

"Very, very deep," Karen confirmed. "No-one's gonna be digging up those sticks anytime soon."

"And what about the rest of the houses," Nyah asked reaching for a plate of salad.

"The two that were already burned out were knocked down. Cassius went to every house, but he said they were all clean, that they didn't need exorcizing or whatever it was he did.

"You can't exorcise memories, though," Nyah said.

"No," Karen agreed. "And thankfully –," she held up her palm displaying the scar from the knife that Yannek had sliced her skin open with. "- I have no memories of getting this souvenir."

Nyah swallowed hard and looked down. "When I saw you – in that circle. I swear, I – I . . ."

"Hey, it's over," Karen soothed, reaching out to put a hand on her knee. "And for me, it never even happened. Don't dwell on it Nyah. It's all in the past now."

On cue, his attention clearly focused on the emotions that rolled from her, Dean pointedly turned away from his own conversation to mouth an 'Are you okay?' at her. She smiled back and Karen turned to follow Nyah's gaze.

"He'll kick my ass if he thinks I'm upsetting you," Karen said and then cringed when Dean turned his gaze onto her and waved a single warning finger.

"Stop teasing," Nyah said loud enough for Dean to hear. "I'm fine."

He winked at them both and then returned to his conversation.

"Young love," Karen sighed wistfully.

Nyah rolled her eyes and leaned back onto her elbows. "So do you remember other things from when I was gone?"

"Some," Karen nodded, squinting into the distance as if the memories were there for viewing. "I remember bringing you to the mall that day. It was confusing. You were smiling at me and it sort of . . . woke me up a bit. I had a sense of being trapped and not being able to do anything about it. But after that, the memories are just a bit blurry and mixed up. I hunted a lot of small animals for Simon – not sure why those memories are so vivid compared to others – but the rest, well, I don't want to scratch at them too much. I know that my experience wasn't anything as bad as Michael's and Blake's and I keep telling myself that it wasn't me, whatever I did – or didn't do – wasn't me, so . . ." She trailed off with a small shrug.

"You think Michael's going to be okay?"

"In time, yes," she answered definitively. "He has to forgive himself first. And understand that it wasn't him that took those lives."

Silence settled for a while. Nyah sat back up and ate the rest of the salad while Karen finished her fruit. The sounds of playing children drifted around them accompanied by bursts of laughter from the different groups scattered around the field. It was comforting and peaceful, and Nyah knew that even if her father's house was still standing she wouldn't have wanted to ever return to Blackwater Ridge. Knowing that her pack were on the verge of breaking apart was difficult, but everyone needed to start afresh; all their lives had been brutalised by Simon Northfell and they all deserved an equal chance to recover in whatever way they felt right.

"So –," Karen smiled once she had wiped her sticky fingers clean. "Mr Alpha – ," she whispered, leaning in conspiratorially, "– I'll bet he didn't wait too long to mark you once you got home."

"Karen!" Nyah squealed and leaned forward to smack her arm.

"Oh come on!" Karen laughed, falling backwards. "You have to tell me!'"

"I will not," Nyah said, appalled, but still laughing.

Karen sat up again, plonked her elbows on her knees and then dropped her chin into her palm. "But it was amazing – right?"

Nyah sighed and brushed some crumbs off the skirt of her dress. "Yeah," she shrugged nonchalantly. "It was okay."

"Okay?" Karen spluttered, "- a hot wolf like that and it was only okay?"

"Fine," Nyah laughed. "It was amazing. No – it was more than amazing." Glancing around she let her gaze linger on her handsome mate for a few seconds. For so long she had bitterly regretted the day that she had landed in Shoreton. Now she wouldn't change it for anything. Despite everything that she had been through, despite the fear, the pain, the loss – everything – she felt like the luckiest girl alive. "It was amazingly super-fantastically awesome," she whispered, pulling her smile back to Karen. "Times ten."

Karen clapped her hands together. "I love a happy ever after!" she cried.

"It's not a happy ever after," Nyah said wisely, "it's just a beginning – a very happy beginning."

THE END

About the author

Julie Embleton was born and raised in Dublin, Ireland. She graduated from the National College of Art and Design with a bachelor's degree in graphic design in 1994 and then promptly left Ireland to find her fortune in London within the hotel industry. Three years later she realized that the fortune she sought was an urban legend so returned home to Dublin where she continued to experience an eye-opening education in hotels.

It was when she left the unsociable hours of hotel management behind that her neglected passion for writing began prodding for attention once again. In secret, she began scribbling away and finally decided to brave a step into the literary world with Bound, the first book in the Turning Moon series.

The always unpredictable journey of life now has her living in the seaside town of Skerries, Co Dublin with her amazing daughter and ridiculously cute cat, where she is happily buried in the creation of her next book.

If you've enjoyed this book perhaps you'd like to review it at your favourite retailer? Thanks for your support!

Julie Embleton

Want to read more from this author?

Now Available

Released

Book 2 of the Turning Moon series

Available at all good online retailers.
Read on for a free sample of Released!

Released

Book 2 of the Turning Moon series

Desperate to escape the memories of the horrific acts committed against his former pack, Michael Vincent has spent the last year running as a lone, tormented wolf. Fearful for his weakening humanity he returns to human form, but chooses to live in solitude, deep in the Rochfort Mountains. When he discovers his mate, a fragile hope slowly begins to ease the burden of the guilt he bears, but the evil that splintered his former pack is casting its shadow anew and Michael is reunited with his pack mates as they brace to confront a terror they had thought long buried.

Prologue

He ran, and beneath him, the earth bled. Mud-slick ground churned under his paws, warm like a river of thick, oozing blood. Above him, trees strained towards the ruby-hued night, their limbs strung with scarlet needles, their towering trunks layered in flayed flesh, dried to a brittle finish by the relentless icy winds. Even the moon hanging low and swollen above the mountain peaks in the depthless sky was stained with the angry hue. When he ran like this - ran until his heart hammered towards explosion, ran until his spittle turned to sour foam, ran until sweat weighted his thick coat and stung his eyes - the rage owned him, possessed him even, and in its terrible purity, gave relief.

He tore through the undergrowth, branches and thorns snatching at his coat, nature appearing to plead with him to stop. He wasn't ready to stop. The end only came when his scalding breaths no longer held enough strength to fill his lungs and his screaming muscles seized into inoperability. Then he would crash hard against the unyielding ground and surrender to exhaustion.

At first, the end used to come within a few hours. Now, it took longer. These gruelling marathons had him so fit that he had to pound for hours and hours before relief would begin to settle upon him - not that he deserved relief, he didn't deserve one good thing in his life after what he'd done.

A jagged memory pierced his mind: Eddie Stone, a strong and proud wolf, the man who had been his friend, his pack-member, suddenly staggering backwards, his eyes wide with fear and disbelief, his blood-slick hands clutching wildly at the wide gash in his neck, his mouth working to ask why, but only able to produce a rush of bubbling, scarlet blood. He had done that. He had cut his pack-members throat, slit it at the exact point that would produce the most blood. And he had then held a chalice against the gaping wound, had slammed Eddie against a wall to force him still in order to fill the cup, just as he had been ordered. 'You were possessed!' a faint voice reminded him 'you weren't in control!'

He snarled the voice away, only to hear it being replaced by Leanne Stone - Eddie's mate, screaming at him to stop before he visited the same death upon her. 'Michael, no, no, NO!' Hearing his name sounded foreign to him. He couldn't recall when he had last uttered it or had heard someone say it, and that was what he wanted. Michael Vincent didn't deserve to exist. He was a vile, murderous piece of scum. He should have been ripped to shreds by his surviving pack members and had his limbs flung into the farthest corners of the earth.

Propelling himself forward he welcomed the cramps burning through his legs. His panting breaths were weakening, straining to fill his lungs and feed his blood. Oblivion was coming and he greeted it with a long, mournful howl.

The earth was bathed in red. Michael Vincent surrendered and crashed into its embrace.

One

"Day three." Michael firmly scored a line through the date on his hand-written calendar. The single page, showing only two weeks' worth of dates, was set out on the table in front of him, his empty dinner plate having been shoved aside to make space for the scrap paper. Today was always going to have been the hardest day, and while there was another three hours before midnight, the primordial urge to phase into his wolf-form was definitely weaker than it had been the previous night. He placed the pencil back on the table and held out his hands, palm down before him. A slight tremble was still evident, but nothing as intense as earlier. The ringing in his ears had passed sometime in the early afternoon too - around the same time that his spine had quit twitching to spasm. Curling his hands into loose fists he rested them on the table top and sat back in his chair to glance around. His surroundings were cleaner, more habitable than yesterday, and now that he'd a small fire going, warmer too. Staying in human form for the first self-imposed period of two weeks demanded that he live like a human - even if he had to do so in this rented, thin-walled, two-roomed hunting shack. Once two weeks had passed he would allow himself to phase into his wolf for a few hours, but he had to be careful; he had to ensure that he stayed in control and didn't wander far - both mentally and physically.

His empty plate bore no evidence of the rice, beans and tinned tuna meal he'd devoured - a far cry from what he had been dining on for the last few months - but weaning himself off the meat was a vital step in his recovery. Ripping into fresh kill every mealtime had only nudged him closer and closer to surrendering entirely to his animal side and the fact that a human had nearly been one of those meals three days ago . . .

The horrific memory threatened to replay and he smashed it away by jerking up out of his chair and grabbing the empty plate. The water sitting in the plastic basin was icy cold, but he scrubbed the plate clean and then did the same for the other few pots and dishes, giving the task his full attention. With the dishes then dried and returned to the tiny cupboard above the fridge he turned to face the room, knowing that he needed to keep himself busy until he was tired enough to sleep. Michael grimaced at the efficiency that lay before him. The few pieces of furniture that filled the living space had been straightened and cleaned; the threadbare armchair sitting in front of the wood-burning stove, the veneer-topped kitchen table with its single wooden chair, and finally, a tall gun cabinet, which although empty, had been repositioned in an attempt to make a partition between the poky bed and the rest of the room. Even the wooden floor had been swept clean. There was one job left however; the stove was riddled with rust, and earlier on he had found a stumpy wire brush in the lean-to where his jeep was stored at the side of the shack.

Happy to be close to the warmth Michael dropped to his hunkers before the stove and began scrubbing at the flaky surface. For the first while his mind was occupied with removing the rust from the intricate pattern that ran in a wide band around the stove's width, but then, as he progressed to the flatter sections his thoughts began to wander.

He was, he had to admit, quietly pleased with himself. He hadn't truly believed that he would make it this far without phasing back into his wolf form. Yes, it was only day three, but considering that he'd been wolfed out for the last four months, making it to day three was a big deal. There were stories, urban legends even, of werewolves that had stayed in their wolf form for so long that, eventually, all traces of their humanity had vanished. It was rumoured that once it happened the wolf would become feral and any living thing - human, fellow werewolves, even vampires - wouldn't stand a chance if attacked. There were all sorts of nightmarish tales that kids loved to whisper to each other at night; the vicious wolf Hancock who had lost his mate in a pack fight and swore revenge. Hancock had turned wolf to track the killer, vowing that he would not return to human form until her death was avenged. He never found her murderer however, and legend says he still roams the land, slaughtering entire packs in one night, no known man or beast able to stop him. As a kid, Michael often wound up his younger brother at night-time, swearing blind that he could see a huge wolf prowling around the outside of their house, the moon highlighting the streak of grey fur that ran from Hancock's nose to tail. Legends always held a grain of truth he reminded himself, pausing to blow a fine film of red dust away. He may not have turned as wild as Hancock had, but the proof that his humanity had begun to fade had been undeniable when he'd wanted to pounce on that girl. It was the jolt he'd needed to snap himself out of the mental state he'd allowed himself to sink into. Her scream had wrenched him right back to Blackwater Ridge and the horrific acts he'd carried out there. Never again, never, did he want to cause fear like that in any person.

Michael shuffled sideways to work on a new section of the warm cast-iron, taking a moment to lean back and see the difference already made. He wasn't going to dwell on the incident with the girl. He couldn't. He had to look towards the future and try to leave what was in the past behind. Peace would never be made with what he had done; the lives he had taken would never be paid for, even taking his own life - something he had considered for a long time - would not make amends. Guilt owned him now, its clammy presence resided in his bones and had the right to do so until Mother Nature called time on his life, the life he had no idea of how he should live. This was the one thought that had been heavy on his mind. How did he deserve to live now? He needed to find some sort of neutral state, a place where he was neither happy nor remorse-ridden. Happiness he definitely didn't deserve, and remorse, as he'd already learned, allowed him to be swallowed by his animal side, which in time would smother his humanity. If his humanity evaporated he would feel no more guilt. He had to feel guilt. So what would he do?

He scrubbed harder at the metal, a layer of powder spilling onto the floor by his knees. Today had felt right for some reason. His mood had been balanced, despite still having to struggle with his caged wolf. What was it that had made him tolerable to himself? He had done nothing but wake, eat and work. He had just . . . what? Michael stilled as the answer came to him; he had existed. That was it. That was all he had done today - existed. And that was what he would do from now on. He would wake, eat, work and sleep - nothing more. He didn't deserve anything more, or anything less. 'Existing' was the perfect compromise. No comfort, no joy, just basic existence.

"Exist," he murmured, and with an accepting nod returned to scrubbing at the rusty stove.

Two

Genna Clancy set her address book on the bar counter and flipped it open at the 'X' section. She didn't know a single person whose surname ended in 'X', 'Y' or 'Z' so scribbling her many lists in the tail-end of the little book made perfect, non-wasting-of-money sense. Determinedly clicking her pen she leaned over the page and added the value of her latest pay cheque to the end of the column marked 'Money In'. In the neighbouring column - 'Money Out' - she filled in her expenditure from the last couple of days; rent, food and her favourite magazine 'Catering World'. Betty Kirk, the owner of Kirk's Homestore ordered it in especially for her every month. She kept it in its plastic wrapper and made a big deal out of presenting it to Genna every time she came in to buy it, and every time Genna felt obliged to offer gushing thanks. Although, considering that most of the magazines that Betty sold were of the male sport/hunting/fishing and 4x4 theme, Genna's catering publication probably seemed exotic.

She quickly added up her columns and then pulled a face. If she didn't eat for the next three days she'd hit her target for expenditure and saving this week. She could absolutely go three days without buying food. A girl could live on bar nuts alone. And if she sucked on some lemons she'd get plenty of Vitamin C - so no worries about scurvy.

The door to Black's bar squeaked open and Bob Kincaid ambled in. As usual, he had a newspaper tucked under his arm and he made a beeline for his favourite table in the far corner. Genna waved a hello back and closed her address book. "What'll it be, Bob?" she called from behind the bar, already dropping three ice-cubes into a tumbler.

"Let me see," he called back in his tobacco-destroyed voice. "I think I'll have . . . a beer."

"One beer coming up," she said, pressing the tumbler against the Scotch bottle optic.

"You know -," he began, and she mouthed his words in tandem as the first measure of amber liquid splashed over the ice, "make that a Scotch instead."

"A single?" she asked, filling the glass with a second shot.

"Of course," he replied, and then, "well . . . why not make it a double."

She placed the glass in front of him a moment later. He had his paper spread open on the table and was peering over the rim of his glasses at the headlines. He'd sit here for the next hour and a half, work his way through five shots of Scotch - two doubles and then a single, cos, good God above, three doubles would be sinful at this hour of the day - and by the end she'd know exactly what was going on in the world. Which was of benefit, she told herself, aiming a swipe with her cloth at one of the table tops as she crossed back to the bar. With Bob reading out the contents of his newspaper to her every day she didn't need a TV or a radio. See? Another way in which she was able to save money.

The recital began and Genna allowed herself to slip into standby mode. It meant propping her butt on the shelf wedged between the sink unit and the decrepit glass washer, not the most comfortable perch, but from it she could see a strip of glass in the outer door so if any customers, or the boss, Tony Black, happened to wander in, she'd have enough time to straighten up and look busy. Not that keeping Bob Kincaid in Scotch was going to keep her any way near busy, but she didn't want Tony to wonder if he was only paying her to wedge her butt on a shelf while she thought about being in places that weren't his bar in the sleepy town of Rochfort.

Bob read out a headline and loudly gave his own opinion on how no-one needed to be told how depressed the economy was; everyone was acutely aware of it. She agreed with the first of many automatic 'uh huh's' and decided that she'd start her mind-wanderings with a good old ponder on what her best friends Shaun and Tina might be doing at that moment.

Shaun and Tina had escaped Rochfort last August and were now ensconced in college life, far, far away from her. She would have been with them only her financial restraints had held her firmly in place and would continue to do so until the balance in her bank account moved from hundreds to thousands. Their Hospitality and Tourism course sounded amazing. Tina had filled her in on every little detail of their classes and the only time she'd felt like spitting with jealousy was when Tina had told her that they were to take an eight week block in cookery after Christmas. Genna's dream was to be the head chef in her own restaurant. When she wasn't serving the good people of Rochfort in Black's bar she was working in the kitchens of the local retirement home as a general, do-a-bit-of-everything chef. It was only a few shifts a week, and what she served wasn't what her dream restaurant would serve, but it was cooking, and she loved it, so for now, it would keep her sane.

She was lucky; two good-paying jobs within walking distance of her rented cottage was more than most people had. And if she stuck with her plan she'd be out of Rochfort before three years were up. Three years . . . that was a long time. Would she still be sane after another three years of Bob's daily news reports, three years of the same old grind in Black's bar, three years of cooking food that wouldn't even make the front cover of '101 reliable dinners for those without teeth', and three years of counting every single coin that passed in and out of her bank account? Probably not, she decided, grabbing a fistful of nuts from a bag under the bar. She'd be completely bonkers by then. But rich and bonkers - so that would make up for it.

A buzzing from somewhere below jerked her into unwedging herself off the shelf. Her mobile was ringing. Scrambling through her bag she whipped it out, smiling as she saw Tina's name flashing on the screen. "Hey Tina T!"

"Hey Genna C, how's you and your things?" Tina's voice greeted. "What's happening in Sleepyville?"

"Nothing and some more nothing. Tell me about you, what's going on there?"

"This is a quick hi. I've a lecture in five minutes, but I had to call you with some juicy news."

"Tell me," Genna begged, wishing she could squeal aloud instead of keeping her voice at a suitably respectable level.

"Shaun has a hot date tonight."

"No way!"

"Yes way! There's a guy in our accounting class who's been flirting with him and he asked him out last night."

"Does he seem nice? Is he decent?"

"I think so, I hope so."

"So do I. Aw, Tina, that's brilliant!"

"I know. Imagine; our little man Shaun is all grown up."

"Tell him to ring me with all the details tomorrow."

"I will, don't worry. He's already having a good spaz-out over what to wear."

Genna gave a sad sigh. "I wish I was there, Tina T."

Tina blew a sigh too. "Me too. I really do. It sucks without you here."

"It sucks without *you* here. Sleepyville is worse than ever with you both gone."

"Oh, God," Tina groaned in sympathy. "I'll bet. Have you been doing anything besides working?"

"Not much. I stayed with Mom last weekend, which was nice. Mom says hi."

"Tell her I said hi back."

"Actually," Genna suddenly remembered, "it wasn't all nice. Wait 'til I tell you what happened." She took a quick glance over her shoulder at Bob. He was stuck into his newspaper, but there was only a sip of Scotch left in his glass. She really didn't want to be interrupted while she told Tina her only bit of news so she turned her back on him and prayed he wouldn't call out to her. "I took a walk into the forest on the

Saturday morning. I didn't go far," she said quickly, knowing that only strangers to the town were stupid enough to wander deep into the forest that hemmed the edges of the massive mountain range looming over the town. "But next thing I heard snapping twigs and when I turned around there was this massive wolf standing right behind me."

"Whoa," Tina breathed. "Seriously?"

"I nearly pee'd my pants," Genna said. "I swear to God this thing was huge."

"What did you do?"

"I freaked," Genna replied. "I went to run, fell flat on my ass and ended up screaming."

"And what did it do?"

"It ran off."

"Bloody hell, Genna, that is not funny."

"I know! I was shaking so much when I got back to the house that Mom had to give me a brandy."

"Wow," Tina said. "It's been years since I've heard of wolves coming that close to the town."

"I know, and it absolutely scared the life out of me."

"It's scaring the life out of me," Tina said earnestly. "Promise me you won't go near the forest again."

"You needn't worry. I have no intention of going anywhere near it."

A muffled knocking sounded out from the background of wherever Tina was calling from and a second later Genna could hear Tina's name being called. "Damn, I have to go," Tina sighed. "I'm sorry. I'll call you later, though. Half eight okay?"

"Yeah, perfect. My shift in Willow Lodge ends at eight."

"Okay, talk to you then. Mind you and your things."

"You mind you and your things," Genna replied back customarily. The line clicked dead and she closed the phone, glad that she had got to talk to Tina, but feeling the familiar tug of loneliness for her friends. "Shaun has a date," she said to herself quietly, turning back around to stash her phone in her bag. "Lucky guy," she sighed. "I get stalked by a wolf and he gets a date."

Three

Bright green shoots were poking through the last remaining patches of snow before Michael surrendered to the fact that he had to leave the mountains and visit the town. One near empty bag of rice was all that remained in the kitchen cupboard - that, and a half jar of mustard. Nothing, no matter how much he wanted it to, would make either of them into a decent meal. Not looking forward to a single thing about the trip he yanked the tarp off his aged jeep and was almost disappointed when the engine turned over first time.

Rochfort looked exactly the same as it had on his previous visit; one long, wide main street flanked by nondescript shop fronts that, try as they might, could not inject any life into the place. He stopped for fuel first, inviting no-one to engage with him as he filled the tank and then promptly paid. He intended to remain equally detached in the store, wanting to just grab what he needed, pay, and then leave again.

It was all going to plan until he reached the counter. The tattooed guy ringing through his shopping was as uninterested in conversation as Michael was, but then an older woman appeared from nowhere and he suddenly found himself the centre of attention.

"Excuse me," she said, stepping right into his personal space so as to get a good look at him, "aren't you the young man staying in Charlie Simmonds old shack?"

"Yes," he said reluctantly, frowning at tattoo guy who had stalled scanning his shopping to have a good stare too.

"Michael," she stated. "You're Michael Vincent."

Michael turned to look at her. "Who wants to know?" He recognised her then; she was the woman that had served him the last time he had been here. The owner, he guessed as she announced her name.

"Betty Kirk, and I have mail for you," she announced happily, and hurried through the flyer-layered door behind the till. Tattoo guy was still staring when Michael's darkening frown landed back on him. "Could you -?" he began, shoving a tin of kidney beans at him to make him finish ringing his shopping through. How could he have mail? No-one knew he was here, no-one, he assured himself, yanking his wallet from his back pocket as the last of his items beeped across the finish line. Before the total blinked up on the screen Betty Kirk was back and holding out a large brown envelope. "Here you are, dear," she smiled.

His full name was written on the front of the envelope, nothing else, except for the 'Strictly Private and Confidential' stamp that filled the entire upper left-hand corner. He didn't want to take it. He wanted to say that it wasn't him, Michael Vincent wasn't his name, but his hand was automatically reaching out in response to her shoving it towards him and before he could stop it the envelope was in his hand.

"It's been here a while," she told him, shaking out a bag and placing what was left of his shopping into it. "Only Charlie said you were still up there I would have thought you were gone. How are you surviving in those mountains anyhow?" she asked, "we've had the harshest winter this season. Haven't we Roy?"

"Uh huh," Roy answered, lazily scratching at the back of his neck before announcing the total of the shopping. "A bitter one."

"I manage," Michael muttered to them both, dropping the envelope onto the till belt so he could pull notes from his wallet. He quickly slapped them into Roy's waiting hand.

"I can't imagine there's much heat in that shack," Betty pressed.

"There's not," Michael answered, gathering up the two bags of shopping in one hand and sticking out his hand to encourage Roy to scoop his change out of the till drawer with a little more speed.

"And what about the animals up there? I'll bet you've clapped eyes on a few of them."

"A few."

Roy handed over the change. Michael grabbed it, jammed it into his back pocket and turned to walk away.

"Don't forget this!" Betty reminded him, snatching up the envelope. She helpfully wedged it into one his bags before he could swing it out of her reach. "Thanks," he ground out, stepping around her and barrelling out the door.

Feeling a rising temper prickle hotly across his skin he flung the bags onto the passenger seat of the jeep and loudly slammed the door shut. He then marched around to the driver's side, wrenched open the door and climbed in. The door banged shut with another vicious slam.

"Don't open that envelope," he ordered himself on release of the breath he'd sucked in to try and soothe his swelling temper. "Do not open it." For a long moment he sat rigidly still, his hands gripping the steering wheel and his eyes fixed blankly on the crowded window of the store front. "It can only be bad news," he said eventually. "People only go to great lengths to get information to you when it's bad."

A can settled in the plastic bag, shifting the contents to one side and shoving the envelope further forwards. From the corner of his eye he could see it offering him an inch more of its dog-eared corner. "Dammit," he muttered, and with a surrendering sigh snatched it up and ripped it open.

It took him a long moment to understand what he was holding in his hands. He read the words over and over, and while he understood their meaning, he didn't understand how it made sense. His old pack land, Blackwater Ridge, was his. He was holding the land deeds in his hands and his name was printed all over them. Michael Vincent was the owner of the entire lot, all of it, every last inch of land. He didn't understand. He flipped the thick document over as if the answer would be written on the back. He then did the same with the envelope, peering closely at the writing and looking for anything that might suggest where it had come from, even sniffing it for good measure. It was as he was lowering the envelope from his nose that he looked up and caught the eye of Betty peering through her cluttered store window at him.

"Tony Black left it in here for you," she answered a moment later, pretending she'd been busying herself with lining up tins on a shelf as opposed to staring out her shop window at him once he'd marched back in and straight up to her. "He never said where it came from, just knew that you'd be more likely to come in here than his place."

"Who's Tony Black?"

"Tony Black," she replied, as if it was the most obvious thing in the world. "Black's Bar," she expanded, pointing towards the window. Michael only realised then that there was a bar on the opposite side of the street.

When he swung the door open Tony Black's bar was empty except for an elderly man reading a newspaper at a table in the corner and the girl behind the bar itself. A TV was on behind the bar, but the sound was muted. The only noise was the hum of the fridges stocked with bottles. "Is Tony Black here?" Michael asked, cutting off the girl before she could finish drawing breath to greet him.

"No, he's out," she replied. "Can I help you with anything?"

Michael held up the envelope. "Someone left this here for me a while back. I need to know who it was."

The girl looked at the envelope and then back at him. "Sorry, it wasn't me that took it. It must've been Tony."

"And he's not here."

"No, not for another hour anyway."

"You sure you didn't see who left this?" he asked again, holding it closer to her face and then giving it a shake as if it might jolt her memory. "Did you even hear of someone asking about me?"

"No, sorry."

"You sure?"

"Yeah."

Michael lowered the envelope. "It was a while back, a couple of weeks, maybe even more. Think hard."

"No, I didn't hear anything."

"What about a-."

"Sir," she cut across him patiently. "I'd remember if someone had been looking for you."

"You would?" he said cautiously.

"Yeah," she said, breaking out a smile. "In a town like this, a stranger looking for another stranger would be big news, big exciting news for Sleepyville."

"Right." Michael rolled the envelope into a tube and tapped it irritably against the side of the bar. This Tony guy would have to remember who gave him the envelope. If as the girl said it was 'Sleepyville' surely he'd be able to clearly recall the -.

"Coffee?" A hand rested on the envelope, halting the incessant rapping. "Or maybe something to eat?" the girl asked, pointedly looking at where her hand had stilled the tapping. "Food might be better than caffeine."

Michael slid the envelope out from under her hand and held it down by the side of his leg instead.

"There's a really good omelette on the lunch menu," she continued. "I make it myself, and I eat it, so I can guarantee that it's -."

Not caring for food, or her thoughts on it, Michael turned his back to her and looked to where the older man was still poring over his newspaper. The place wasn't spacious. If he sat at a table away from the bar he'd be within talking distance of the old-timer instead. Why did everyone in this damned place want to engage him in conversation? He glanced down at his watch. Another fifty seven minutes to go.

Michael realised that he suddenly didn't care who had brought the envelope. What difference would knowing make anyway? He didn't want Blackwater Ridge and being the new owner of it didn't change how he felt about the place. It could stay the way it was for all he cared; an abandoned, derelict place, haunted by unadulterated evil.

With the decision made he left the bar and returned to his jeep, carelessly chucking the envelope onto the floor of the passenger well as he revved up the engine. If he'd been thinking straight he should've bought a years' worth of supplies. Having to come back down into the town within the next twelve months was already pissing him off.

His mood had not improved by the time he got back to the shack. Dumping the shopping on the kitchen table he decided that he needed to take a run. The only way he could clear his head and figure out what to do about returning the land deeds was if he burned off some of his nasty mood first.

Michael paid little attention to his path as he began to run. Instead he focused on who could have sent him the envelope. It was only one of two people: Tanya Stenson, the widow of Alpha Alan Stenson, or, Nyah Morgan, the daughter of Harper Morgan; the Alpha who had preceded Alan for many decades. Alan's tenure as Alpha had only just begun when he had been killed, and as Lycan Law placed huge weight on the mourning period, it was unlikely that the formal business of land transfer to Alan from Alpha Morgan had even been discussed. If, by some chance it had however, he knew that Alan's widow Tanya wouldn't have wanted the land. She had fled Blackwater Ridge with their young child and unborn baby, the intention to never return carrying her far, far away. It made sense to assume that if she had been given ownership she would have hurriedly transferred the land to Michael in order to be rid of it, but he knew that wasn't the case. Nyah Morgan had sent him the deeds - he was sure of it. As the only remaining member of her family the deeds had automatically transferred to her after her father's death. Alan wouldn't have even entertained the idea of disrespecting her father's memory by accepting ownership of the land any sooner than the usual six month waiting period that preceded land transfer, so Nyah was, or until now at least, had been the owner. . . unless . . .

The thought was disturbing enough to bring his feet to a lurching halt. Simon Northfell had been the last Alpha to reign over Blackwater Ridge. Although his crazed plan to create hybrid demon-werewolf pups had ended in him being sucked into some kind of hell dimension there was always a chance that he could come back, and as he had been disrespectful enough to blatantly ignore Lycan Law in the past, he may have insisted on Nyah transferring the land to him long before the six month wait had ended. What if he *had* somehow gotten out and was trying to lure Michael back to wherever he now was? Michael had been an obedient puppet to him before, maybe he would be again . . .

"No!" The vehement shout ricocheted through the surrounding trunks. 'I won't let that happen again,' he swore silently, bunching his hands into fists and slamming them against the sudden pressure building in his skull. Simon Northfell had made him perform the most horrific acts, the memories of which were returning in all their appalling glory again. "Stop," he pleaded to the force spilling the images into the void behind his closed eyes. "No!" Simon's pinched face wavered before him, his mean lips shifting into a leer. "Michael," it taunted.

Spittle flew from between Michael's gritted teeth as he crashed to his knees on the hard forest floor. "Stop!" he pleaded louder, pounding his fists against his head to hammer out the brutal images. Once again Eddie and Leanne Stone's faces were before him, their choked screams making him retch. Another flashback tore across his mind to silence their screams, but the memory was just as sickening; Nyah was before him, pacing his kitchen floor in Blackwater Ridge, begging him to believe that her instincts about Simon Northfell were right. "I'm not crazy!" she was pleading with him, "I'm not! Simon Northfell is up to something and allowing him to become Alpha of this pack is the worst thing that can happen!" The fear that Michael had allowed to overwhelm him that day swelled through his being again and he shook his head violently from side to side, wanting to dash his brains against his skull to stop the vivid replay of how he had turned away from the girl he had known for nearly twenty years to so cowardly submit to Northfell. And then he was back in his old pack house daubing bizarre symbols on the walls, his mind caring only for the orders made by Northfell as the blood of his pack members dripped between his fingers while he painted. "Stop," he sobbed, "please!" Falling forwards, Michael raked chunks of earth under his fingertips as he fought to stop the onslaught. Every one of his senses seemed to be reliving the nightmare; the rusty tang of werewolf blood stung his nostrils, the choking fumes of the nameless concoctions Northfell had burned during his voodoo rituals made him cough and retch, even the cold, clammy sensation of where the talisman Northfell had controlled him with rested against his chest made him want to tear his skin off. "No, no, no," he screamed, scoring his nails against where the necklace had once hung. When Northfell's face swam before him again he fell back, shielding his face with his arm as he tried to scramble away. He landed awkwardly on the hard ground and the jolt shocked him into realising what was happening. The chaotic terror was too much. His wolf reared and he let out a single cry. The cry morphed into a snarl, and not caring for where it might end, Michael allowed his wolf to take control.

Released is now available at all good online retailers

Made in the USA
Charleston, SC
12 April 2016